ALL THAT I AM

GRACE HARTWELL

BOOK ONE OF THE HESITANT HUSBANDS SERIES

For Laurie Judd
Without your suggestion, this book would never have been written.
I am forever grateful.

~

And in memory of Christopher Weed, my real life romantic hero. I love you with all that I am, and miss you with all that I have.

But in a crowd of thousands, I'll find you again.

PROLOGUE

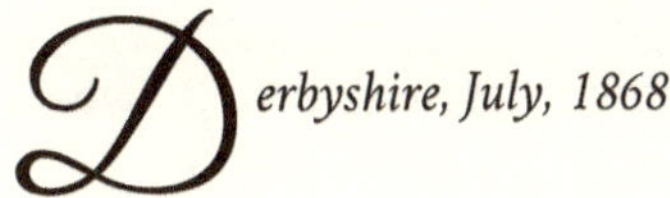

erbyshire, July, 1868

THE SOUND of shattering glass pulled Leighton from sleep.

The scream that followed yanked her bolt upright.

What was happening? Leighton sat, paralyzed, as the sounds of scuffling feet and men's angry voices reached her ears. Furniture was being knocked over as whoever had broken into the house fought with…whom? Her parents? The servants? She slipped out of bed and crept to the door, but she froze when her mother cried out.

"No! Leave her alone!"

The desperation and panic in her mother's voice signaled danger, and when footsteps pounded on the stairs, Leighton backed away from the door, her heart in her throat. She glanced frantically about, and when her eyes fell on the tapestry on the far wall, and she made a mad dash for it. She dove behind it and shoved open the door that led to the secret tunnel. She was no sooner safely ensconced in the tunnel than the sound of men bursting into her room rever-berated on the other side of the hidden door. She tried desperately to overcome her ragged breathing as she tiptoed over to the tiny peephole. She could just see her mother, her arms held roughly by two terrifying-looking men, face streaked with tears, hair falling from its pins. There was a third man in the room, out of Leighton's line of vision. The sound of his angry snarl carried through the wall.

"Where is she?" he demanded.

"I don't know," her mother sobbed. Leighton gasped when the man struck her mother hard across the cheek.

"Do not lie to me, Mrs. Courtwright. Where *is* she?"

"I don't know," she repeated, desperate. "There are hundreds of places she could be hiding!"

But Leighton knew her mother knew exactly where she was.

"Please," Kate begged, her voice fearful. "Please, leave us alone. My husband just thought he was protecting—"

"You expect mercy?" The deadly calm in his voice sent chills down Leighton's spine. "Your family for mine, Mrs. Courtwright. What's fair is fair."

"No!"

"Your husband should have thought it through before he opened his mouth," the man snapped. "Forget about the girl," he said to the others. "She's in the house somewhere. She won't get away—I will hunt her down myself. Make no mistake about that." And then, "Kill them. And burn the house to the ground. We'll smoke the girl out or she can die here."

Leighton clapped her hands over her mouth to stifle a scream.

"No! NO!" Her mother was sobbing. "Please! Don't do this. *Please!*" Leighton watched helplessly as the two men dragged her mother from the room. "Leighton! Leighton!"

she screamed, the sound of her voice fading as she disappeared from view. Silent tears streamed down Leighton's face, and her throat ached. Blood roared in her ears as she sank to the floor, trying to comprehend what was happening. Who would want to hurt her parents? And why would they want her, too? She was only fourteen, a good girl. What had Papa done to—

A pungent smell met her nostrils. *Smoke.* They'd already set the fire! She sucked in an unsteady breath and squeezed her eyes shut, trying to thwart the rising panic in her chest. Panicking wouldn't get her out alive. She forced herself to think.

London. Papa had told her they were leaving for London in the morning to visit an old friend of the family. A Mr. Mac...something. No matter, it would come to her. The thought of traveling to London alone made her stomach clench, but she wasn't safe here, and she'd only put neighbors and friends in danger by going to them for help. Perhaps this person they were to visit had some idea of what was happening. She would find help in London, she was sure of it. She just had to get there.

She would need money. She had quite a bit of pin money saved, and she could sell her jewelry if she had to. She stood on shaky legs and peeked through the peephole once again. She saw nothing but flames licking the walls in her room. She was running out of time. She moved to the door and rested her hand on the latch. "Lord help me," she whispered, before tugging it open. She poked her head around the tapestry and immediately choked on the smoke, but she was alone. Taking a deep lungful of musty tunnel air, she shoved the tapestry aside and raced to her wardrobe, yanking out a valise and stuffing whatever clothing she could into it, followed by her sturdiest pair of boots and a cloak. Smoke clogged her throat as she stumbled to her dresser, eyes burning, and emptied her jewelry box into the valise as well, followed by her pin money. She spun around to make her escape, but the portrait of her parents in the small frame by her bedside caught her attention. Pain squeezed her chest, and she hesitated a moment, suddenly realizing that she might never see them again. Without another thought, she dashed toward the bed, which was now engulfed in flames. She shielded her face from the heat and fumbled around till her fingers brushed the frame. It was hot, and it scalded her fingers as she grasped it and ran for the passageway, only to skid to an abrupt halt. The tapestry, too, was now in flames, blocking her route to safety. She glanced behind her. She could still make it out the door, but to what end? She would be captured for certain. Frantic, her eyes darted around the the room until she spied a heavy wool blanket on a chair in the corner. She snatched it up, tossed it over her head, and dove for the tapestry. She used the blanket to shove the flaming tapestry aside enough so that she could slip behind it and squeeze through the door, dragging her valise behind her. She quickly shed the smoldering blanket and tamped out the flame that had ignited on the hem of her nightgown. She collapsed on the stone floor, gasping for breath, limbs trembling, eyes watering. She allowed herself only a moment of collection before she felt around for her boots. Her hands were shaking so badly she could hardly put them on her feet. Blinded by tears and hampered by the darkness, she stumbled her way along the tunnel for what seemed like forever, panic threatening to overtake her at any moment. Finally, when she thought she would never make it, she burst forth into the moonlit orchard, a short distance away from the house. She gulped in the fresh night air, trying in vain not to cough. The acrid scent of smoke clung to her skin and clothes, and she was covered in filth from the tunnel.

A chill crept down her spine, and she glanced around,

unable to shake the feeling someone was watching her. She slipped further into the protective shadow of the trees and donned her cloak, knowing her white nightgown would act as a beacon in the moonlight. Leighton turned to look back at her once grand home. Flames shot through the windows, the blaze lighting up the night sky. She could hear the shouts of the servants awakened by the melee, barking orders and trying to reach those who would be trapped. Muffled sobs wracked her body. Her entire life, gone in only a few moments. And for what purpose? Were her parents really going to be killed? Or had the man just said that to draw her out of hiding? She refused to let herself believe she would never see them again. "I will find you, Mama, Papa," she vowed, choking back a sob. "I *will* find you." She prayed for a miracle to save them, and then turned and headed for the secret tree house in the woods where she planned to spend the night. Tomorrow she would be bound for London.

A safe harbor awaited her.

CHAPTER 1

 ondon, 1876

THERE WERE sixteen pairs of eyes focused on Aidan Lockwood, Earl of Ashby, waiting for him to say something. Anything.

The odor of cigar smoke hung thick in the air, the cloud in the room echoing haze in his head. He tried to pull words together in his brain, but after an evening of drinking with his friends, they were proving a bit more elusive than he cared to admit.

After a moment's careful thought, Aidan raised his glass in a toast and said, "To my dear friend, William Everett, on the eve of his nuptials. May a temporary loss of sanity lead to a lifetime of happiness." He winked at William. "Congratulations on finding someone willing to marry you," he finished with a grin.

A roar of laughter broke out among the men, and those nearest Everett pounded him on the back.

"Spoken like a true bachelor," Will said, shaking his head, amusement twinkling in his blue eyes.

"Best wishes, my friend," Aidan returned, clinking his glass of whiskey with Will's. "Better you than me."

Will chuckled. "You're just jealous."

"Hardly, my friend. Though Miss Barrington is a lovely woman," he amended hastily.

"When *will* it be your turn, Ashby?" Donovan MacKavoy chimed in. "You can't keep running around breaking hearts with that scoundrel, Mayfield, forever, you know."

"I'm still running around with you, aren't I?" Aidan saluted him with his glass. "I could be asking you the same thing."

"Yes, but I'm only twenty-four." Donovan grinned. "You're getting old."

More laughter. Aidan narrowed his eyes. "Twenty-nine is hardly old, MacKavoy. I've a few good years left in me yet."

"You'll be thirty in three days," Donovan reminded him. Aidan sipped his whiskey and shot him a dark look over the rim of his glass.

"Come now, Ashby," Donovan pressed. "You can't tell me there isn't some young lady who's tempted you at least a little bit thus far."

Snickers could be heard round the table. The truth was; he did have to marry. Sooner rather than later. He had an obligation to continue the family line. The problem came in finding the right sort of wife. He mentally filed through the names of all the simpering young ladies who had been thrust at him in every ballroom across London over the past nine years. He didn't want just any debutante. He needed someone who understood him. Someone efficient, respectable, and trustworthy...someone with a good mind. Perhaps even a healthy dose of spirit. But most importantly, he needed someone who would accept that he could never offer her love. He had no intention of marrying for love.

The sticking point was that in a desperate moment, he had promised his dying father that he would do exactly that.

"Not a one," he replied, a hint of resignation in his voice. Oh, how he dreaded the upcoming season. "Besides, you all know I have to get my sister married off first."

"Coward," Will muttered.

"What was that?" Aidan eyed his friend.

"He said you're a coward, Ash," Marcus Walker, the newly-minted Viscount Thorpe, replied blithely, grinning. There was a moment of stunned silence, and a flicker of warning skittered across Aidan's face. The men glanced around the table uneasily, until Donovan reached over and removed the tumbler of whiskey from Marcus's hand.

"That's enough for you, Thorpe," he said.

"Oh, come now," Will chided, his words slurring slightly. "Despite what you may think, Ashby, falling in love is actually a wonderful thing." He hiccuped.

Aidan rolled his eyes. "If it means turning into a sop like you, I want no part of it."

"Ashby, Ash, my silly little friend," Will said, clapping him on the shoulder as he leaned in to impart his sage advice. "When are you going to learn that you don't have a choice in the matter?"

"Blast, you sound like my sister!" Aidan sputtered. Enough of this. Time to steer the conversation away from his situation and put the focus back on the reason they were all there. He stood abruptly, the chair shrieking as it slid across the floor. Aidan glanced at his friends and shot them all an unsteady grin. "Gentlemen, find me a woman with a sharp mind and a sharper wit who isn't more interested in gowns and gossip than family and friendship and I promise you, I'll make her a bride." *What on earth was he saying?* Dear God, he must be drunker than he thought. "I'm quite sure Everett, here, has found the last one in London. Which brings me back to the point," he said, raising his glass again. "To my good friend, Ev. May you and Louisa find all the happiness your hearts desire. God bless you both."

"Hear, hear!" General shouts of congratulations rang out, and Will's eyes met Aidan's across the table. He nodded toward Aidan in thanks, and a small smile touched Aidan's lips, his eyes filling with warmth. Will and Aidan had been through much in life together, and Aidan couldn't be happier to see him with a good woman. Louisa suited Will perfectly.

"Gentlemen, the hour grows late," Aidan said, swaying just slightly. "I fear I must be getting Everett on his way or his fiancée will have my head when he falls asleep at the altar."

There was general protest, but the men bid each other good evening amongst more laughter and congratulations, and then finally Aidan and Will were out in the peace of night, away from the noise and stale air. It was a brisk evening, the March wind whipping about them in a sudden gust. There was an ominous storm brewing, the thunder rolling down the cobblestone street. Aidan paused and smiled genuinely at his lifelong friend. "Are you ready for this?"

Will grinned. "I can't wait." He paused. "You know, Ash, I meant what I said. I want you to be happy."

"I don't have to be in love to be happy, Ev."

"I've known you almost my whole life, Ash. You're a care-taker. What are you going to do when when your sister *does* marry? I think you need someone special in your life. I remember the person you were before your father—"

"Don't."

Will sighed. "Mark my words, Ash. When you least expect it, love is going to slam into you so hard you won't even know what hit you, and you will be powerless to stop it." Will grinned. "I speak from experience."

Aidan opened his mouth to protest when a scuffle across the street caught his eye. A man had latched onto a woman by the elbow, and she was clearly unwilling to be led away. Aidan squinted.

"Oh, for the love of—is that Smythe?"

Will followed his gaze. "'Fraid so."

It was so like Smythe to pick on a weaker human being. The man was an absolute weasel.

The woman he had in his grasp was struggling in earnest now. It was enough to propel Aidan across the street. "Excuse me just a moment, Ev. Send Jack for the carriage, will you? I'll only be a minute."

"Don't go getting into trouble. I need you tomorrow."

"Rest easy. I'm just going to send Smythe scurrying on his way like the dog that he is," he replied, stepping into the street. He had a deadly sort of calmness in his voice that Will recognized immediately.

"That's what worries me!" Will called after him. He sighed. "Always the bloody hero, aren't you?" he muttered to himself, chuckling. Aidan couldn't resist a damsel in distress. It made no difference to him that she was clearly the poorest of the poor—she was a woman, and one being bothered by a man Aidan couldn't tolerate under any circumstances. Will didn't budge from his spot in front of the club. He wasn't about to miss the show.

The couple was so involved in their tug-of-war that they didn't even hear Aidan approach.

"I believe the lady asked you to let go of her."

The struggle stopped instantly as Smythe snapped his head around to see who had spoken. "Well, well, well. Who do we have here?" He straightened up a bit. "Go away, Lockwood," he sneered. "I'm busy."

Aidan ignored the snub of using his surname rather than his title. "I can see that. However, the lady does not appear to want your company."

He turned to bestow a smile on the woman, and found himself staring into the most arresting blue eyes he had ever seen. The air left his lungs in a rush, as though he had been punched square in the chest. In the gaslight, he couldn't quite ascertain their exact shade, but they were impossibly large and framed by sooty lashes. The woman's face, however, was smudged with dirt, her dark hair pulled back into what could only be described as a rat's nest of a chignon that was coming loose from its pins, and her clothes were hopelessly over-sized. Yet she wore the expression of a woman ready to do battle with the both of them if necessary. Despite her body language, the fear in her eyes told him all he needed to know. He was not about to let Smythe lead her away. "My apolo-gies, Miss," he said, nodding to her. "Do speak up if I am incorrect."

She remained silent and wide-eyed. Aidan ignored her look of disbelief as he reached out and gently took her wrist in his hand, while he dug his other fingers into Smythe's elbow joint and squeezed.

"Might I suggest, Smythe, that you honor the lady's request and be on your way?" Despite his choice of words, it was not a suggestion. He squeezed a little harder—just for emphasis, of course.

Smythe gave in to the pain Aidan was causing him and released his grip. He stumbled back, glaring at Aidan. "She ain't no lady. Why is she of any concern to you?"

Aidan glanced at her. Anger flashed in her eyes, yet she appeared ready to bolt. Clearly, she trusted Aidan no more than Smythe. "A lady, rich or poor," Aidan began, turning back to the weasel, "should choose to accompany a man, not be forced into it."

Smythe looked from Aidan to the woman and back again, obviously in a dilemma. Aidan released his hold on her wrist and clasped his hands behind his back. "This is the part where you beg her pardon and bid us 'good evening'. And might I suggest you not let me catch you in this situation again, Smythe. Next time I may not be in such a good mood."

Aidan's threat was not an empty one, and Peter Smythe knew it. One word from the Earl could send him to prison—or worse—for the crime he'd committed against Aidan's father. Hatred radiated from him as he turned his loathing glance on the girl.

"Beggin' your pardon for the misunderstanding," he ground out, nodding to her. He shot a black glare at Aidan, spun on his heel, and stormed off down the street. Aidan turned to the mystery woman.

"Are you all right?"

She nodded, clearly apprehensive. "Thank you," she managed. She tightened her threadbare wool cloak around her, her glance darting around the street. She edged away from Aidan.

"What are you doing out at such a late hour? It's dangerous."

"I..." She fished about for something to say. "I was supposed to meet a friend." She shifted on her feet, warily looking at the sky when lightning flashed. "I must go." She tried to move past him, but he stepped in front of her.

"Can I escort you somewhere safe, Miss?"

Her lovely eyes widened in surprise. Aidan knew he should let her pass, but those darned eyes were drawing him in, compelling him to stand his ground. There were secrets in those eyes, and Aidan dearly loved a mystery.

"No. But thank you for coming to my rescue." She moved away.

"Wait. What is your name?" This was absolute madness.

Aidan knew he should have just sent Smythe on his way and been done with it, but he couldn't make himself leave her. She regarded him for a moment, seeming to assess whether or not to impart this information. The wind tossed loose strands of hair about her face, and she reached up a pale hand to keep it under control. His pulse quickened as her lips parted, perhaps with a reply, but it never came because she was interrupted by a shout from across the street.

"Ashby!" Will called, pointing to his pocket watch. "I'm getting married in nine hours. I need to be there!"

Aidan turned to Will, laughing. "You'll be there, you miserable swine!"

"I also need to be awake!"

Aidan waved him off and turned back to the woman, but she was gone. He spun about, looking all around him, but she was nowhere to be seen. He was quite alone in the lamplight.

"*Ashby!*"

"Coming," he shouted back, with one last glance around. How had she moved so quickly without him noticing? It was just as well, he supposed. The scene had surely been witnessed from the club, and there would be plenty of talk tomorrow. He jogged across the street back to where Will waited.

"Are you through playing the hero?" Will grinned.

Aidan chuckled. "Some hero. The damsel in distress ran away!" He studied the other side of the street for a moment, scanning it for any sign of the young woman with the arresting eyes. "You didn't happen to see where she went, did you?"

"No, I turned away to send Jack and Browning for the carriages. I'd like to get home before the rain comes. Oh, and before I forget, let me give this to you for safe keeping." William handed Aidan a piece of paper. "It's my marriage license. I can't be trusted with it." He grinned. "Don't forget to bring it with you tomorrow."

Aidan chuckled. "I'll do my best to remember." He reached out to take the license from his friend, but a sharp gust of wind whipped it from his hand. "Bloody hell!" Aidan swore. He watched as the paper flew into the street on a demonic course for the gutter. He raced into the street after it, so intent on catching it that he barely noticed the flash of lightning that struck nearby, spooking a team of horses and sending them careening down the street. They were heading straight for Aidan.

Heedless of the approaching danger, Aidan chased the license for nearly half a block before triumphantly snagging the elusive parchment. William, who had initially frozen in panic, was just catching up to him.

"I hope this isn't an omen," he called. Aidan laughed and turned back toward the curb. It was only then that he heard the pounding of hooves. He glanced up and saw the horses heading directly for him, but it was too late.

"Ashby! Look out!"

William leapt from the curb with the intention of pulling Aidan to safety, but Leighton reached him first. She launched herself at him, slamming into his body and sending him sprawling to the ground, taking Will with him. But she couldn't regain her footing, and one of the horses crashed into her, sending her flying through the air. She landed in a motionless heap several feet away from where the men lay entangled on the ground. The team and empty carriage clattered on down the street, disappearing into the night.

"Christ, Everett, are you all right?" Aidan asked as he moved his weight off his friend and staggered to his feet. He was dizzy from his slight overindulgence at the club, and he'd smacked the side of his face on the cobblestones, but he was otherwise uninjured.

"Never better," William replied shakily. He reached up to take Aidan's outstretched hand. "You?"

"Just surprised," Aidan said, helping William to his feet. "Who—?"

He turned around in confusion, just realizing someone had pushed him out of the way. He glanced about him, and his heart nearly stopped as his eyes came to rest on the figure lying crumpled on the cobblestones.

"Mother in heaven," Aidan whispered. He grabbed his friend by the shoulder. "Ev, fetch a doctor!"

William stared in stunned silence at the tangled heap in the street for a heartbeat, then took off running for the nearest help. Aidan sprinted over and knelt down beside the woman on the ground, pulling her knotted hair from her face, which was already starting to bruise. Blood was coming from…somewhere. "Damn it all to hell!" He began searching for her injuries, cursing his lack of medical knowledge.

Men who had seen the accident through the window of the club poured out onto the street, forming a crowd around them as Aidan frantically tried to rouse her. "Miss? Miss! Can you hear me?"

The driver of the runaway team finally reached the group, gasping for air. "My lord, I'm so sorry," he wheezed. "The storm spooked 'em an' I couldn't hold on." He bent over and put his hands on his knees, sucking in gulps of air. "My God, my God," he chanted between gasps, his frightened gaze taking in the lifeless woman on the cobblestones. Someone in the crowd assured him that he wouldn't be held responsible, but Aidan didn't even acknowledge him.

"Stay with me, now," he whispered, brushing his fingertips down the young woman's cheek. Will came rushing back, pushing through the crowd to Aidan's side. "I sent Browning for the doctor. He'll meet us at your place." He stopped as he got his first glance at the woman's face. "Isn't that the girl you were just talking to a minute ago?"

"Yes," Aidan snapped, continuing his efforts, and trying not to recoil in horror when he touched her hair and found his hand covered with blood. "Dear God," he whispered, a chill shuddering through him. "Where the bloody hell is Jack with the carriage?" he shouted, struggling to his feet.

"He's coming round the corner now," Will said. The crowd moved out of the street to make way for the oncoming carriage. William stared at his friend. "Ash, you could have been killed," he said quietly.

"I know that," he replied testily.

Will glanced down at the crumpled body on the cobblestones. "She saved your life."

"I know that, too," Aidan snapped. "I'm hoping to return the favor. Help me get her into the carriage."

She weighed almost nothing. He was shocked to see how thin she really was, and Aidan briefly wondered how she had possessed the strength to knock his six-foot frame off his feet. They moved her as little as possible and laid her across one of the seats. Aidan wedged himself against her so she wouldn't roll off, and then they took off at full speed toward his home. The men spoke not a word to each other the entire way.

CHAPTER 2

The door to Lord Ashby's house crashed open, stunning the normally unflappable butler into open-mouthed silence as Will and Aidan exploded into the foyer. Tibbs recovered quickly as Aidan flew by with a woman in his arms—and certainly not the type his lordship usually brought home. Will was right on his heels.

"Lord Ashby! What on earth—"

"Mrs. Bartlett," Aidan bellowed, ignoring the butler and charging up the stairs. "Mrs. Bartlett!"

"Here, my lord," she called, appearing at the top of the stairs. She caught a glimpse of filthy clothing and matted hair as Aidan rushed past her to the nearest guest room. "What on earth happened?"

"Get some linens. She's bleeding badly." Aidan laid her on the bed while the housekeeper yanked linens from the drawer. She bent to apply them to the girl's wounds, but she seemed unsure of exactly where they were.

Aidan snatched the linen from her hands. "Here," he said, putting it behind the girl's head and applying pressure. "Fetch some warm water."

Mrs. Bartlett went and returned swiftly, and began to clean the blood from the gash on the woman's forearm. After a few moments of silence, she glanced at her employer.

"My lord?"

Aidan met her questioning eyes and sighed. "She saved my life by throwing herself in front of a runaway carriage."

Mrs. Bartlett stopped what she was doing and stared at Aidan. "My dear," she breathed. "Are you hurt?"

"I'll be fine," he replied, perfectly aware that he was a frightful mess. He could feel blood trickling down his cheek, and if the throbbing was any indication, he'd be sporting a right fine black eye tomorrow. He glanced down at his ruined shirt and neckcloth. The coat was dark, and might be able to be saved. Richards was going to kill him, but if anyone could get the blood out of his coat, it was his valet.

This was definitely not how this night was supposed to have ended.

The sound of another carriage pulling up outside drew his attention. He turned to Will, who had been so silent that Aidan had forgotten he was there. "Ev, can you—"

"I'll fetch him," Will said, and fled the room. Aidan allowed himself a small smile. His friend was not fond of the sight of blood. He dipped his hands in the basin of water, dried them with a rag, and stepped into the hall to greet Dr. Lambert.

The doctor wasted no time in climbing the steps, but he put his hand on Aidan's chest when he tried to follow him into the room. "I can do this better without you, Lord Ashby," Dr. Lambert said. Aidan began to protest, but Will pulled gently on his arm and dragged him back toward the stairs.

"Tibbs, brandy, please," he ordered as he shoved Aidan into the study, despite his protests. "Ash, you know she is in good hands and you will just get in the way."

"What," Aidan began, "What on earth possessed her to do such a thing? She could have been killed!"

"I'm sure she was thinking the same thing," Will replied.

"Shouting a warning would have been sufficient."

"Ash, you were concentrating so hard on chasing my marriage license that you didn't even hear the horses. Hell, I didn't even hear them! Do you really think you would have heard her?"

"Still—"

"Enough!" Will said firmly. "She saw someone in danger and just reacted. I'm sure she was planning to get out of the way as well, she just didn't make it."

"But why would she risk her life for a total stranger?"

"Was she supposed to just let you get killed? Count your blessings that she was quicker on her feet than either one of us."

Tibbs arrived with the brandy, which Aidan ignored. Perhaps if he hadn't been drinking, he would have noticed the horses racing toward him and he wouldn't be in this mess. Funny how he didn't feel even slightly intoxicated at the moment.

He knew Will was right, but the whole situation still seemed surreal. And what was it that he had interrupted on the street? The fear and desperation in the woman's eyes had taken Aidan aback. Those sapphire orbs held an intriguing story in them, and Aidan burned to know what it was. Now he was responsible for this woman, a complication he did not need in his well-ordered life.

Half an hour later, Dr. Lambert entered the room. Both men leapt to their feet.

"How is she?"

"No breaks in the legs, but there are some broken ribs and she may have fractured her shoulder as well. It's hard to know for sure until she wakes up. If she wakes up."

Aidan's brows slammed together. "If?"

"The girl suffered a pretty nasty blow to the head. It could be days or weeks before she regains consciousness. There's just no way to tell. Other than that, she's got scrapes and bruises on the outside, but I don't know what's happening on the inside. She was hit quite hard. She could be bleeding internally. If that's the case, she may not survive the night."

Aidan's stomach somersaulted. How could that be? This woman had saved his life, and he may never know who she is. "I see," he said quietly. "So what you're telling me is that there is nothing to be done but sit and wait to see what happens."

"I'm afraid so. I did leave Mrs. Bartlett with a bottle of laudanum for the girl. If she does wake up, she'll be in a good deal of pain and she'll need to be kept quiet until she starts to heal. She's in for quite a recovery period. Mrs. Bartlett is washing and dressing her wounds now. I'll be back tomorrow to check on her."

Aidan nodded. "Thank you for coming so quickly at such a late hour."

"My bill will be enormous." Dr. Lambert flashed a smile, trying to add some levity to the situation. "Lord Ashby," he said more seriously. "You're a very fortunate man to be standing in front of me tonight."

"I know," Aidan replied quietly. He shook hands with Dr. Lambert and had Tibbs show him to the door. Aidan turned to Will.

"*Christ.*" He shoved a hand through his hair. "Days? Weeks? What am I supposed to do with her? I'm leaving for France on Thursday!"

"I'm sure Mrs. Bartlett can handle the situation."

Aidan groaned. "This is not happening. The busiest time of year for me and I have a female house guest for an unde-termined amount of time. Oh, I can't wait to see the gossip columns tomorrow!" He slumped into a nearby chair. In a matter of seconds, his quiet life had been turned upside down. "What if she dies?" he said quietly. "I don't even know who she is."

"She's not going to die, Ash. Have faith. All will be well, you'll see."

Aidan regarded his friend with a frown. "How can you be so bloody optimistic all the time? It must be exhausting."

Will grinned. "One of us has to be. And I choose to believe that good is rewarded. She'll pull through and you can thank her for saving your arse. I know I will."

Aidan dropped his face to his hands, momentarily forgetting his injuries. He yelped the moment his hand contacted his cheek. "Damn it!" He sighed, glancing at the mantel clock. "Everett, your fiancée will have my head if you don't show up to your wedding on time tomorrow…or should I say later this morning? I think perhaps you should be on your way so you will be well rested."

"Are you going to be all right?" Will looked doubtful.

"Of course. And I wouldn't miss your wedding for the world, if you are worried about that."

Will smiled, loath to leave his friend. He had known Aidan long enough to know that he would heap an enormous amount of guilt upon himself because this woman was hurt due to his own foolishness. Will also knew him well enough to know that he would do everything in his power to make it up to her. He gave Aidan's shoulder a reassuring squeeze. "Believe, my friend. And take care of yourself tonight. I'll show myself out."

Will left and Aidan let his head fall back against the chair. He let out a shaky sigh. He spied the glass of brandy on the table, grabbed it, and took a huge swallow, desperate to stop the trembling in his limbs that had just appeared out of nowhere. How could he have been so stupid? How could he have been so unaware of the danger? Had he been so enchanted by those beautiful blue eyes that his senses had immediately taken leave of him? This woman intrigued him. Who was she? There was something about her that didn't quite fit, though he couldn't put his finger on it. He wanted to know more about her. No matter that she was obviously destitute, she was brave, and he owed her his life. If she hadn't lost her own.

Mrs. Bartlett finally came downstairs to get him. "I bathed her as best I could and dressed all of her wounds, my lord. I put her in one of Mary's nightgowns so we can wash her clothes, though I don't think it would be much of a loss if they simply disappeared. Now, I think we'd better tend to you before you see her."

Aidan glanced at her and shook his head. "It can wait."

He pushed past her and strode out the door. He hated to just brush her aside, but the need to see his guest temporarily quashed his guilt and drove him up the stairs two at a time. He paused on the threshold of the room, staring at the tiny frame of the woman lying unconscious on the bed. She had a large bandage wrapped around her head and another around one forearm, but she looked much better than she had an hour ago. He approached her quietly, as if he might wake her. Now that her eyes weren't distracting him, he could see she had fine features, despite the swelling in her face. She was very pale, with long, dark hair that surrounded her in a mass of tangled chocolate curls. She had delicate eyebrows and a petite nose that made Aidan want to run his finger down it. Her skin was clear, but held a slightly gray tinge to it, and she had dark circles under her eyes, as though she hadn't slept in days. Her full, perfectly proportioned lips seemed to hold a hint of a smile even though she slept. All in all, he thought she could be an attractive woman.

Mrs. Bartlett came in behind him. "Have a look at this, my

lord," she said, drawing back the covers to reveal the woman's ankle. Around it was a tattered ribbon that held a gold charm. Aidan bent down to study it. It appeared to be a Celtic knot. It seemed oddly familiar to him, though for the life of him, he couldn't think why, nor could he fathom the reason she even had it. As his eyes took in her rail-thin frame, he thought it would have served her much better had she sold it for food. Looking down at her, he couldn't imagine how this half-starved creature had actually knocked two men to the ground in one shot.

"I want to know the instant she wakes up, no matter the time, is that clear?"

"Yes, my lord. I'll be with her the rest of the night. Mary will take over in the morning."

"Very good." Aidan nodded. "Thank you, Mrs. Bartlett," he added.

She nodded, understanding in her eyes. "And might I remind you to tend to your cheek before bed? You will be quite a sight at the wedding tomorrow if you don't."

Aidan gave her a small smile. In so many ways, she had become his mother figure. "I promise, I will." He turned and headed for the door.

"I also took the liberty of ordering you a hot bath. I thought perhaps you might be in need of a good soak," she called after him. "And some ice for your face," she added.

He paused on the threshold. "You are a saint, Mrs. Bartlett." He smiled at her. "Good night."

"Good night, my lord."

He left the room and went to his own bedchamber, stripping off his coat as he walked. By the time he reached his destination, he had managed to get his neckcloth untied as well. His valet, Richards, appeared from out of nowhere, and paled visibly when his eyes came to rest on Aidan and his bloody attire.

"Sorry, old chap." Aidan stripped off the ruined shirt, which was now beginning to stick to his chest as it dried. He handed the shirt and tie to Richards. "I'm afraid you'll have to burn these. And see if you can get the blood out of this," he added, handing him the coat as well.

Richards held the bloodied linens between his thumb and forefinger and eyed them distastefully. "Very good, my lord."

"That will be all for this evening."

Richards's head snapped up. "But, my lo—"

"I am well, Richards. I thank you for your concern. However, I very much want to soak in that bath and sink into bed. I can manage that on my own."

Richards looked crestfallen. "As you wish, my lord." He slipped quietly from the room.

Aidan removed the rest of his clothing and checked his face in the mirror. Good God, he looked worse than he thought. There was a small gash running from his left cheekbone to his temple, and the flesh surrounding it was swelling rapidly. The purplish hue did not bode well, either. He sighed, wrapped some ice in a cloth, and then sank gratefully into the tub to let his mind wander over the night's events. Who was this mystery woman who was willing to risk her life for that of a stranger? And what was it about her that had compelled him to stay even after Smythe had left? It was disconcerting to him.

He wasn't sure exactly what he was going to do with her now that she was here, but his sister would be home in a few days. Lainey would know how to handle the situation.

Holy hell, his face hurt.

CHAPTER 3

Two days. Two blasted days and the girl hadn't so much as moved. Aidan was quite sure his behind had left a permanent impression on the powder blue velvet chair he'd been sitting in watching her for those two days. He had cut a spectacular figure at the wedding with a purple, swollen face, and as a result, he was now being forced to endure continual, probing questions from everyone he knew, which was *really* beginning to grate on his nerves. Speculation was running rampant about town. And to top it all off, he couldn't seem to get any work done because he found himself constantly drawn to this woman's bedside. He and Gavin Mayfield, his best friend and business partner, were about to head to France for two weeks for a purchasing trip. Aidan wanted to know who this woman was before he left, and he wanted to be damn sure she didn't die while he was gone.

He leaned over his charge, peering intently at her. She looked ethereal, lying there with her dark hair spread across the pillow, tangled mess though it was. He studied her every feature, intrigued by her very presence.

"It's time to wake up now, young lady," he whispered. "I need to know who you are."

It was growing late. He frowned, watching the firelight flicker over her pale face. He was just about to give up for the evening when the girl startled him by suddenly opening her eyes. Aidan froze, not sure if she was really awake. She seemed to be staring blankly at nothing in particular. He leaned in a little closer to her.

"Hello, there."

She blinked, and her gaze shifted and locked with his. He wasn't prepared for the raw fear he saw reflected in her eyes. They went round, and she bolted upright, screaming both in terror and at the pain the movement caused her. Aidan reached out to try to help, but it only caused her to shrink away from him, crying out again.

"Miss, it's all right, it's all right," he soothed, frantically trying to calm her. "I'm not going to hurt you. You're safe here."

Mrs. Bartlett flew into the room, snatching the bottle of laudanum from the dresser as she sailed past. She gripped the girl's uninjured shoulder and talked her into lying down again. The young woman groaned in pain as Aidan helped her lie back. Her breath came in ragged, short bursts as she gulped for air.

"There, there, Miss," Mrs. Bartlett soothed. "You need to be still. You had quite an accident."

The terrified girl looked from her to Aidan and back again. Aidan backed away a little so he didn't appear so threatening. She clutched the sheets to her chest, squeezing her eyes shut against the pain wracking her body. A shattered moan tore from her throat, making Aidan wince.

"Mrs. Bartlett, the laudanum, please." He moved closer to the bed and tried his best to calm his guest. "Don't be frightened, Miss. Everything is all right. My name is Aidan Lockwood. We met a few nights ago on the street…do you remember?"

LEIGHTON REGARDED the man in front of her and blinked, trying to clear the fog in her head. His face seemed vaguely familiar, but it was hard to think through the pounding in her head. It hurt to breathe, too. *What was wrong with her?* Every inch of her body seemed in agony. She closed her eyes for a moment, trying to recall her last memory. There was a storm brewing, and a bitter wind stirring everything in the street. A man who wouldn't let her pass. A bolt of lightning, horses spooked…and a different man standing in their path. The kind stranger who had smiled at her with friendliness in his eyes. The very same eyes that had looked down at her a moment ago. Oh, the pain she felt! It was making her positively nauseous. She opened her eyes with some effort and struggled to bring his image into focus. Yes, she remembered him. He had saved her from Peter Smythe. But was she now in just as dangerous a situation? She tried to speak, but nothing but a few squeaks came out, so she simply nodded instead.

"Drink a little of this," the woman beside her said, holding a spoon containing a small amount of what smelled like brandy to her lips. Leighton complied, nearly gagging at the surprising bitterness. "That's a good girl." She was rewarded with a sip of water to chase away the aftertaste. Leighton watched the man by her bedside warily as she tried to piece together her hazy memories.

"Can you tell me your name?" he asked gently.

Was there cotton stuffing in her head? It was hard to put a coherent thought together. When she finally spoke, she wasn't sure it was her own voice. "E…Elizabeth," she mumbled, using her middle name as she had for nearly eight years now, just as she did her grandmother's maiden name. As far as she was concerned, Leighton Courtwright was dead, and it was best if the rest of England thought that, too. There was only one person in the world Elizabeth trusted enough to tell her real name to, and that was Betsy. "Elizabeth Townsend."

"Miss Townsend," Aidan said. "Do you remember what happened?"

Elizabeth closed her eyes and thought hard, trying to clear the fog. "There…there was…a carriage," she said slowly. "You were in the way."

"Yes, that's right," Aidan smiled. "You pushed me to safety."

A faint smile touched her lips. "I knocked you down," she said listlessly, forcing her eyes open. "Were you hurt?" She could see now the damage to his face.

Aidan chuckled lightly. "Just a little." He was gazing down at her with something in his eyes that Elizabeth could not discern. He pulled his chair closer to the bed and sat, studying her. "You saved my life, Miss Townsend," he said softly. "I am forever in your debt."

Elizabeth blinked, not sure she was hearing things correctly. Men did not put themselves in debt to Elizabeth. They usually wanted something from her. Surely she must be dreaming. Or dead. No, that hardly seemed likely. She was in too much pain to be dead. She was certain a knife must be lodged in her side. She shifted to make the pain go away, but only succeeded in making herself wince.

"Please, Miss Townsend, you must lie still. You have broken ribs, and Lord only knows what else you have done."

She watched him with a guarded expression. Whatever that woman had given her was making her feel very strange.

"I will send for the doctor in the morning. He will be

pleased to know you have awakened." Aidan paused, seeming at a loss of what to say. "Miss Townsend, it is my wish that you remain here until you are fully recovered. It is the least I can do in return for your selfless act. Is there some family I may contact so as to inform them of your whereabouts?"

The question was an innocent one, but it sent a thread of yearning through Elizabeth's heart. Family. She longed to be able to tell this man that there was, indeed, someone who would be missing her, but the truth was, she was alone. The echoes of that harrowing summer's night eight years ago still rang in Elizabeth's head. She would never forget that man's voice as long as she lived. *Your family for mine, Mrs. Courtwright...Kill them...I will hunt her down.* But she'd never stopped believing that her parents were alive, and hopefully looking for her, too. So far, her search had been fruitless. But it was difficult to search when one had to stay in hiding.

"Miss Townsend?" Aidan prompted.

"No," she said quietly, jarred from her memories. "I have no one left." She closed her eyes against the memory as her head began to pound in earnest.

"I can see you need to rest," Aidan noted. "I shall take my leave of you now. Perhaps we may continue our conversation when you are feeling better." He stood to go, but not before he tried to allay her fears one more time. "You are quite safe here, Miss Townsend. Mrs. Bartlett, here, will oversee your care, and Mary has been assigned to you should you need anything." He nodded to Mrs. Bartlett and slipped from the room.

"Get some sleep now, dear," Mrs. Bartlett said, running a cool cloth over Elizabeth's forehead. "Are you comfortable enough?"

Elizabeth floated on a sea of bliss. She couldn't tell if the pain was finally starting to ebb or if she just couldn't be bothered to care about it anymore. She barely managed a mumbled answer before she slipped into oblivion.

CHAPTER 4

"N...no more." Elizabeth clamped her lips firmly against the spoon that was trying to pass them. She'd had enough of feeling fuzzy and detached from her body. She would deal with the pain. It reminded her she was still alive.

"Miss Townsend?"

Elizabeth cracked an eye open to find a young girl of about fifteen peering anxiously at her. She managed a weak smile.

"I don't want any," she mumbled, trying to reassure the girl.

"Beggin' your pardon, Miss?" The girl looked uncertain. "Are you sure?"

Elizabeth nodded.

"Can I get you some tea, Miss?"

"Please," Elizabeth croaked, not sure if the word sounded the same out loud as it did in her head. Everything was so difficult. She could barely open her eyes let alone put a coherent sentence together. She tried desperately to shake the fog that surrounded her like a shroud—not an easy task when all she wanted to do was sleep. She felt hands slip behind her head to help her drink, the cooled tea feeling wonderful on her parched throat. She couldn't remember the last time she'd had a decent cup of tea. Truth be told, she couldn't remember much of anything at the moment.

"Are you comfortable, Miss? Warm enough?"

"Yes, thank you," Elizabeth managed. She forced her eyes open to look at her companion. Through the haze, Elizabeth could see that she was a thin girl with huge brown eyes that twinkled, and mousy brown hair that was pulled back in a simple style. Her fair skin was covered with a smattering of freckles. She was staring at Elizabeth and wringing her hands.

"What's your name?"

"Mary Bartlett, Miss. The housekeeper's great-niece. I've been helping tend to you."

"I see." Elizabeth still couldn't tell if she was speaking clearly. Her tongue felt so thick, and the words didn't seem to want to come off of it. "Where am I again?"

"You're at Lockwood House, Lord Ashby's residence, Miss. Don't you remember? You've spoken to him several times now."

"Oh…yes, that's right," Elizabeth said sleepily. The man who'd been sitting by her bedside. Had they actually spoken? She couldn't remember. She just knew that he'd been floating at the edge of her consciousness, a ghost of a man.

Something filtered through her cloudy mind. "*Lord Ashby?*"

"Yes, Miss. That's right."

Gracious! She was in a *nobleman's* guest room? Mary must have seen the surprise on Elizabeth's face, because she rushed to reassure her. "He's a very kind man, Miss. You needn't worry. He'll take very good care of you."

Elizabeth grimaced. Kind men were rather like unicorns.

Mythical. She hadn't met a truly kind man in eight years. He did, however, deserve credit for caring for her while she recuperated.

"He'll be wantin' to talk to you. We haven't gotten much out of you these past days."

"Days?"

"Yes, Miss. You've been sleeping on and off for three days now."

"Three days? Goodness." Right now, going back to sleep sounded good. Anything to get rid of this haze. She didn't like this feeling one bit.

"You look like you could still use some rest," Mary noted. "Are you hungry at all?"

"I'm…not sure. Maybe a little."

"I'll bring you toast and some tea. Auntie said it would be best to start you off with something plain. How does that sound?"

"That's lovely, thank you," Elizabeth mumbled, already nodding off.

"Very good, Miss. I'll let you rest."

Elizabeth was asleep before Mary crossed the threshold.

It was much later in the afternoon when Elizabeth awoke again to find Lord Ashby himself sitting by her bedside. Good heavens, but the man was diligent. Elizabeth blinked to clear her blurry eyes and found that the fog that had surrounded her earlier had dissipated a bit. Unfortunately, the pain had increased, and she couldn't stifle the groan that accompanied a slight shift in position.

"How are you feeling, Miss Townsend?" Aidan asked, frowning slightly.

She studied him for a moment. He was much better

looking than she remembered. He had a finely chiseled jaw and high cheekbones, one of which was discolored with bruising. His straight nose led her eyes down to full, beautifully shaped lips. The man exuded confidence, elegance, and power, an intoxicating and very dangerous mix. Even sitting in the chair with his legs casually crossed, he resembled a panther about to pounce. He had a thick mass of dark hair that fell in perfect waves, curling about his ears and giving him a hint of a roguish look. It was a bit longer than was fashionable, but it suited him, Elizabeth thought. She hadn't seen him smile yet, but she had the feeling that when he did, it had a devastating effect on every female within twenty yards.

But it was his eyes that most intrigued her. They glittered with intelligence, and seemed to take in everything at a glance. They were a rich brown, so full of depth that Elizabeth thought she might completely disappear in those whiskey-colored pools.

His very intent gaze was leveled on her, awaiting an answer. Elizabeth sighed. "Everything hurts."

"Are you sure you do not want anything for the pain?"

Elizabeth held up her hand. "No, no more. I've lost three days as it is."

"Five, actually," he pointed out. At her look of disbelief, he said, "You slept for two days before you woke up and knew you were in pain. Do you remember anything?"

"Not since our first conversation."

Aidan regarded his guest thoughtfully for some time. Elizabeth waited, wondering what he could possibly be thinking. Was he sizing her up? Trying to decide how best to put her to use? Or was he pondering how he would let her "repay" him for all the trouble she had caused him? She shuddered.

He knit his brows together and frowned at her. "You are

still looking at me with apprehension in your eyes. Do I frighten you?"

Truthfully, *all* men made her uneasy. She wanted desperately to say no, she wasn't afraid of him, but her silence gave her away.

"I see." He leaned forward in his chair. "Well, at least you're not screaming this time." He flashed her a smile, and Elizabeth saw that she'd been right. *Devastating.*

"Miss Townsend, you have nothing to fear here. My staff will attend to your every need. Is there somewhere I may send someone to fetch you some clothing? I'm afraid what you were wearing is no longer suitable for the light of day."

Had it ever been? Elizabeth thought of the tiny room she rented that contained what few belongings she had. She couldn't risk going back there now that Smythe knew she was in town. What little there was would have to remain there indefinitely. She shook her head, embarrassed.

"Well then, it appears I will need to supply you with some new clothes." He stood up. "You are a guest in my home and are free to move about as you so choose…that is, whenever you are able. Shall I have Mrs. Bartlett arrange a tray for you? You must be hungry."

Elizabeth simply stared at him, mouth slightly agape. How had she gone from sleeping on a bug-infested straw mattress in a closet-sized room to lying in a comfy feather bed with a nobleman promising her food and clothing? And what was he going to want in return? "Why are you doing this?"

Aidan blinked. "I owe you my life, Miss Townsend. It's the least I can do."

Elizabeth shook her head slightly. "I cannot accept such charity."

Aidan raised his eyebrows in surprise. "It's hardly charity, Miss Townsend. How much do you think my life is worth?"

"That's not what I meant, my lord."

"My lord? Well, I guess that secret's out," Aidan said dryly. He went to the dresser to retrieve a hand mirror. He came back to the bed and held it so Elizabeth could see herself. "Tell me, Miss Townsend. What do you think *your* life is worth?"

Elizabeth gasped. She looked horrifying! She hardly even recognized herself because of the swelling. She was a mess of scrapes and bruises. Heavens, had she hit the ground face first? She reached up to touch her cheek, but even that small movement caused her pain. She flinched, and Aidan didn't miss it.

"Charity, indeed." He placed the mirror on the bedside table. "You've broken some ribs, Miss Townsend, and possibly fractured your shoulder. The doctor said you'll need at least six weeks, perhaps more before you're really feeling better. Until then, you'll be experiencing some discomfort."

That was putting it mildly. She noticed that he had a fierce-looking abrasion of his own that was still discolored. She gestured vaguely at it. "Did I do that?"

Aidan chuckled. "That, and then some. You're much stronger than you look, Miss Townsend."

"Not strong," she corrected him. "Just desperate."

"I'm very grateful, all the same." He clasped his hands behind his back. "You didn't answer me before. Are you hungry?"

Elizabeth paused for a moment before nodding. Being hungry had become a way of life for her—no one ever actually asked her if she was or not, and she had to think a moment before she knew the answer.

"You must be thirsty as well. Would you like some water?" He didn't wait for her reply before pouring some from a pitcher near her bedside.

He handed her the glass, which held perfectly clear water,

not the turbid kind she was used to drinking in the city. But she was so weak she couldn't hold the glass without trembling violently. He reached out and closed his fingers over hers. "Here, let me help you."

Elizabeth had frozen and was staring at the large, warm hand covering hers. He had beautiful hands. Strong hands that seemed to infuse their strength into hers. Her heart thundered in her chest as he slid his arm behind her shoulders and propped her up so she could drink. She was acutely aware of the solid muscle supporting her as she drained as much of the water from the glass as she could.

When she was finished, Aidan gently withdrew his arm, leaving her with the most peculiar sensation of loss. His simple gesture of kindness had sparked a vague memory of what it was like to feel...comforted. It was a foreign sensation. She blinked up at him, and the fleeting moment passed.

"If you'll excuse me, Miss Townsend," Aidan said, clasping his hands behind his back. "I have an appointment I must attend. I will be leaving on a business trip tomorrow, but fortunately, my sister is also due home tomorrow, and you'll be left in her capable hands. I trust you will get along just fine. I'll be sure to introduce you before I leave." He stopped in the doorway. "I'll have Mrs. Bartlett bring you a tray. Should you desire anything else, please don't hesitate to ask. Good day, Miss Townsend." He nodded and was gone.

Elizabeth stared after him in complete disbelief.

Well.

Perhaps she should have thrown herself in front of a carriage long ago.

CHAPTER 5

The next morning, Elizabeth awoke to sun streaming in the windows. The fog was finally gone from her head, and the light supper she had eaten last night had bolstered her some. She was sure now that she hadn't been dreaming. She really was lying in a huge, comfy bed, the likes of which she hadn't seen since she was much younger.

Whatever stroke of fate had sent her here, she was eternally grateful for it. Lord Ashby seemed friendly enough, although she could trust no man. She couldn't quite figure him out. He seemed to be genuinely concerned for her welfare, but she couldn't imagine why. She'd met many wealthy people like him in her new life, and every single one of them had let her know that she was nothing but the dirt beneath their feet. Why should he be any different? He was a peer, for heaven's sake! He should be looking further down his nose at her than anyone else ever had.

She tried to sit up, but it hurt too much. She was tired of lying on her back, but it seemed she was destined to remain there a bit longer. She sighed. Recuperating was going to be boring.

The door opened and Mary waltzed in. "Ah! You're up. Mornin', Miss Townsend. I was just coming to wake you. Can I get you some breakfast?" She came in with a tea tray and set it on the table in front of the fireplace.

All at once, Elizabeth realized how hungry she was. "I would love some, thank you."

"Very good, Miss." She set about putting a log on the fire to chase the chill away. "His lordship has asked the doctor to come and check on you today. He'll be here after breakfast. And Lady Elaine is coming home today. It'll be good to have her home again. You'll like her, Miss. She'll be good company while his lordship is away."

"So I've been told."

"Let me help you sit up, Miss Townsend. You can't very well eat like that, can you?" She brought the tea tray over to the bedside and then helped Elizabeth to a sitting position, which was no easy task. Mary poured a cup of tea and handed it to Elizabeth, who could barely hold it.

"Don't you worry, Miss," Mary smiled. "We'll be getting your strength back in no time. Just look at you, half starved, y'are. I'd best be fetching your breakfast so we can fix that." She winked at Elizabeth and disappeared. No matter how wary Elizabeth was of the mysterious man that owned the house, she liked his staff immensely.

Mary returned a short time later with a breakfast tray, and sat down to help Elizabeth eat. Elizabeth couldn't believe how pathetically weak she was.

"I'm sorry you get stuck helping me," she told the girl. "I'm usually much more self sufficient." She nibbled on some dry toast.

"Don't trouble yourself, Miss Townsend. I don't mind a

bit. Besides, it's my job." She grinned cheekily. "I'm training to be a lady's maid like Meg some day."

"Who is Meg?"

"Her ladyship's maid, Miss. And my best friend. She came to us last year and we became friends straightaway."

"It must be nice to have a good friend to work with you."

"Aye, Miss, it is. Makes the work more fun." She paused, knitting her brow. "Your friends must be worried about you, Miss Townsend."

Elizabeth eyed the chatty maid. Perhaps Elizabeth could make use of her, if she could trust her. "I only have one friend, and at the moment, I don't know where she is. I suspect we are worried about each other."

"Oh," Mary said softly. "I'm sorry to hear that. Is there anything I can do to help, Miss Townsend?"

"Perhaps, Mary. We'll see. But let's keep this just between us for now, all right? And please, you don't need to call me Miss Townsend."

"Beggin' your pardon, Miss?"

"My name is Elizabeth."

Mary's mouth dropped open slightly. "It wouldn't be proper for me to—"

"I may be his Lordship's guest, but I assure you, I cling to the bottom rung of society's ladder." Elizabeth smiled. "I could use a friend at the moment."

Mary toyed shyly with the plates on the tray. "I would like that." She glanced up at Elizabeth. "Perhaps…perhaps Miss Elizabeth, then."

Elizabeth smiled warmly at her and carefully sipped her tea. "If that suits you, it suits me as well."

Now, if only she could draw a breath without stabbing pain in her side!

≈

Aidan was in his study when he heard the carriage pull up in the drive. An unconscious smile played across his lips. Although he did his best to keep his heart walled up, his sister was the one person who could find the chink in his armor, and the house had been unbearably silent while she'd attended a friend's lying-in in the country. He wouldn't admit to himself how much he had missed her.

Tibbs entered the study. "Lord Ashby, Lady Elaine has arrived," he announced.

"Yes, I see. Thank you, Tibbs." He returned a sheaf of papers to the desk and left to greet his little sister.

She was in the front hall peeling off her gloves. She turned and flashed him a smile. "Hello, brother dear."

"It's about time you returned," he replied, kissing her cheek. "You stayed away too long."

"I just want to make sure you appreciate me," she said coyly. She pulled back from him and noticed his bruised face. "What on earth happened to you? Good heavens, were you in a *fight*? Can you not behave while I'm gone?"

Aidan chuckled. "I was not in a fight. I had a bit of an accident."

"An accident? What on earth happened? Are you hurt?"

"I'm fine. I do have some news to share with you, however."

"What is it?" she asked, knitting her brow in concern.

"Nothing to worry about. Come sit with me in the study while I tell you the whole sordid tale. Thanks to my stupidity, you very nearly didn't have a brother to come home to."

"What?!"

"Study, please," he said, ushering her inside. "Tibbs, some refreshments for our weary traveler."

~

"So she's here? Now?"

"Yes, and I'm afraid she's not in very good shape."

"I should think not." Lainey tried to absorb the story Aidan had related to her. She wanted to slap him for being so careless. He was all she had left. "But she will live?"

"Yes, it appears so. She began refusing the laudanum yesterday, so that's a good sign."

"My word, Aidan," Lainey said, shaking her head.

"I'd like to introduce you if she's awake. Mary's been assigned as her lady's maid, but I was hoping you could aid in her care while I'm away. She'll be restricted to bed rest, but I thought you could—"

"Entertain her?" Lainey interrupted, a smile coming into her eyes. "You know I'd be happy to do so."

"I am hoping that you will be able to get her to relax a little." Aidan sighed. "She doesn't seem to feel safe here, and apparently, I frighten her enormously."

Lainey stifled a grin. "I do repeatedly tell you that you need to smile more. You always have that scowl on your face. Perhaps if you had a woman who—"

"Lainey."

"Well, you promised Father—"

"I know what I promised. Father was a tortured soul. I would have said anything to make him happy in his last moments," Aidan snapped.

Lainey raised her eyebrows. "Gracious me. It seems I've hit a nerve." She rested her palm against his cheek. "I just miss my brother. The one who always had an easy smile and laughter in his voice. When did you get so serious, anyway?"

"When I became an earl and the responsibility of running a business and the estate fell upon my shoulders. Not to mention the care involved in having an unmarried sister," he said pointedly.

Lainey sighed and rolled her eyes. "Not now, Aidan. We

have more important things to worry about. Be a dear and introduce me to your guest," she replied, effectively changing the subject.

Aidan frowned at her as he offered her his arm. Lainey had been engaged two years ago, but the gentleman had unexpectedly broken it, and Lainey's heart as well. She had shown no sign of interest in any man since then. His sister was living proof of another reason not to give your heart to someone else for safekeeping. He sighed. "Very well. Shall we?"

Lainey put her hand in the crook of his elbow as he led her upstairs and knocked on the door of his guest's room. Mary's voice came from behind the door.

"Come in."

Aidan poked his head around the door. "Is Miss Townsend awake?"

"Yes, my lord."

Aidan stepped into the room, followed by Lainey. Elizabeth warily turned her head toward her visitors and Aidan's heart gave a little squeeze. Was he really that frightening?

Mary dropped a curtsey. "Welcome back, Lady Elaine. Did you have a pleasant journey?"

"Yes, Mary. Thank you." She smiled, knowing what the girl wanted to hear. "I'm sure Meg would love to see you."

Mary's face lit as she shifted from one foot to the other, and Aidan had to bite back a chuckle at the girl's anxiousness to be off. He smiled slightly and raised his eyebrow. "You'd best not keep her waiting, Mary."

Mary looked as though she might explode. "Yes, Lord Ashby." She dropped another hurried curtsey and practically flew from the room. Aidan turned his attention to the woman lying in bed.

"Miss Townsend. Mrs. Bartlett tells me you have refused further medication. How are you feeling this morning?"

"Less foggy, thank you."

"And the pain?"

Elizabeth gave him a half smile. "Hmm…less fog, more pain. But I can cope with it."

"I see." Aidan hesitated, studying her for a moment. Silence stretched between them before he seemed to abruptly remember that Lainey was standing beside him, and he turned to make introductions. "Lady Elaine Lockwood, may I present to you Miss Elizabeth Townsend? Miss Townsend, this is my sister, Lady Elaine."

Lainey moved forward to clasp her hand over Elizabeth's. "Miss Townsend, how can I ever thank you for saving my brother?"

Elizabeth smiled weakly. "I think your brother has taken care of it."

"Yes, he's very generous like that, isn't he?" She smiled at her brother. "I don't know what I would do without him, Miss Townsend. You must be his guardian angel."

"I'm quite positive I am no one's guardian angel, my lady, but I am glad I could be of assistance, as he was of assistance to me."

"Yes, so he told me. Despicable man, that Mr. Smythe." She patted Elizabeth's hand. "Don't you worry, Miss Townsend. You and I are going to be great friends, I'm sure of it. We'll get you all better before you know it."

Aidan cleared his throat. "I hate to interrupt, ladies, but I must be on my way." He kissed Lainey on the temple. "I won't be away more than a fortnight, though I doubt you'll even notice that I'm gone. I leave you in good hands, Miss Townsend," he said, turning his dark gaze on her. He gave her a brief nod and headed for the door.

"Try not to step in front of any speeding carriages," Elizabeth chided.

Aidan froze at the door, then slowly turned around.

"Are you…are you *teasing* me, Miss Townsend?" he said, raising an eyebrow.

Elizabeth shrank back into the pillow and regarded him warily. Perhaps it was best not to tease a peer. "Maybe just a little," she admitted weakly.

The faintest trace of amusement played across his lips, tugging at the corners of his mouth. "Hm. Good day, ladies," he said, and then he was gone.

Lainey turned to Elizabeth, who still had that frightened look on her face. "Don't let him fool you, Miss Townsend. He may look intimidating, but my brother has the most wonderful heart I know."

CHAPTER 6

 aris, France

AIDAN STARED out his hotel room window at the street below. "What do you suppose they are doing right now?"

Gavin propped his feet up on the table and leaned back on the sofa, linking his hands behind his head. "If I know your sister at all, she's probably regaling your guest with every embarrassing story from our youth that she can remember."

Aidan turned from the window in horror. "Gad, you're right! Hadn't thought of that." He poured them each a brandy, handed one to Gavin, and joined him by the fire. "Cheers."

"I can't wait to meet this girl," Gavin said, taking a good swallow. "She must be quite something if you are thinking of her so very often."

"Not so often," Aidan defended, sinking further into the comfortable leather chair.

"Aidan," Gavin said, casually crossing his ankles. "You've made some mention of her every day since we arrived."

Aidan's gaze snapped to his friend. "Have I?" When Gavin nodded, Aidan shrugged and sipped his brandy. "I can't help it, I feel responsible for her injuries. I did something incredibly stupid and she got hurt."

"Are you sure that's all you feel?"

"I owe the girl my life, Gav. I'll admit, she's on my mind. She's...an enigma." Aidan let his head fall back on the chair. "What the hell am I supposed to do with her? Let her wounds heal and put her back on the street?"

"You know you wouldn't do that. Besides, Lainey wouldn't let you even if you wanted to."

"My point exactly. So what do I do with her? I can't just set her up in a house. She's not my mistress, for God's sake. She's a complication I don't need in my life."

Gavin studied his friend. "I don't know, Aidan. I think you need a good complication."

"A woman is not a good complication." Aidan waved his glass in Gavin's direction. "Especially this one."

Gavin was silent for a moment. It was clear this girl had really ruffled Aidan's feathers. The question was, why? "I'm sure Lainey will have some idea of what to do with her. You needn't worry about a solution."

"I suppose." He frowned. His life was infinitely messier than it had been just a week ago.

Gavin swirled his brandy, letting the crackle of the fire fill the silence. "When are you planning on marrying, Aidan?" he asked without warning.

Aidan snapped to attention. "I beg your pardon?"

"I'm serious. You need an heir. You just turned thirty. Do you want to be an old man when you have your first child?"

"Of course not."

"Then what is it? You're not looking for love, so what's holding you back from just choosing someone?"

Aidan's jaw tightened. "A promise." He leaned forward and rested his elbows on his knees, studying his drink intently. He should never have made that blasted promise. "Besides, you know I need to get Lainey settled first," he said, shaking off the memory. "It's my duty as her brother."

"With all due respect, that is a lousy excuse."

"Lainey needs a husband."

"Just as you need a wife," Gavin pointed out. "Lainey will settle down when she wants to and not a moment before. You gave her that choice. She's more concerned about you right now."

"Gav, my sister is a romantic. She wants someone to sweep me off my feet, and that's not going to happen."

"Well, it sort of did. Perhaps not with the results Lainey wanted, but Miss Townsend *did* knock you down." He waggled his eyebrows at Aidan.

"Miss Townsend? Are you drunk?"

Gavin laughed. "I'm jesting, of course. But you gave me such an opening." He plunked his feet on the floor and leaned forward. "All Lainey wants is for you to be happy."

"Why do people keep insisting I'm not happy? I am perfectly content."

"That's a very different thing entirely." Gavin's blue gaze fell on his friend. "You were a very different man in your youth, Aidan. We all miss your ready laughter."

Aidan regarded him for a long moment, lost in thought. "Things change," he finally said.

"Yes, I know. The weight of the world fell on you when your mother died."

"I was just a child myself, but suddenly, all the responsibilities fell to me. You must remember. My father was useless! Lainey and I were forgotten entirely. She was eleven, for God's sake. She needed her father. And he wasn't there. He just—" Aidan stopped and glared down into his drink, a muscle twitching in his jaw. Several seconds ticked by before he could speak past the lump in his throat. "Have you ever watched someone die from a broken heart?"

"Actually, I have," Gavin said quietly.

Aidan sighed, scrubbing his hands through his hair. He was such an arse. How could he have forgotten Gavin's own mother? "Of course you have. Please forgive me for such a careless remark."

"Aidan." Gavin reached over and squeezed Aidan's forearm. "You've done well. Your estates are profitable. The business has thrived. Your good name weathered Lainey's broken engagement scandal with nary a black mark. You will do right by her, we all know you will. You gave up your youth to responsibility, and you are a great success. It is time to relax and find happiness once more."

Aidan's brow furrowed. "When did you become so philosophical? Is there something you're not telling me?" His eyes widened in alarm. "Oh good God, you're not in love, are you?"

Gavin burst out laughing. "Gad! Perish the thought!" He shrugged. "Perhaps I've let Lainey bend my ear a little too much lately."

"Ah, my meddling sister."

"She's worried about you. Be glad you have someone so special to care for you."

"I am. And you're right, I suppose. It is time to get serious about searching for a wife. Trouble is, I haven't met anyone I even *like* enough to consider. Debutantes were just the thing when I was twenty, but I've matured a bit since then. Now I just find them annoying."

Gavin chuckled. "Perhaps you should look beyond the debutantes, then."

"You mean widows?"

"Maybe. Or perhaps women who once might have been considered not so suitable a match for an earl. You said yourself, times are changing. Pedigree isn't quite as important as it used to be. I'm sure there are any number of governesses who would be thrilled to marry above their station. All intelligent women, which I believe is one of your criteria."

"A governess? Are you daft?" Gavin's expression told Aidan he was serious. "I can't marry a governess! I'm an earl, for Chrissake."

Gavin burst out laughing at his friend's indignation. "You may be an earl, Aidan, but sometimes, you are also a pompous arse!"

Aidan's eyebrows nearly disappeared into his hairline.

Then he roared with laughter and grinned at his friend.

"Bugger off."

CHAPTER 7

ondon

ONE WEEK LATER, Elizabeth took her first steps out of bed. She was supported on either side by Mrs. Bartlett and Lainey, for she could hardly stand on her shaking legs. She mentally cursed her weakness for the hundredth time.

"You're doing wonderfully, Elizabeth. Keep going," Lainey encouraged. The two women had, at Lainey's insistence, dispensed with the formal form of address. It had taken quite a bit of coaxing to get Elizabeth to call Lainey by her given name, but Lainey was not a woman who was easily deterred.

"I can already tell we are going to be good friends, Elizabeth, so we might as well save ourselves the trouble of being so exceedingly polite," she had said. "And absolutely none of my friends call me Elaine. I hate it! So it will have to be Lainey or nothing, as I will cease to answer to anything else."

That had settled it. It went against Elizabeth's upbringing to use the Christian name of someone she barely knew, but truth be told, she was glad to have things on the familiar level. However, she wasn't at all sure how Lainey's brother would take to her using the name Lainey's friends and family used.

They had talked about Aidan in his absence. Elizabeth was not entirely convinced Lainey's glowing reports weren't simply sibling bias, but Mrs. Bartlett and Mary seemed to hold him in high regard as well. He appeared to be a well-respected man, despite the fact that he "dirtied his hands" with trade, which even Elizabeth knew was frowned upon among peers. But he clearly had a successful business if this guest room was any indication of his wealth. No matter what her companions thought of him, Elizabeth was terribly glad that he wasn't around to hover over her and make her nervous.

Elizabeth had taken great care over the past week not to reveal much about her past at all, though Lainey had tried to get her to talk. Elizabeth always answered as honestly as she could, but gave very vague answers, letting Lainey fill in the blanks in her mind. Elizabeth hated to hide things, especially since she and Lainey had grown close over the past seven days, but she didn't dare tell anyone the truth—the Lockwoods would have her tossed out on the doorstep in no time at all. Plus, she'd been prevented from meeting Betsy, and therefore hadn't gained any information as of yet. Elizabeth was desperately worried that something had happened to her —she was a sweet girl who had a talent for uncovering information, but it was sometimes a dangerous pursuit. She was the only friend Elizabeth had known in London, so when Elizabeth had received Betsy's letter saying she may have discovered some information pertaining to Elizabeth's parents, she had returned to London immediately. She had tried to keep a low profile for several days, and was supposed to have met Betsy the night of the accident, only she had run into Smythe instead. *That wretched man!* Elizabeth worried that Betsy may have encountered foul play, and that Smythe had had something to do with it, and now here she was, trapped in this house in her invalid bed, not able to do a thing about it. The longer she stayed here, the closer she came to being discovered. She knew people had witnessed the carriage accident, possibly even Smythe, and he knew people of all classes. He could out her at any moment. All it would take was one word whispered in someone's ear in St. Giles, and the tale of Elizabeth's London past would wend its way through the grapevine up to the *ton,* and scandal would land itself on the Lockwood's doorstep. She'd either hang for what she'd done, or the man who she was sure had been chasing her for years would finally catch up with her. She was desperate to leave before any damage was done to this family who had taken her in and cared for her. She willed her body to heal faster.

She made it as far as the chair by the fire and gave up. Her legs were shaking so badly she had to sit down, but the bending motion hurt her side.

"For heaven's sake," she growled. "I can't even sit down on my own. Nothing seems to want to work!"

"Beggin' your pardon, Miss, but that's to be expected. You came to us half-starved, took a beating, and then spent the past two weeks lying in bed," Mrs. Bartlett pointed out. "Did you really think you were just going to pop up and be on your way?"

"No," Elizabeth grumbled. "It's just frustrating. I'm used to being independent."

"Well," Lainey said, "I guess it's about time you just relax and enjoy having someone take care of you."

"I'm sorry, Lainey. I don't mean to sound ungrateful for your hospitality, it's just...well..."

"I understand, Elizabeth. But you are making good

progress. Dr. Lambert will be here soon, and he'll be happy to see that you are up and about. I'm sure you'll get your strength back in no time."

Elizabeth sighed. "I hope so, because I'm going to go mad lying in that bed!"

~

FOUR MORE DAYS HAD PASSED. Dr. Lambert had been pleased with Elizabeth's progress and had bound her ribs to make her more comfortable. Her shoulder seemed to be healing, and although she still couldn't lean much weight on it, she could move it a little. Cook made sure their guest was well fed, and Elizabeth was beyond grateful for the meals that were prepared for her. She hadn't eaten this well since she had fled her burning home, and the effects of good nutrition were just beginning to show.

Mary strode in with the morning tea, Lainey right on her heels.

"Good morning, Miss Elizabeth. Did you sleep well? Wait till you see what a lovely day it is outside!" Mary set the tray down and threw open the balcony door. Elizabeth felt the slight brush of warm air float over her.

"Goodness, that feels heavenly! But how unusual for this time of year."

"Perhaps spring will come early," Mary observed, taking a deep breath.

"Perhaps." Elizabeth fell silent as she looked from Mary to Lainey and back again.

"What is it that you need, Elizabeth?" Lainey asked. "I can tell it's something."

Elizabeth glanced down at the sheet as she twisted it in her fingers. "I was hoping...if it wasn't too much trouble...I haven't had a real bath in a very long time, and would desperately like to soak in one. I thought it might help ease the ache in my muscles, and Dr. Lambert said my wounds were healed enough to—"

"Elizabeth!" Lainey laughed. "Don't be ridiculous! You may take a bath whenever you so choose. You do not need permission."

"But I do need help…I don't want to be a bother."

"Stop. Mary, have Meg help you prepare a bath for Miss Elizabeth. Make sure it's hot, and put some lavender oil in it, too—no, make it lilac," she mused, a mischievous glint coming into her eyes. "It suits her more."

"Yes, ma'am. Miss Elizabeth…"

"Yes, Mary?"

"Might we also see to your hair? Beggin' your pardon, but it's a frightful mess."

Elizabeth laughed out loud, grabbing her side. She loved Mary's straightforward ways. "Yes, I'm sure that it is. It may take you hours just to get a comb through it."

"I've never met a head of hair I can't handle, Miss."

Elizabeth giggled as Mary dashed from the room. Lainey helped Elizabeth sit up straighter and stayed with her while she ate her breakfast. Mary and Meg bustled in and out of the room while the two women chatted.

"You know, Elizabeth, we're going to have to get you some clothes. My brother is due back in a few days. Now that you can get out of bed, it wouldn't do to have you wandering about the house in a nightgown."

Elizabeth turned pink at the thought.

"You can borrow some of mine until we can do something about that."

"Oh, Lainey, I couldn't—"

"I insist."

"Miss Elizabeth, we're ready for you," Mary announced. She and Lainey helped Elizabeth out of bed and they slowly made their way into the bathing room, where they removed her nightgown and bandages and assisted her into the bathtub. Elizabeth sank down into the hot water gratefully as Mary took the soap and cloth and began to scrub gently. Elizabeth was in heaven. She closed her eyes and let the heat ease the ache from her body and the lilac soothe her senses. If she died in this very spot, she'd be happy.

When Mary was done bathing her, she moved on to Elizabeth's mass of dark tresses. Mary lathered her hair, rinsed, and began with the comb. She sat and worked diligently for the next half hour while Lainey entertained Elizabeth with more stories of her youth.

"It sounds like your brother was a bit of a scoundrel," Elizabeth mused, a lazy smile on her face.

"He still is a scoundrel, if you ask me. He just hides it better now."

Elizabeth laughed. "I'll keep that in mind." She paused, not sure if she should ask the question in her thoughts, but her curiosity overwhelmed her. "Tell me, Lainey, how is it that someone like Lord Ashby isn't yet married? He's titled, and it seems he's wealthy...and he's...erhm..."

"Attractive?" Lainey's eyes danced.

Elizabeth stared down at the bath water to hide her embarrassment and shrugged her good shoulder. "I would think that he would be descended upon at every moment."

Lainey waved her hand. "He is. He and Gavin both are. But they both manage to resist. I don't know what Gavin's excuse is, but I know Aidan is determined to not fall in love."

Elizabeth's eyes widened. "Why on earth would he want to avoid love?" That was all Elizabeth had ever wanted.

"I'll let him explain it to you. I think he's being ridiculous. And of course, he doesn't realize that he has no choice in the matter anyway." Lainey laughed. "Nevertheless, he's looking for a specific kind of woman, and he just hasn't found her.

Yet," she added, sending a sideways glance at Elizabeth. "Someday he may surprise himself and discover that what he thinks he wants and what he really needs are two very different things," she mused.

Lainey didn't supply any more information, so Elizabeth was left wondering what type of woman *would* interest Lord Ashby. She didn't wish to be any more impertinent than she already had been, so she changed the subject. "You mention Mr. Mayfield's name often. Is he an old friend of the family?"

"I've known Gavin my whole life. He's Aidan's best friend and his business partner. He's quite charming, as I'm sure you'll see when you meet him. The two of them are a couple of heartbreakers, if you ask me. Many scheming mamas have tried to snare them for their daughters, but they refuse to be caught. I swear, men can be such bloody idiots about love."

She grinned cheekily, and Elizabeth giggled while Mary stated that Elizabeth's hair was finally free of tangles. She lathered and rinsed it again, and then pronounced Elizabeth presentable.

Getting in the tub had been the easy part, Elizabeth soon discovered. She gritted her teeth, but still yelped as they hauled her out of the tub and wrapped her in a towel. Once she was dried off and rebound into her bandages, Lainey helped her into a simple cotton wrapper that absolutely hung on her. Lainey laughed out loud.

"Well, it's not exactly a perfect fit, is it?"

"It is just a hair too big, I think." Elizabeth giggled.

"No matter. You'll fill it out soon enough." Lainey held her arm out to Elizabeth. "Come and sit by the fire while I brush your hair."

CHAPTER 8

idan arrived home later that afternoon, grateful to be off of ships and trains, and out of carriages at last. Tibbs met him at the door, taking his coat and hat.

"Welcome home, my lord. I trust you had a good trip?"

"I did. Quite successful."

"Good news, sir. Will you be wanting some refreshment?"

"Yes, I think that would do nicely."

"Very good, sir. Lady Elaine is having tea on the balcony. With Miss Townsend."

"Miss Townsend?" Aidan couldn't keep the surprise from his voice.

"Yes, sir. Your guest."

"Yes, Tibbs, I am aware of who she is. She's doing much better, then?"

"I'll let you be the judge of that, sir. Will you be joining them?"

Aidan paused. "Tea sounds lovely," he said, already heading for the balcony.

"Very good, sir," Tibbs replied to the air.

~

ELIZABETH HAD MUCH BEEN on Aidan's mind the entire ten days he'd been gone. Curious, that. He had tried to pass it off to Gavin as concern for her welfare, but if he were being honest with himself, he'd have to admit that it was something more than gratitude. She fascinated him. She was a mystery he needed to unravel, a story begging to be told. And he was very much looking forward to hearing it.

He went out to the balcony and followed the sound of Lainey's voice, stopping short when he rounded the corner.

Elizabeth was sitting facing him, but he went unnoticed. She was snickering at whatever Lainey had said to her, and Aidan realized it was the first time he had seen her smile. It lit up her entire face and captivated Aidan so completely that it rooted him to the ground.

The change in her since he had seen her last was almost too much to comprehend. There were still shadows under her eyes, but her skin had taken on a more natural color. The early afternoon sunlight touched her hair, lighting it on fire with cinnamon highlights peeking through the dark strands. It had obviously been washed and brushed till it shone. The mats were gone and it now hung in loose waves about her shoulders and halfway down her back. Aidan's belly tightened as he watched her. For once, her eyes held nothing in them but laughter.

That is, until they fell on him.

"Good afternoon, ladies."

Elizabeth's smile vanished from her face instantly. Lainey, however, launched to her feet and ran to hug her brother.

"Welcome home, brother dear. You're early! How was your trip?"

"It was good, thank you. I trust you two have gotten to know each other a bit?" he smiled, glancing at Elizabeth. She was staring at him like he was about to rush at her with a knife.

"Oh, yes!" Lainey exclaimed. "We've been taking good care of her. See how well she looks!"

"Yes, I see," Aidan said softly. "How are you feeling, Miss Townsend?"

She blinked. "Better than when we last spoke. Thank you."

She said nothing more. Aidan couldn't stop looking at her, Lainey forgotten at his side. She cleared her throat.

"Well," she said, breaking the silence. "I wish I had known you were coming home today, Aidan. I promised Anne I would call on her this afternoon."

"Then go you must," he said, kissing her temple. "Will you be home for dinner?"

"I promise. Then we can finally catch up with each other."

"I look forward to it. May I see you out?"

Lainey turned to Elizabeth. "Forgive me, Elizabeth. Will you excuse me? I'm sure Aidan will keep you company."

Aidan watched Elizabeth's eyes widen in alarm. For heaven's sake. Clearly he was still frightening. He offered his arm to Lainey and nodded to Elizabeth. "May I join you in a moment?"

Elizabeth looked panic stricken, but she managed a tight smile. "Of course."

"Excellent." Aidan was ready for some answers.

"So what have you been able to learn of our houseguest?"

"Not much, I'm afraid," Lainey replied. "She's not very forthcoming with information."

"She's hiding something?"

"Most definitely. But it's not that she's necessarily hiding information to be secretive; it's more like she's afraid to

reveal it, if that makes any sense. She's been through something terrible, Aidan, I just know it."

"The question is what?"

"I haven't any idea. But she can't have always been so
poor. She's very well educated."

"Yes, I've noticed."

"And she has good manners. She was taught how to
behave properly, that's for sure. She's quite fascinating, actually. But then you'll find that out for yourself, won't you?" she
grinned. "Go easy on her, brother. She's as skittish as a
rabbit."

"Yes, I've noticed that, too," Aidan said, pursing his lips in
thought.

"And you simply must make arrangements for Mrs. Essex
to come and fit her for some decent clothes. Mine are too big
for her, and what she arrived in is nothing more than rags,
though she wouldn't let me throw out that moth-eaten cloak
of hers. It must have some special meaning to her. She'll need
some morning gowns, and of course a tea gown and a dinner
gown. Something suitable for company, just in case. Oh,
and—"

"Aren't you late for your engagement?"

Lainey giggled at his obvious hint. "Fine. I'll see you at
dinner."

"Give Miss Hastings my best." He kissed her on the
temple and saw her to the waiting carriage. Once she was
safely on her way, Aidan headed back out to the balcony to
join Elizabeth.

THE INSTANT AIDAN came round the corner, Elizabeth
stiffened. While Lainey had been gentle in her quest to find

out more about her, Elizabeth wasn't too sure the earl was going to be as easy to handle.

"May I sit?"

Elizabeth nodded, eyeing him. He chose the seat opposite her and leaned back in a deliberately casual pose. "I am much relieved to find you better, Miss Townsend," he began. "I fear my guilt would have followed me all my life had you not improved."

"I am no one to be so concerned over, my lord," she replied. "And I was merely returning a favor. What happened was my own doing."

"But you wouldn't have been hurt had I been paying attention." He paused. "Then again, I suppose neither one of us would have been in danger had you not run away."

Her cheeks flamed. "I'm sorry," she said, unable to look him in the eye. "I was afraid."

"As you are now."

Her gaze snapped up to meet his. The retort she had ready died on her lips when she caught sight of his sorrowful expression.

"I don't bite, Miss Townsend."

"I…I beg your pardon?"

"You are looking at me like I'm a rabid animal about to attack," he pointed out. "I'm actually a decent man once you get to know me."

A nervous twitter burst forth from her lips. "Forgive me, my lord. I have not known many decent men in my life. They all make me rather nervous."

Aidan nodded. "I can certainly understand." He took a sip of tea. "So are you from London, Miss Townsend?"

"No. I came by way of Kent." She bit her lip. It wasn't exactly a lie; it just wasn't the whole truth. She had to be careful to give both brother and sister the same information, but they were intelligent people and it wouldn't be long before they became unsatisfied with her vague answers.

"Do you have family there?"

"No," Elizabeth replied. "I've been on my own for quite some time. My parents died when I was young."

"I'm sorry to hear that. Mine have both passed on as well." He set the cup in its saucer. "Miss Townsend, if you don't mind my asking, how old are you?"

"I will be two and twenty in June." She paused. "And you?"

He raised his eyebrows, but he answered her. "I just turned thirty. Three days after we met, actually." He glanced about and noted with some surprise the book lying on the table near Elizabeth. "Do you read, Miss Townsend?"

She nodded. "Anything I can get my hands on, though that hasn't been much, lately."

He leaned forward and studied her intently. "Miss Townsend, forgive my being forward, but you seem rather well-educated for someone of your…circumstances," he finished lamely.

Elizabeth gave a small laugh. "My father believed everyone deserved an education, no matter what their station in life." That statement was entirely true. Her father had made sure each one of his servants knew how to read and write, and learned anything else he could teach them.

"Was he a teacher?"

"No, but he was very smart. Actually, he was a business-man. Something I hear he has in common with you," she added, grasping the opportunity to change the subject.

"Ah, I see Lainey has been talking."

"Yes. I've learned quite a bit about you in your absence," she teased.

"I see I have some catching up to do, then."

"Tell me about your business," Elizabeth said, desperate to steer the conversation away from herself. "I thought noblemen didn't usually engage in such lowly pursuits," she said with a small smile.

"Normally, they don't. My father was a businessman before he was a peer. He had started a business importing silks and other luxury fabrics, and by the time he was three-and-twenty he was turning a healthy profit. The earldom was quite unexpected. And though he was very proud of his title, he was a working man through and through, and he refused to give it up. When he passed, I took over everything."

"Do you like it?"

"Yes, actually, I do. It keeps me busy and gives me purpose. I get to travel and meet all sorts of people, and even Lainey helps every now and again. Plus, I'm very popular with the ladies in town." Elizabeth's mouth dropped open at his candid words and he couldn't help but chuckle. "I'm teasing you, Miss Townsend."

"Oh! Of course. Because of the silk. For dresses." She couldn't seem to stem the flow of stupidity, so she gulped her tea to stop the babbling, hiding behind the comfort of the cup. What was it about this man that rattled her so? She hadn't meant to reveal that bit of information about her father. It had just tumbled from her lips in a moment of nervous chatter. Lord Ashby seemed genuine, yet Elizabeth had never known a good man in her life, other than her father, and she didn't want to trust that he could really be so kind. It was still early yet. She had learned long ago that people were never what they seemed at first.

Aidan broke into her thoughts. "Speaking of dresses, my sister tells me I have been remiss in your care. Now that you are up and about, you'll need some decent clothing to wear. I'll arrange to have Mrs. Essex pay you a visit as soon as you feel up to it so she can get you some dresses made. She's the best dressmaker in town—I think she's made just about everything Lainey owns."

"Oh no, you needn't bother!"

"I insist. For heaven's sake, I have made my fortune in fabric. What would people say if I didn't at least clothe you properly?"

"But—"

"It's the least I can do. And I do get a good discount," he added wryly.

Elizabeth smiled. For such a serious-looking man, he did seem to have some sense of humor. "I have no doubt." She thought a moment. "I do know how to sew. Perhaps you could send Mary to purchase something secondhand at the market that I could alter to fit." It would also be a good opportunity for Mary to ask after Besty.

Aidan raised his eyebrows in surprise. "An accomplished seamstress as well?"

"It's how I earned a living in Kent," she admitted. "And I wouldn't go so far as to say I'm accomplished. I took in mending and laundry, hardly a highly skilled trade. It was hard work for very little pay, but it kept a roof over my head and some food on the table."

"I see." Aidan regarded her silently, a myriad of indiscernible emotions flickering across his face. "Miss Townsend, I appreciate your thoughtfulness, but you need only to focus on getting better. It's just a few dresses. I would like to do this for you."

"But I really can't accept—"

"I would like to do this for you," he repeated, leaning forward. "To thank you." The words were softly said, but his tone brooked no argument.

Elizabeth squirmed in her chair. She had sold most everything she had to travel to London, and what was left probably wasn't going to land her respectable work. She desperately needed money at the moment. What was one or two work dresses to this man? She didn't want to be beholden to him, but she really had no choice. "Very well, then. Thank you for your generosity. But I will pay you back."

Aidan shrugged. "As you wish. I'll send a note over now." He stood to go. "If you'll excuse me, Miss Townsend, unfortunately I have to catch up on all the estate business I missed while I was away. And, you look rather tired."

"Yes," she sighed. "I still don't have quite the energy I should have."

"It will come back, Miss Townsend. Give yourself some time. You're looking much better already." He nodded to her. "Good afternoon."

With a slight bow, he turned and left, and Elizabeth exhaled slowly. Well, that had been...interesting. Lord Ashby had been looking at her as though she were his favorite baked treat before he'd recovered himself and slipped on his lordly demeanor. But for those few seconds, she'd seen a surprising vulnerability in his eyes. Perhaps he wasn't the man on the inside that he wanted everyone to see on the outside. There were cracks in his reserved façade, and for a moment, Elizabeth allowed herself to wonder who this man would be if he let down his guard.

But only for a moment. There was no point in trying to get to know him. She would be on the run again soon enough—there was certainly no place in her life for an earl.

The sun was getting lower in the sky, and the temperature was beginning to drop, so Elizabeth gathered her book and went back into her room to lie on the chaise by the fire. She'd only read a few sentences before she fell fast asleep.

CHAPTER 9

A few days later, Elizabeth asked Mary to put her hair up and help her with the wrapper Lainey had given her. With Lainey's permission, she had made some alterations to it so that it now fit her appallingly thin frame... more or less. Elizabeth studied herself in the mirror. It was always a shock to see the pale, malnourished person who had taken over the vibrant girl she used to be. She did her best to avoid mirrors. They only reminded her of everything she had lost.

She slowly limped her way out of the room. It felt odd to be wandering about a total stranger's house alone, but she couldn't bear to be trapped in that room one more minute, and her host did say she was free to look around as she pleased.

He was a different sort of man, this Lord Ashby. He still came to visit with her every day, and they had gotten to know each other a little. Elizabeth still couldn't quite make out his character. He had an air of seriousness about him that didn't seem like it was his true nature, because when he did smile his face lit with a brillliance that made Elizabeth's heart flutter. He exuded the self-confidence of the upper class, but he never used it to make her feel small. He could be charming, polite, and proper, then in the next instant, he could look at her so intently that her breath would be stolen completely away.

He was exactly the kind of man she feared most.

Yet there was something about him that drew her in, an energy that ignited the air around him. She had felt so oddly protected when he had stepped between her and Smythe. And the way he had looked at her on the street...it had completely unnerved her. It was like he could see right into her soul. She'd trusted a man like that once.

Trust was a luxury she could no longer afford.

She was struggling to get down the stairs, puzzling about the man who had come to her rescue, when all of a sudden, he was there again, repeating his performance.

"Miss Townsend? May I be of assistance?"

She started and turned to face him, trying not to grimace at the stab of pain the sudden movement caused. "I couldn't stand one more minute of lying in that bed—comfortable though it is," she added apologetically.

"I see." Aidan nodded. "Being a restless soul myself, I can certainly understand your predicament. But are you sure you are ready to be up and about?"

"Ready or not, here I am. Lainey had mentioned you had a library I might like to visit. I didn't think that would be too taxing."

"Except for the trip there," he said, amusement twinkling in his eyes. "Please, you must let me assist you before you fall."

"Oh, no, that's not necessary. I can—"

"I insist," he said, laying her hand on his arm. "I didn't pick you up off the cobblestones only to have you fall down my stairs and break your neck."

His hand was warm over hers, and it rattled her to have him so close. Her pulse began to pound in her ears, and she had no choice but to lean on him because her legs were beginning to shake with the effort of her descent. Surely her physical weakness was what was causing her knees to wobble. *Wasn't it?*

As if sensing her dilemma, Aidan said, "You do realize that you will have to come back up these stairs at some point."

Elizabeth laughed in spite of herself, unconsciously bringing her hand to her aching side. "I have all day."

"Perhaps I should endeavor to not make you laugh." Aidan's brows knit together in concern.

"Oh please, my lord, I beg you not to be more serious!" Elizabeth turned scarlet at the look of surprise on his face. "I…I mean…I'm sorry," she stammered. "I just meant that I dearly like to laugh."

"And perhaps I could use more of that as well?"

"Oh. Well. Perhaps." She gave him an overly bright smile and glanced down the stairs. Too many more to go. She envisioned sliding down the banister just to get away from Lord Ashby faster. She giggled at the thought.

"Do I make you nervous, Miss Townsend?"

"What? Ah. Well, erhm…" Hysterical laughter threatened to bubble up out of her throat. She knew the answer was painfully obvious, but she could see he was still going to force her to admit it. "As a matter of fact, yes, you do."

"And why is that?" He smiled. "I think we've established that I don't bite."

"True." Elizabeth searched her mind for some reason to give him. "I…I've never known an earl before. I'm afraid my behavior might not be proper enough for you." Oh, for heaven's sake, was that the best she could do?

He turned to face her, and leaned so close she could smell the soap he used to shave. "Miss Townsend?"

She swallowed hard. "Yes?"

"You are a terrible liar." He held her gaze for a few heartbeats before he straightened, and they continued down the stairs.

Elizabeth's heart was thumping like a scared rabbit's. Surely he could feel her pulse racing right through the sleeve of his coat. There would be no hiding the truth from this man for very long.

They finally arrived at the bottom of the stairs. "Ah, here we are, safe at last," he said, keeping his hand securely over hers. "How did you fare?"

"I am…surprisingly tired," Elizabeth admitted. She wasn't sure how she was going to get back up the stairs once she'd selected her book.

"Then perhaps you should allow me to escort you to the library. To ensure your safety," he added.

She was about to protest, but he gently guided her away from the stairs. A sheen of perspiration dampened her brow. *From her exertion, of course. Definitely not because she was on the arm of a handsome man.* She allowed him to lead her down the hall toward the back of the house. The warmth he provided seeped through the muslin of her dress as she leaned heavily on him, accepting his strength. How he could make her so anxious and yet comfort her at the same time?

"I'll have Mary bring you some tea in the library, if that is to your liking," he said, breaking into the silence.

"That sounds lovely, thank you." She glanced about her, just beginning to notice how large his house was. "You have a splendid home, my lord."

"It's been in the extended family for generations, though my father only inherited it in his mid-twenties. Perhaps not as fashionable an address as Mayfair, but I prefer the space it affords me. And the peace. London proper is far too crowded and noisy—the outskirts suit me just fine."

"I completely understand. I've never been much of a city girl myself. I much more enjoy the freedom of the country."

"Were you raised in the country?"

"Yes."

Aidan waited, but no further information came. "Whereabouts?"

"North of here." Elizabeth smiled, her eyes crinkling in amusement.

"There's a lot of country north of here, Miss Townsend."

"Yes, I know."

"You'll have to be a little more specific, I'm afraid."

"You can't possibly expect me to reveal all of my secrets, my lord. I would lose my mysterious air," she teased. *Please stop asking questions!* she wanted to scream.

He stopped walking and turned to gaze down at her, a smile playing at the corners of his mouth. "Correct me if I'm wrong, Miss Townsend, but I don't believe you've revealed *any* of your secrets thus far. Except that you *have* secrets to reveal," he said, the velvet in his voice reaching out to her in an intimate caress. He pinned her with a stare and she flushed, realizing that she had just openly admitted that she was hiding something. He leaned a bit closer to her. "Did I mention how much I like to solve mysteries?"

And just like that, the intense Lord Ashby appeared and stole her breath away. She shrank back from him, cursing herself for getting too chatty. *Damn him and his ability to fluster her!* He flashed her a devilish grin and slipped his arm past her to open the door to the library. He stepped back and gestured for her to enter.

Elizabeth gasped as she entered the room. Shelves of books surrounded her, the floor-to-ceiling windows letting in plenty of natural light. The room was appointed nicely, definitely to a man's taste, but it was welcoming and inti-mate, dotted with comfortable-looking leather chairs and thoughtfully placed tables, a cozy fireplace at one end. She wanted to live in here and forget every horrible detail of her life. It was why she liked to read so much—she could escape everything in a book.

"Is this agreeable to you?" Aidan asked from behind her. She turned to answer him, realizing for the first time that he was a full head taller than she was, which left her staring at a rather broad chest. He was standing too close. She caught another whiff of his soap. Sandalwood. Definitely sandalwood.

"It's heavenly." Was she talking about the library or the way he smelled? She wasn't entirely sure.

"Excellent. Then I trust you will have enough to keep you occupied while I attend to some business in town."

"I think I can find something to do," she said, her expression one of mock seriousness.

"In that case, Miss Townsend, I shall take my leave of you. Have a pleasant day." He sketched a shallow bow and turned to leave.

"Lord Ashby?"

He turned at the door. "Yes, Miss Townsend?"

"My…my name is Elizabeth. I appreciate your propriety, but you needn't address me as Miss Townsend."

Aidan frowned. "Does it offend you?"

"Of course not. I just…I am…no one, and yet you treat me as though I were a proper lady. I'm used to being just 'Elizabeth.'"

He paused, studying her with that dark gaze of his. "Miss Townsend, I assure you. You are, indeed, someone. A very selfless someone who didn't give a thought to her own safety when she saved the life of a very drunk and very stupid man, and you are every inch a lady. Do not sell yourself short." He hesitated a moment more before saying, "You may call me Aidan if you wish. Or Ashby. But truth be told, I prefer Aidan."

Elizabeth shook her head. "That would be most improper, my lord."

"And yet you call Lainey by her given name."

"Lainey is different."

"How so?"

"Well, she's a woman, for one thing. And I believe we've become friends, so that makes it acceptable."

"I see." Aidan looked down at her, an expression on his face she couldn't discern. One side of his mouth curved up slightly. "Perhaps one day you and I will be friends as well. Good day, Miss…Elizabeth."

CHAPTER 10

The rain had stopped, and it was another fairly warm day for March, so Aidan decided to walk home. As he strolled along, he thought of Elizabeth, as he seemed wont to do every day. It bothered him to his very core that he should be so preoccupied with her. He was usually very focused on business, with a drive to succeed, yet this morning's meeting with Gavin had been agonizing. He couldn't stop his mind from wandering to thoughts of her, the feel of her hand on his arm, the essence of lilacs in her hair...how *was* it that she managed to smell like his favorite spring bloom? It was uncanny.

Perhaps it was the mystery that surrounded Elizabeth that made him want to talk to her every day, to try to peel away another layer of secrets so he could find out who she really was.

But did he want to know? Was she right about what she had said this morning? Would knowing ruin all the intrigue, or was it more than the mystery that made her so compelling? He knew one thing for sure. He hated the way she looked at him with mistrust in her eyes. No matter how kind he was to her, no matter what he could possibly think of to do that would put her at ease, she always had that same look in her eyes, and it irritated him to no end. She was afraid of him, and he couldn't fathom why.

He was so lost in thought that he collided with someone on the street. "I beg your pardon." He looked up and was met with an unwelcome but familiar face. The muscles in his jaw tightened. "You again."

"Lockwood. So soon we meet again," Peter Smythe ground out. "Heard you took home the girl you stole from me."

"I don't recall taking anything that belonged to you, Smythe. And the name's Lord Ashby."

"Yer fancy title don't mean a thing to me, Lockwood. Neither did your father's."

"Apparently his friendship didn't mean anything to you, either."

A flicker of anger flared on Smythe's face. Peter Smythe and Thomas Lockwood had been boyhood friends long before Aidan's father had unexpectedly inherited his title. Peter had never been as smart or as well liked as Thomas, and as they grew up, though Thomas tried to keep the friendship alive, it became more and more apparent that they were not destined to travel in the same circles. When Thomas became a peer, Peter had to hide the jealousy it caused even though it ate away at him inside, because he recognized the value of having a titled man for an acquaintance. All friendship had ceased, however, when Peter fell desperately in love with Marianne, yet she chose Thomas instead of him. He thought Thomas had plotted to steal her away from him, and his lofty title had secured her attentions. Peter's jealousy erupted into rage and bitterness, and he secretly plotted to seek revenge on Thomas. Peter Smythe had spent a lifetime hating his former friend, and when

Thomas died, Peter's hatred passed on to Thomas's son. Aidan wondered if Peter even remembered why he was still so angry.

"You'd best watch yourself, *my lord*," Smythe ground out. "You may have gotten more than you bargained for with that one." He snorted. "T'would serve you right. Like father, like son." He stalked away, leaving Aidan puzzled.

What on earth had he meant by that? Did he know Elizabeth? Lord help him if Smythe was the one he had to turn to for help in discovering her identity. He was the last person on earth Aidan wanted to deal with, for anything.

He decided to try asking the person in question directly, and he would start by inquiring about that gold charm she had around her ankle.

AIDAN WAS NOT surprised to find Elizabeth curled up in his favorite chair, sound asleep. He had often succumbed to slumber there himself.

She looked like an angel lying there with a book tipped up on her chest, her bare feet poking out from beneath the hem of her dress, her head tilted to the side, and one arm hanging over the edge of the chair. Her hair flowed loosely about her shoulders—she had obviously taken the pins out after Aidan had left. Clearly, she preferred to have her tresses free. Aidan preferred them that way, too. A man could really tangle his hands into hair like that.

What the hell? He shook his head to clear it and was about to turn away, not wishing to disturb her, when her eyes fluttered open and locked with his. She blinked in confusion, and then realized she had fallen asleep in Aidan's library. She sat up with a start and a wince, and he held up his hand.

"Don't get up. I just came to check on you."

"I'm sorry. I shouldn't still be here."

"It's quite all right. I trust you found everything to your liking?"

Elizabeth blushed. "Apparently so."

"May we talk?"

"Of course," she replied, eyeing him warily.

Aidan seated himself in the chair opposite her. "I ran into Peter Smythe on my way home from Mr. Mayfield's this morning. He seems to claim some acquaintance of you. Do you know him?" It was clear that she did from the way her face drained of the small amount of color she had at the mention of his name, but Aidan waited for her answer.

"Not...not well," she admitted, her gaze flicking around the room. "I met him long ago. He had a certain...fondness for me that I did not return."

"Why does that not surprise me?" Aidan said wryly. "It seems Smythe has faced such difficulties most of his life." He paused. "How did you meet?"

Elizabeth looked distinctly uncomfortable. "I was a server in a tavern when I was young. He used to frequent the place."

Aidan regarded the woman in front of him and tried to picture her working in a tavern. He had been in many in his lifetime, and even the tamest were a bit dangerous. A knot formed in his stomach at the thought of her working in those that were further into the slums of London. It would explain why she looked at him with such mistrust. He could only imagine how she'd been treated. "He seemed to think I would have my hands full with you under my roof. Am I to understand that you are a bit of a hellcat?"

The laughter that burst forth from Elizabeth was music to his ears. She grabbed her sides and then turned worried eyes to his. "Have I given you that impression, my lord?"

"Hardly," he returned. "But I have the distinct feeling that your true nature is being hidden from me at the moment."

Elizabeth smiled hesitantly. "Just a precautionary measure, my lord."

"I see."

Elizabeth studied him. "You do not like the man, either. You have had past dealings with him?"

"I inherited his hatred. He and my father were good friends once."

"What happened?"

"They both fell in love with the same woman. She could only choose one of them."

"Your father."

"Yes. Smythe never forgave him. My father always believed in the good of people, and either wasn't aware of his scorn, or chose not to see it. He hired Peter Smythe as his overseer...I suppose he thought it would help to make things better. Instead, Smythe put everything he had into learning about business and after a few years, began embezzling money from my father. Small amounts, at first, to see if he could get away with it. He did, for a very long time, working with the bookkeeper and allowing him to keep part of the money in exchange for his silence. He never expected his employer's son to be as mistrusting as his father was faithful. About a year before my father's death, I figured it out. I gathered all the evidence and confronted Smythe with it. I could have had him thrown in jail, but instead I chose to let him live out the rest of his life with my shadow falling across his path. My father finally saw him for what he was, and it ruined Smythe in society. He's been scrounging around ever since."

"That's why he left without a fight that night," Elizabeth mused. "He doesn't want to tangle with you."

"That would be a good assumption." Aidan eyed her. "Why was he so intent on having you come with him?"

"I don't know," Elizabeth replied uneasily. "Perhaps he

wanted to make me pay for shunning him all those years ago. He doesn't sound like the type to grant forgiveness."

"That, he's not," Aidan said, leaning back in the chair. "Miss Town—Elizabeth," he corrected, enjoying the feel of her name on his tongue. "When you first arrived and Mrs. Bartlett was tending to you, she noticed the charm you wear about your ankle. It seems oddly familiar to me. What is it?"

Elizabeth's eyes grew huge in her face. She obviously didn't think he knew about it. She immediately tucked her feet beneath her skirts, a gesture which Aidan understood. Wearing the charm around her ankle was probably the only way to keep it safe, living as she had.

"It's a Celtic knot. The symbol of love." Elizabeth's eyes filled with tears, and Aidan felt his heart twist.

Had she been in love? And if so, where was he now? She always answered his questions so vaguely. What was she hiding? He burned to know the secrets of her past, her childhood, and everything there was to know. He desperately wanted her to trust him enough to tell him those stories. And he had no idea why. "Where did you get it?"

"It was given to me by someone very dear to me," she said softly, a faraway look coming into her eyes.

Clearly, that was all she was going to tell him. He didn't press her, because the unshed tears that stood in her eyes threatened to spill over, and he had no desire to make her cry. He glanced at the book in her lap. "Who are you reading?" he asked instead, changing the subject.

"Jane Austen."

"Ah. Talented woman, that one. Or so my sister says."

"You've never read her, have you?"

Aidan grinned guiltily. "Not my sort of literature."

"You don't know what you're missing." Elizabeth smiled. "If only I had such talent! To be able to create such vivid characters that you can't help but fall in love with them, and stories that capture you and pull you right in to their midst...to be able to write so well that the reader is sad when the book ends..." Elizabeth trailed off, heaving a wistful sigh. "You should really read this sometime," she said, holding up his sister's much beloved copy of *Pride and Prejudice*. "Unless, of course, you're not secure enough in your manhood to withstand a romantic story," she teased.

Aidan raised his eyebrow and she paled. "I beg your pardon, my lord. That sounded disrespectful and it wasn't intended to be."

A warm smile creased his face. "No insult taken. I rather like it when you tease me. I do have a sense of humor, you know. I'm not *all* ogre."

"I never said you were an ogre!"

"You didn't have to. It's in your eyes."

She immediately looked away and her face flamed with color. He was right, of course. He had been nothing but kind to her, yet she had continued to treat him with wariness and mistrust.

"Why are you so frightened of me, Elizabeth?" he asked softly.

She sighed. "It's not your fault, really. You can't help who you are."

"An earl?"

"No. A man."

Aidan's brows drew together and he frowned. *That did not bode well.* "Surely there must be more to it than that."

Elizabeth shook her head. "I have a hard time trusting men. I've not had much luck with them, and I'm afraid it's influenced the way I live my life."

Aidan was dismayed to learn the reason behind her wary eyes, but at least it was something he might be able to change. There was hope. "Just because I haven't read Jane

Austen doesn't mean I've never read romance," he blurted. What the hell had made him say *that*?

Elizabeth's mouth fell open in surprise. "I didn't mean—"

"That is to say, it depends on what you view as romantic," he amended hastily. He stood up and strolled over to the bookshelf that sat between the floor to ceiling windows. "Here," he said, gesturing to a row of books. "All poetry. I've read every one of them. Some of them more than once." Aidan cringed inwardly. Had he just bragged about reading *poetry*? If Gavin were here he'd be howling with laughter. Why, *why* was he so desperate to connect with this woman?

WAS IT HER IMAGINATION, or was Lord Ashby desperate to prove himself to her? Elizabeth wandered over and joined him, eyeing the shelf. There were quite a few books on poetry. Surely he hadn't read *all* of them. "I'm sure you have," she said politely.

He didn't miss the disguised disbelief in her voice. He reached up and handed her a thin, worn volume. "I've read this one so many times I've memorized it."

She raised a skeptical eyebrow but said nothing. He met the challenge in her gaze and smiled, leaning toward her. There was the glint of battle in his eyes. "Go on. I dare you."

"My lord, you certainly don't need to—"

"Page 34. Lord Byron, I believe," he said with a touch of smugness in his voice. All traces of it disappeared, however, when he began to quote:

> *"She walks in beauty, like the night*
> *Of cloudless climes and starry skies;*
> *And all that's best of dark and bright*
> *Meet in her aspect, and her eyes:*

Thus mellow'd to that tender light
Which heaven to gaudy day denies."

He had stepped closer to her, his rich voice reaching right into her heart and making it beat just a little faster. He had a wonderful voice for reading, and for a fraction of a second, an image of him reading to his children filled her mind. Elizabeth cleared her throat and shifted uncomfortably. His eyes bored into her, challenging her to find a poem he couldn't recite. Well, she wasn't about to fold. "All right, then," she said crisply. "Let's see how you do when *I* choose the page." She pursed her lips and flipped to another poem, desperate to wipe that smirk right off his face. Insufferable man. She stopped when she caught sight of a name even she didn't recognize. "One hundred six."

"Ah. My favorite. How ironic."

"Surely you can't know—"

"Give me a kiss, and to that kiss a score
Then to that twenty, add a hundred more."

Elizabeth's eyes flew to the page in front of her. Good heavens, what on earth had she selected? She looked up as Aidan stalked her, pinning her with those whiskey orbs of his. Unconsciously, she backed up until the wall prevented her from retreating any further. Her stomach fluttered, rather like a butterfly cupped in two hands, as he continued in a low, husky voice.

"A thousand to that hundred, so kiss on,
To make that thousand up a million.
Treble that million, and when that is done,
Let's kiss afresh, as when we first begun."

He was so close to her that the only thing that separated them was the book she held in her hands. Elizabeth's heart slammed against her ribcage. He leaned forward ever so slightly, and for a brief moment, Elizabeth thought he was going to do as the poem suggested.

"Shall we continue the test?" he said instead.

She tried to speak, but nothing but a small squeak came out. He shot her a knowing grin, and it immediately sent her temper flaring. "I think you've made your point," she said flatly.

"You see, Miss Townsend. It all depends upon what you consider romantic." He didn't move. He just stood there, staring into her eyes, the heat of his body flowing into hers, making her skin tingle. Was she still breathing?

"Yes. Well. You are very well-read," Elizabeth replied, thrusting the book at him and breaking the spell. "I'm sure Miss Austen won't be offended that you haven't deigned to include her in your repertoire."

Aidan winked and slipped the book from her hands, returning it to the shelf as she skittered away from him. "Just because I hide it from the world doesn't mean I don't have a romantic soul, Miss Townsend. Ogre or not." He inclined his head in farewell and strode to the door.

He paused on the threshold and turned his smoldering gaze on her. A seductive smile curled about his lips. "And incidentally, Miss Townsend," he said, his voice thick. "I assure you, I am most secure in my manhood." He jerked his chin to the forgotten volume on the chair. "Enjoy your book."

He quit the room, leaving Elizabeth to wonder how she hadn't simply turned to dust after the way he'd looked at her. She forced air into her rebellious lungs. It was clear she would have to avoid being alone with Aidan at all costs. The Earl of Ashby was a dangerous man.

CHAPTER 11

What the hell had he been thinking? He'd nearly kissed Elizabeth. Elizabeth! The girl who, a few weeks ago, had been pulled from the gutter. That very same girl, he'd wanted to kiss.

Desperately.

Still.

This was insanity. She invaded his every thought, turning his life upside down. He was Aidan Lockwood, Earl of Ashby, owner of a highly successful business, manager of a profitable estate, and a respected Member of Parliament. He was always in control; always able to make the impossible happen. His life was well ordered, scandal-free, and exactly how he liked it.

Then she exploded into it, and nothing had been the same since. His once quiet house now rang with feminine bursts of laughter, interrupting his thoughts and distracting him completely. It was damn near impossible to get any work done with two women carrying on like that.

But then again, he was glad to see Lainey so happy. She had only been eleven when their mother had died. Aidan did the best that he could with her, but he knew she missed the female companionship that he simply could not offer her. She always said that she had everything she needed, but he knew better. She kept herself so busy because she was trying to fill a void in her life. And right now, Elizabeth seemed to be filling it nicely.

Aidan took a sip of his scotch. The club was packed with men playing cards or sharing a drink with friends. Only Aidan sat alone in a chair by the window, staring out into the street where he had first seen Elizabeth. Memories of that night washed over him, of how close he had come to dying. If it hadn't been for Elizabeth, who could say what would have happened? If he'd been killed that night, then Lainey would have been left alone with no one to look after her. He knew that Gavin would protect her, as any of his friends would, but still...the woman needed a husband whether she liked it or not.

He took another sip of scotch and let it burn its way down his throat. He sighed and closed his eyes, leaning his head back against the chair.

"Drinking alone, Ashby? That's never a good sign with you."

Aidan cracked an eye open to find Donovan MacKavoy looking down at him with an amused expression. "Just trying to enjoy some peace and quiet, MacKavoy. Don't let me interrupt you."

Donovan grinned and took the seat across from him. "What's troubling you, my friend? Is it the girl?"

"Jesus, MacKavoy." The man had an uncanny knack for seeing right into Aidan's head.

Donovan shrugged. "Why else would you be sitting here with that weary look on your face?" A snifter of brandy was delivered to him, and he raised it to Aidan before taking a long swallow. "Has she taken a turn for the worse?"

"No, she's doing quite well. Lainey is taking very good care of her."

"I'm sure she is. She's a good woman, that sister of yours."

"Would you like to marry her?"

Donovan laughed out loud. "I would, but I'm not good enough for her, remember?"

"Did I say that?"

"No, I believe your actual words were, 'Touch her and I'll kill you'."

"Perhaps I was a bit hasty."

Donovan laughed again. "I think not. I'm not ready to settle down, and you know it. And even if I were, your sister doesn't want me. I don't care how much you bemoan the fact that she's still unmarried; you're not going to let her marry just anyone. And after what that fool Danby did to her, she deserves to be blissfully happy."

Aidan sighed, conceding that Donovan was right. Unlike himself, Lainey wanted true love and happily ever after. Truth be told, he was in no hurry to let her go, because then he would be the one left alone.

"But she's not why you're sitting here," Donovan pointed out. "It's the other one."

"By that, I'm guessing you mean Miss Townsend."

"How many other women do you have in your house? Of course I mean Miss Townsend. She's healing well, so what's the problem?"

Aidan didn't say anything. The problem was, for the first time in his life, he felt like he wasn't in control. There were times during the day when thoughts of cerulean eyes assailed him, knocking the breath from his lungs. He took another sip of scotch. The problem was, she was of the poorest class, and he was an earl. The problem was, he wanted to take her in his arms and kiss her until the fear permanently disappeared from her eyes. That was indeed a problem.

"Hell, Ashby," Donovan said, unable to keep the smile from his face. "You want her."

"Mack, for God's sake!"

"Hello, boys. What are we talking about?"

Aidan looked up to see that Gavin Mayfield had arrived. Just what he needed— another prying gaze from which he could hide nothing. "So much for my peace and quiet," he muttered.

Gavin raised his eyebrows. "Am I interrupting something?"

"Yes! My time alone with my scotch!"

"You seem a bit on edge tonight, my friend. What am I missing?" Gavin looked at Donovan, who shrugged.

"We were just discussing how Ash here wants to get his houseguest into bed," he said simply.

"MacKavoy!" Aidan roared. Several heads turned their way. "Jesus! *Jesus,*" he hissed, shoving his hand into his thick mass of hair and sighing loudly. "I do not want to get her into bed."

"Don't sell me a dog! It's written all over your face."

Aidan groaned and put his head in his hands. "I just wanted a drink and some time alone," he whimpered.

"I can see I came at just the right time," Gavin said gleefully. "I've been trying to get Ash to admit to his infatuation since we went to France." He clapped his hands and dropped into a seat next to Donovan. They both looked expectantly at Aidan. He rolled his eyes.

"I am not attracted to her," he lied. "There was just a moment earlier this afternoon when I had a bit of a judgment lapse, that's all."

"Holy hell, did you kiss her?" Gavin practically shouted.

"No," Aidan ground out. "And I'll thank you to keep your voice down."

"So you *nearly* kissed her. But you're not attracted to her." Donovan grinned. Aidan shot him a dark look.

"There's nothing wrong with being attracted to her, Ash," Gavin said. "You are a man, after all," he chided.

Aidan glared at him. "She's a pauper, Gav. And she's in my care. And she's entrusting her safety to me, despite the fact that she seems terrified of me. Three very good reasons why the thought shouldn't have even crossed my mind."

"It's just a natural feeling, Aidan," Gavin pressed. "She sounds quite fascinating from what you've told me. She's an enigma, and you are drawn to puzzles. It must make her very compelling."

"Maybe when she's all better you can make her your mistress," Donovan offered. There was a long pause as both Aidan and Gavin turned to stare at Donovan.

"I take it back," Aidan said, incredulous. "I wasn't hasty at all."

"I told you, you don't want me to marry your sister."

"You offered this louse Lainey's hand in marriage?" Gavin sputtered. "Good God, man."

"Easy, Gav. It's a long story." He drained the rest of his scotch and stood to go. "Gentlemen, if you will excuse me, I aim to get some of that peace and quiet I mentioned earlier. I think I will walk home."

"Oh, good. Can you have Jack bring me home? I came with Thorpe, but from the look of things, he'll be here for hours," Donovan surmised.

Aidan chuckled. "Jack would be happy to see you home. I'll tell him. Goodnight, gentlemen." He turned to go, but then paused. He looked at Gavin. "Come to tea on Friday afternoon. I'll introduce you to Miss Townsend. You," he said, pointing a finger at Donovan. "Stay away from my sister."

CHAPTER 12

A few days later, Elizabeth sat in front of the mirror and fidgeted while Mary did her hair. Gavin Mayfield was coming to tea today and Elizabeth was meeting him for the first time. She didn't know why it mattered to her, but he was the first friend of Aidan's she was meeting, and she wanted to make a good impression. She was wearing a simple cotton morning gown, not particularly suitable for tea, but the only thing she had at the moment.

"There you are," Lainey said from the doorway. "I just saw Gavin's carriage pull—" She stopped speaking when she caught sight of Elizabeth's new dress. "My brother imports the finest fabrics in the world and he ordered you brown calico," she said flatly.

Elizabeth's cheeks flamed. "No, I did. I need a serviceable dress, Lainey. I know it's not fashionable, but I don't need fashionable. I need practical."

Lainey sighed. "I suppose you are right." She eyed Elizabeth. "Eliza, what do you plan to do when you leave us?"

"I…I'm not sure."

Lainey took Elizabeth's hands in hers. "Elizabeth, you can't think we mean to just set you back out in the street."

"I hadn't really thought about it."

"Well, we absolutely will not. You're our friend now. Let us help you."

That was one thing Elizabeth couldn't let them do. "I can take care of myself, Lainey. You needn't worry about me."

"You didn't look like you'd been taking very good care of yourself when you arrived," she replied, crossing her arms over her chest.

Elizabeth conceded the point. "Money was tight. The previous few months had been a little difficult," she admitted. Traveling back to London had depleted her savings quite rapidly, and she couldn't find work once she'd arrived. She'd traded her hair brush for coal, for heaven's sake. Winters were tricky.

"Then let us help you. We can at least find you respectable employment."

Elizabeth hesitated. "I'm not sure how long I plan to stay in London…" she hedged.

"Hm."

What that meant, Elizabeth could only guess. "Aren't we keeping your guest waiting?" she offered feebly.

Lainey shot her a look that said she knew when she was being deflected. She patted Elizabeth's cheek. "You do look lovely in your new dress. It fits you beautifully. But I am going to order something a little more fun from Mrs. Essex tomorrow." She put up her hand to stop Elizabeth's protest. "You may do with them what you wish once you have left, but I insist you have them. Besides, I may have already ordered them." She coughed delicately into her hand. "And once word gets out that Gavin was invited for tea, there will be a line out the door of callers wanting to meet the woman who saved London's most eligible bachelor. You'll need a proper dress to survive the onslaught." She grinned.

Elizabeth went pale. "No! Lainey, that's a bad idea! I don't need to meet anyone. The fewer people who know me, the better."

"That's an odd thing to say."

"Please, Lainey. I can't take callers."

Lainey's worried gaze travelled over her. "Well, you must meet my closest girlfriends. They are a fiercely protective bunch. And I think you need some friends."

THE MEN STOOD when she and Lainey entered drawing room.

"Ah. Ladies. Please join us." Aidan gestured to a nearby sofa. Elizabeth eyed Gavin as he stood to meet her. He was an attractive blond with sparkling blue eyes, a slender build, and height that surpassed Aidan's by an inch or two. He was also, Elizabeth noted, in possession of a winsome smile designed to melt any heart in an instant, which he bestowed upon her as Aidan made the introductions.

"Miss Townsend, I am delighted to meet you at last," he said, bowing slightly over her hand. "May I be the among the first to thank you for your bravery."

"That's very kind of you, Mr. Mayfield. I just happened to be in the right place at the right time."

"She's terribly modest, is she not?" Lainey grinned.

Gavin turned to her, flashing her that charming smile. "Hello, Lainey." He bowed his head and she blushed. "How have you been since your return to London?"

"I've been quite busy, not that you would know. You've been horribly remiss in coming to call, you know."

"Forgive me. Your brother has been keeping me at bay with business."

"Mm hm." But she smiled at him as she took a seat.

Elizabeth was staring at Gavin. She had been studying him during the banter. There was something vaguely familiar about him, though she couldn't quite put her finger on it. He didn't seem like the type to frequent the taverns in the poor section of town, but one never knew. She had seen many a fine gentleman stumble in, looking to drown their sorrows in a place where no one knew them. But still…that didn't seem quite it.

She gradually became aware of three pairs of eyes on her, and she flushed at having been caught staring. But she couldn't help it. "Mr. Mayfield, have we…met somewhere before?" she asked, knitting her brows together in concentration.

"I don't believe so," Gavin replied. "I'm sure I would remember you. You have such lovely eyes. I can see now why Aidan has been so captivated by them." A smile tugged at the corner of his mouth, but he refused to let it manifest itself. He didn't dare meet Aidan's pointed stare, as the daggers that were shooting from his eyes would surely find their way straight to his heart and kill him on the spot.

"I'm sorry," Elizabeth mumbled. "Of course we haven't met. I don't know what I was thinking."

"Gavin has that effect on people," Lainey assured her. "Once you've met him, you feel as if you've known him all your life."

"That's because you *have* known me all your life."

She rolled her eyes as they all sat and Lainey poured for them. The conversation flowed freely, and Elizabeth slowly began to relax, though she still kept an eye on Gavin. She just couldn't place him, and it was driving her to distraction. Gavin was asking a lot of questions, which made Elizabeth uneasy, but she did her best to answer them. Without think-ing, she reached for the pot to pour herself a second cup.

"Aidan tells me you are an avid reader. Poetry, is it?"

The tea she had been expertly pouring a moment before sloshed out of the cup in a tidal wave. She practically dropped the pot in her haste to stem the flow. "Oh!"

"Oh, dear, Eliza. Let me help you with that." Lainey mopped up the tea and handed the cup to Elizabeth, whose face was flaming with embarrassment. "Gavin, must you pester her like that? You're making her nervous!" Lainey scolded.

"I'm not trying to make her nervous, I'm just trying to get to know her. For heaven's sake, Lainey, it was an innocent question."

Elizabeth glanced at Aidan. He looked like he was going to throttle Gavin, who now wore a devilish grin on his face. Aidan shifted his gaze to Elizabeth, and she sent him an accusatory glare. *You told him.* Aidan had the grace to look away, hiding his smile behind his teacup.

"Aidan has also told me you've confessed you love gardens," Gavin continued. "My father has quite an extensive one at our home in Nottingham." Elizabeth stilled. She had grown up in Derbyshire, the next county over. She fervently hoped she wouldn't give herself away if he started speaking of familiar things.

"He calls it his escape," Gavin continued, oblivious. "He saw some terrible things during his years of service—he's a retired colonel, you know. He's served for most of his life, to some great sacrifices, and he's suffered a great deal of loss. I can't even begin to imagine what it was like to be on the battlefield...or even in India, for that matter. I think that's why he tries so hard to surround himself with beauty." Gavin sipped his tea. "He has a most extensive rose garden that he tends to himself. I, however, am not allowed to touch them," he chuckled. "I did *not* inherit his green thumb. Give me twenty-four hours, and I would kill them."

Elizabeth's teacup clattered to her saucer, spilling tea in her lap. She gasped and shot off of the sofa, sending the cup and saucer flying.

"Elizabeth! Are you all right?" Aidan was on his feet instantly. "What's wrong?"

She shifted her gaze to Aidan, unable to find her voice. She tried desperately to act as normal as she could after having just flung tea across the Aubusson carpet. Her stomach instantaneously knotted itself, and she put her hand to it as if to will it to settle. She looked back at Gavin, beginning to tremble. It wasn't his face that had been familiar at all. It was his voice. It was softer now that he wasn't speaking angrily, but it was still the same. *Kill them.* The second she'd heard it, she'd known. Gavin was the man who had given the order that night. Aidan's best friend had killed her family and destroyed her life.

CHAPTER 13

"*E*lizabeth?"

She snapped her gaze back to Aidan. She couldn't let him know. It would destroy him, too. "I…I'm so sorry. I'm so clumsy…I…I'm afraid I'm suddenly not feeling very well." She glanced around her, and they all saw the fear in her eyes. "Ex…excuse me. I'm s-sorry." She fled the room.

The three exchanged worried glances. Gavin looked completely baffled. "What was all that about?"

"I don't know," Aidan replied. "But I mean to find out. Would you excuse me?"

Aidan strode out of the room. *Damnation.* What was with this girl? His quiet, orderly life had taken on more twists and turns since he had met this woman than he had seen in the last five years. He listened for her footsteps or a slamming door to indicate where she'd gone, but no sound met his ears. However, a cold breeze swept over him, and he turned to see that the door to the verandah was open. Beyond it, he could see Elizabeth stumbling through the gardens as fast as she could move.

Of course she'd gone outside.

Because it was raining.

Really, really hard.

"God have mercy on me," he sighed, pausing at the door. A second later Elizabeth was tumbling toward the ground as her legs gave out beneath her.

"Bloody hell." He took a breath and charged out into the rain after her. He was by her side in less than a minute.

"Elizabeth."

She was on her hands and knees, gasping for air. He knelt down beside her, touching her shoulder. "Elizabeth," he repeated.

She screamed and shrank back from him, startled.

"It's me, Elizabeth. It's all right. What is it? What's got you so upset?"

"I'm…sorry," she choked out. "I…" She couldn't finish. Her ragged breaths came harder now, hot tears mixing with the rain on her cheeks. Sobs tore from her throat, and Aidan did the only thing he could.

He sat down beside her and pulled her into his arms, cradling her head against his chest. She clung desperately to him while he spoke to her in soothing tones, smoothing her sodden hair back from her face. Her breathing calmed eventually.

"Come now, we need to get out of the rain before you catch cold." He stood, extending his hand to help her up. "Are you hurt?"

"No…I don't think so." But she didn't move.

"Elizabeth, I will carry you if I have to."

She blinked at him, and Aidan wasn't sure she'd heard him. Her eyes looked vacant, and quite frankly, it scared him. Without another thought, he bent down and swept her into his arms.

"Oh! You mustn't—" The rest of her words died on her lips when he scowled at her. He stared at her for a moment, then she slipped her arms around his neck and let her head fall against his shoulder as he moved toward the house.

He hadn't anticipated that a cold, rain-soaked woman could feel so good in his arms.

AN HOUR and yet another doctor's visit later, Elizabeth sat on the floor of her bedchamber drying her hair in front of the fire. Her mind was racing, trying to figure out how to best proceed. She couldn't very well tell Aidan his best friend was a murderer, and Gavin had shown absolutely no sign of recognizing her. She had to avoid him at all costs. The less she was around him, the less likely she was to do something that would give herself away. She was still too weak to be on the run again. She would have to be extremely careful… which suited her fine, because after her dramatic exit this afternoon, she was quite sure she wouldn't be able to show her face outside of her room again.

A soft knock at the door interrupted her thoughts. "Come in."

The door opened to reveal Aidan lurking on the other side, a dark expression on his face. His hair was damp and tousled, adding to his dangerous aura. Elizabeth's heart fluttered in her chest. She couldn't blame him for being angry with her.

"I hope I'm not intruding," he said, an ominous note in his voice. "May I come in?"

His tone suggested that she had no choice. Elizabeth's heart began to pound in earnest. She didn't want to be alone with him, particularly in her bedchamber. "Of course."

He stalked into the room, leaving the door open behind

him, she noted. He sat on the sofa facing her, leaned his elbows on his knees, and clasped his hands together, looking down at her. "The doctor says you seem to be unhurt except for a minor ankle sprain. Is he correct in that statement?"

"Yes."

"He also says he believes you have suffered a past trauma that set off your episode today." He narrowed his eyes at her. "Is that statement also correct?"

Elizabeth forced herself to swallow. "Yes," she admitted.

Aidan sighed. "Do you want to tell me what happened today?"

"No."

"That wasn't a rhetorical question."

"I know, my lord. It was just...something Mr. Mayfield said...stirred a memory that I was unprepared for," she said softly. "Forgive me, but I cannot tell you more."

"That was a very powerful memory." He studied her a moment. "Elizabeth, are you in danger?"

Her mouth dropped open in surprise. How to answer that? "I...I don't know, exactly. Please, my lord. Do not ask me any more questions. I do not wish to involve you."

"Are you in trouble with the authorities?"

"No! No, it's nothing like that."

"Then what is it?"

I don't want to be found. All she had to do was say it. He would find out eventually anyway, so why couldn't she just admit it?

He was staring at her. She felt like a trapped animal. Goodness, what could he be thinking looking at her like that? He leaned forward just slightly. "If you tell me the truth, perhaps I can protect you."

"At what cost to me?"

"I beg your pardon?"

"What is it that you want in return for your protection?"

She pinned him with her cerulean gaze and folded her arms over her chest. "Men usually want something in return when they offer to grant me a 'favor'," she said, bitterness lacing her tone.

Aidan visibly stiffened, and for the first time, Elizabeth thought she might be mistaken about this particular man. He was quite clearly insulted.

"I simply want to help you, Elizabeth."

Elizabeth shook her head, confusion and question in her eyes. "Why would you do that?"

"Because it is becoming apparent to me that I care about what happens to you. For whatever reason, I feel the need to set your life right again without even knowing what has caused it to go wrong in the first place. You saved my life, Elizabeth," he said, straightening. "I must owe you at least one favor."

"But you have done so much for me already, my lord."

"Hardly." He stood to go, and Elizabeth watched the graceful way he moved as he headed for the door. He paused on the threshold, then stalked back to her. He knelt in front of her and watched the play of firelight across her face. "I changed my mind. I do want one thing in return." He rested his fingers under her chin and forced her to meet his eyes.

His face was so close, his gaze so heated. Surely, *surely* he was going to kiss her this time. "What is that, my lord?"

"Your trust," he whispered. His fingers were so warm on her skin, his touch so gentle. "Perhaps someday you will trust me enough to tell me the truth." He gave her a small, sad smile. "I look forward to that day with great anticipation."

He stood abruptly. An alarming stab of disappointment zinged through her when he withdrew his touch. "You'll be joining us for all meals from now on, Miss Townsend. No more hiding in your room. You are a guest here and will be treated as such." He paused at the door and looked back at her. "And my name, Miss Townsend," he said gruffly, "is Aidan."

Elizabeth stared after him as panic rose in her chest.

She was actually starting to care for this man.

Worse yet, she was beginning to trust him.

CHAPTER 14

"*You* mustn't dawdle, Miss Elizabeth. His Lordship is waiting."

"I know, Mary." Elizabeth hadn't left her room at all yesterday after she had made such a fool out of herself. She couldn't bear to face Aidan, and the feeling hadn't lessened overnight. She had hoped her ankle would be swollen and unusable so she could hide in her room longer, but to her dismay, she had awoken to a perfectly good ankle.

She glanced nervously at her new gown in the mirror and shook her head. She would have to find some way to repay Lainey's kindness. Elizabeth admired the white and blue muslin, glad she had finally filled out enough to give her some sort of curve. An amused smile crossed her lips as she wondered how she was holding up all of this clothing. She'd gotten used to the simple wrapper she had borrowed from Lainey. Now she was clad in a pale blue underskirt and a white and blue pin-striped polonaise with fitted sleeves and an enormous amount of draped material that started at her backside and continued down to the end of the train. She'd lost half her freedom of movement, but she had to admit, she felt attractive for the first time in many years. She smoothed her hand over imaginary wrinkles in her gown.

"You look perfect, Miss Elizabeth," Mary encouraged, grasping her by the shoulders and turning her away from the glass. "Off you go." Elizabeth sighed as Mary shooed her out the door. She dragged herself down the stairs and to the dining room, where Tibbs met her at the door.

"You're looking especially comely this morning, Miss Townsend. The gown brings out the blue in your eyes."

"Thank you, Tibbs. Does it show off my nervousness as well?"

"You have nothing to fear, Miss. It's only breakfast."

Elizabeth giggled. He was right, of course. Perhaps a glass of juice would help to wash down her embarrassment at her behavior yesterday.

AIDAN SAT at the head of the table, reading a newspaper, and wondering if Miss Townsend was going to be brave enough to have breakfast with him. He couldn't begin to imagine what had set her off yesterday, but it made him distinctly uncomfortable. He'd never seen someone so terrified in his life.

The door opened and the lady in question appeared. He flicked his gaze up to her, and his lungs practically seized. Damn. When the hell had she gotten so beautiful? "Good morning, Elizabeth."

"Good morning, my lord."

He stood and waited for her to take her seat. She reminded him of a cautious doe the way she reluctantly crept into the room. Once seated, she fidgeted with the silver that rested by her plate, clearly quite agitated. Aidan used the paper to hide his amusement. A faint but becoming blush stained her cheeks as she stared at her empty plate.

"I trust you slept well?" Aidan said, folding his paper and putting it aside.

"Yes, my lord." She glanced nervously about the room. "Will Lainey be joining us?"

"She's having brunch with Miss Sutherland, and she wanted to stop at the market first."

"Oh."

He watched as Elizabeth's hope of his sister's being a buffer between them died instantly.

"She can't save you, you know," he said, barely able to keep his laughter at bay. Her head snapped up, alarm in her eyes, and he lost his battle. Laughter burst forth from his chest.

Elizabeth's mouth dropped open.

"Don't look so offended, Miss Townsend. You'd laugh, too, if you could see your own face." Merriment sparkled in his eyes.

"You're not cross with me, then?"

Aidan's face grew more serious. He sighed. "Elizabeth, I cannot pretend your behavior yesterday was not troubling, and the cause of some discomfort to my guest and myself, but I am not angry with you. At least, not anymore." A footman filled Elizabeth's plate, and when he stepped back, Aidan continued. "I apologize for losing my temper with you. I am not accustomed to having my questions avoided—I get an answer when I pose a question. You have mystified me from the beginning with all your secrets, and I dislike not knowing anything about you. You are a guest in my home, and I need to know that my family and my staff are safe in your company. Since you promised me yesterday that you are in no trouble, I will let the matter drop for now until you feel that you can confide in me. I understand your unwillingness to trust someone after the life you have led, and I shall endeavor to earn that trust." He reached for his coffee and resumed eating. Elizabeth sat motionless for a good half a minute, apparently struck mute by his words. "Elizabeth? Are you going to eat today? You must build up your strength, you know."

Elizabeth blinked. "I…I'm sorry." She picked up her fork and bent her head over her plate. "You aren't going to question me about my past?" she asked the plate softly.

"For now."

"You trust me?"

He nodded once. "I do."

She turned her eyes to his. "How do you give your trust so freely?" she asked in wonder.

"I suspect I haven't been hurt as badly as you."

They looked at each other in silence for a long moment.

"Thank you," Elizabeth finally said into the silence. She smiled faintly, then stabbed at a piece of meat.

She was so damned exquisite. Aidan suddenly found that the appetite he had this morning was not for what was on his plate. His body was remembering how she'd felt pressed up against him, how he'd delighted in having her arms around his neck. How she always smelled like lilacs.

He stood abruptly, startling her fork right out of her grasp.

"Oh!" She gasped, desperately gathering the bits of food that had been strewn across the table. "I'm so sorry."

"My fault entirely. I didn't mean to startle you." If Aidan didn't get out of this room right now, he was going to haul her out of that chair and have *her* for breakfast. "Elizabeth, would you feel up to a tour of the portrait gallery this morning? I fear I have an appointment, but I have time to share a little of my family's history with you if you are so inclined. Then you may break your fast in peace."

"That sounds lovely, my lord. I would enjoy that."

Aidan sighed. "Aidan."

"I beg your pardon?"

"Aidan. My name. It's Aidan."

"Yes, I know."

Aidan smiled. "You have no intention of using it, do you?"

"None whatsoever." Elizabeth grinned, a sparkle in her eye.

"You will." It was not a command, but rather a promise, softly spoken and delivered with a look that caressed her. He offered her his arm and they left the room.

THEY WALKED in companionable silence for a bit. "Tell me about your parents, my lord."

"Ah, my parents." He absently covered Elizabeth's hand with his, sending a jolt through her. His hand was warm, reassuring on hers. "My father was a brilliant man. I, of course, told you the story of how he married my mother. Theirs was an unusual sort of marriage in that they actually loved each other deeply, something that is not always the case, particularly for their generation. He had a passion for three things in life: family, numbers, and astronomy. But nothing was more important to him than his family. As I said, he began to import fabrics in the late 1830s, and then a distant cousin died and the earldom came to my father unexpectedly. People scoffed at him for continuing with his business, but he loved it so much he couldn't think of staying away from it. He was a bit of a restless man, I think."

"A trait he seems to have passed on to you," Elizabeth teased.

Aidan chuckled. "I'm afraid you're right. My father and I were very much alike. When he died, I took over the business, not wanting to let his life's work disappear. Mr. Mayfield and I have taken it from a profitable venture to a *very* profitable one, what with most every shop in London and other major cities carrying our fabrics now."

She shuddered at the mention of Gavin's name. She had spent most of last night trying to figure out how she was going to avoid him without arousing suspicion. She prayed he wouldn't be calling very often. The season was about to start and that meant a very busy few weeks for both him and Aidan. She was hoping the business would keep them out of the house and away from her. "I'm sure your father would be very proud of you."

Aidan nodded. "I hope so." He paused to open a heavy oak door, and then showed Elizabeth through. They were in the family portrait gallery. The hall was long and narrow, tastefully designed with dark oak and a rich red carpet runner that ran the length of the great hall. The ceiling had to be at least fifteen or twenty-feet high, Elizabeth guessed, with windows that graced the top edge of the outside wall to let in plenty of light, but placed so as to not put the paintings in direct sunlight where they would be damaged. The oil portraits themselves were the largest paintings Elizabeth had ever seen. It was quite clear that the Earls of Ashby had come from a long line of money.

He reclaimed her arm as they wandered along down the row of paintings, Aidan giving as much history about the people in them as he knew. They stopped at a portrait of a woman in a tall powdered wig and an elaborate dress with side hoop panniers that made her appear several feet wide. Elizabeth giggled.

"How on earth did they ever get about in those things?"

"That's my cousin's great grandmother when she was presented at court. That wasn't an everyday dress."

"But still...you have to admit the fashions of a hundred years ago are a bit silly."

Aidan turned to her with an amused smile on his face and pointedly regarded the poufs of fabric that had replaced her backside. "It would be my guess that a hundred years from now, people will think corsets and bustles just as silly."

"I hardly think so," Elizabeth sniffed. "I'm the very height of fashion, thank you."

Aidan chuckled. "For now." They moved to the next painting. "Perhaps this is more to your liking. This is my grandmother."

They were looking upon a portrait of an alluring young woman reclining on a chaise wearing a flowing, empire-waisted gown. The simple style suited her to perfection, and she looked so serene sitting there that Elizabeth felt almost intrusive gazing at her. "She's quite lovely."

"And spirited as well. I believe Lainey has inherited much of her mischievous personality."

Elizabeth laughed. "I'd have to agree." Her eyes darted to the next portrait, and she gasped in delight. "Is that *you*?"

Aidan's rich baritone rumbled deep in his chest. "Yes, that's me. This is the last family portrait that was painted before my mother died. I was fourteen, and Lainey was eight. And those, of course, are my parents."

Elizabeth studied the painting. It was expertly done, so realistic that Elizabeth half expected the people to reach out to her. Aidan's mother sat with a placid expression on her face, her arm around her daughter. She was an attractive blonde, with soft blue eyes and a willowy figure. Aidan's father was just the opposite, a well-cut figure with a brooding expression in his eyes that Elizabeth had seen on Aidan. His passion showed in those eyes. He was resting a protective hand on his son's shoulder while his other was draped around the shoulders of his wife. Elizabeth noticed that even at the age of fourteen, Aidan was showing a hint of the good-looking man he would grow into as the years passed.

"Your mother is so pretty," she said softly. "What was she like?"

"My mother…had love for everyone. She was a kind soul, and gentle, yet fiercely protective of her family. She was the laughter and light in this house," he said, sorrow touching his voice. "It left when she did."

Elizabeth pulled her gaze away from the portrait and turned to look at Aidan. There was an odd mix of love and sadness in his eyes. Elizabeth touched his arm, a current of understanding flowing between them. She knew exactly how he felt. Aidan looked down at her a moment, and Elizabeth felt the first stirrings of genuine friendship.

She smiled and moved to the last two portraits. They were hung side by side, one each of Lainey and Aidan. "How old were you here?"

"This was my twenty-second birthday. I'd become the earl not six months prior, and Lainey insisted we must have a portrait. Lainey was eighteen here, just before her debut."

"You look so much like your father." They were both strikingly handsome, but Elizabeth didn't want to tell him she thought so. She went back to the family portrait. "Lainey was an adorable child."

"Personally, I think she's still adorable, but then again, I am biased." Aidan watched Elizabeth study the portrait. "I wish I could see what you looked like as a child," he said softly.

Elizabeth turned to him with the achingly sad expression in her eyes that came every time she thought about her child-hood. "Would that I had a likeness to show you."

They regarded each other in silence, the air seemingly

charged between them. He started to reach out to her, but Tibbs's cough interrupted his thoughts.

"Pardon me, my lord, but it's ten o'clock. You asked to be informed."

"Right," Aidan replied, letting his arm fall back to his side. "Thank you, Tibbs." He turned to Elizabeth with an apology on his lips. "If you'll excuse me, I have a meeting with Gavin this morning. Actually, that's quite how the next few weeks are going to go. We have to get everything into the shops in time for the season, so I'm afraid I won't get to spend much time with you this week."

"Lainey is good company, and you are hardly responsible for my entertainment."

"Even so, I'm afraid I'm not being a very good host."

"I think I can forgive you." She smiled.

"Brilliant. I'll make it up to you at some point." He offered his arm to Elizabeth. "May I show you back to the dining room?"

"Actually, Mrs. Dunn promised to show me how to make an apple pie today…if that's all right with you," she added sheepishly.

He grinned down at her. "Of course! Provided I get to sample your efforts."

Elizabeth blushed. "We'll see."

Aidan raised a brow. "To the kitchens, then. Minx." He winked, and inside, Elizabeth went all fizzy.

Oh, this was trouble.

CHAPTER 15

It was a beautiful early April day, the warm sun encouraging the flowers to make an appearance. Richard helped Aidan shrug into a charcoal gray morning coat before he headed down to breakfast. Lainey was already seated at the table, and he bent to kiss her on the cheek. No sooner had he settled in to read the morning paper when Elizabeth joined them, rivaling the radiance of the spring day in a floral-sprigged muslin gown. Another of Lainey's purchases for her, it was white with purple floral sprays and trimmed in deep purple ribbon at the square-cut neckline, cuffs, and overskirt. Lace flounces ended the three-quarter length sleeves, giving him a peek of her creamy skin. What would it be like to press a kiss to the inside of that wrist? Would he feel her pulse flutter under his lips?

"Good morning, Elizabeth," he said, standing and shaking off the mental image before he embarrassed himself. "You are looking well." *Like sunshine after three weeks of rain is more like it.*

"Thank you. Good morning, Lainey."

"Morning, Eliza." She poked at her soft-boiled egg while

Aidan reclaimed his seat and dabbed at his mouth with his napkin. For a horrifying moment, he thought he was actually drooling.

"My brother's right. Purple is most becoming on you."

"Thank you. I must admit, you both have spoiled me with this wardrobe."

"Nonsense," Aidan said flatly, immersing himself in the front page of the paper. The two women glanced at him, then exchanged smiles over the table. True to his word, Aidan had been extremely busy for the past few weeks, but when he was home, he made sure he spent time with Elizabeth. Much to his relief, she had lost that look of fear in her eyes, and was no longer uncomfortable around him. She even went so far as to seek him out in the library one evening for his recommendation on a book. They had wound up sitting companionably by the fire as he read her more poetry. He had steered clear of the romantics, and she had hung on every word. Aidan could not remember ever having had a more enjoyable evening.

The three chatted comfortably while they ate, and all the while Aidan stole glances at Elizabeth when she wasn't looking. She had grown so damned captivating he could hardly keep his eyes off of her. She had finally put on some weight, and her ivory skin glowed with health. The visible injuries had faded, though her bones were still healing. Soon, she would be well enough to be on her way, though to where, he still had no idea.

He had never met anyone quite like her. She was smart, much smarter than she believed herself to be, and she had a vibrant sense of humor. Aidan had laughed more in the past few weeks than he had in the past few years, a refreshing and much-needed change.

As he watched the banter between her and Lainey, he

realized that it seemed like she was part of the family. Like she had always been there. Like she belonged there.

He gradually became aware that it had grown quiet, and he glanced at his sister, who was pointedly watching him stare at Elizabeth, with one dainty eyebrow raised. A mischievous smile lit her face. "Aidan, it's such a lovely day out, and Elizabeth is faring so much better now. Perhaps you should take her on a tour of the nearby park today." She turned to Elizabeth. "There's the most darling pond there."

Aidan took in Elizabeth's shocked expression. He, too, was surprised by Lainey's suggestion.

"Park?" Elizabeth's voice was shrill. "As in, out in public?"

"Oh yes, but not to worry, it's quiet. Nothing like Hyde Park. It's just a little bit of a thing, hardly anyone goes there. But I adore the pond. And the fresh air would do you good."

"I…I think it's a perfectly…lovely idea," Elizabeth stammered. "You *must* join us, Lainey." There was a slight note of pleading in her voice.

"Oh, no," she replied, shaking her head. "I have far too many calls to pay today. I couldn't possibly find the time. You'll have quite an enjoyable day with Aidan, I'm sure."

"But—"

"Now do be mindful of Elizabeth, brother. I can't have you wearing her out. Do you think you can sit a horse, Eliza? It would be a very tiresome walk for you at this point in your recovery."

Elizabeth was staring at Lainey with her mouth hanging open in dismay. Clearly, she was not as in love with the idea as Lainey was.

"I…I think I can manage it," Elizabeth said into the silence that had fallen as they awaited her answer. "Though I haven't been on a horse since I was a young girl."

Aidan narrowed his eyes at his sister. "Lainey's mare is very gentle. She would be a good choice."

"How thoughtful you are, brother," Lainey gushed. "See, Elizabeth? He will take good care of you. You can borrow one of my bonnets and a pair of gloves, and I think what you're wearing will do nicely. No need for a riding habit if you're just taking the horses for a walk. You do have the time today, don't you, Aidan? I should have asked before I got Elizabeth's hopes up."

Aidan was already mentally rearranging his schedule. "Of course," he replied, knowing full well that to refuse now would be impolite, and that he had been maneuvered into doing exactly what Lainey wanted. "Would you care to accompany me today, Elizabeth?"

She was trapped. "I think I should like that very much. Thank you."

"Splendid!" Lainey clapped her hands together. "Oh, but it is a shame you are not well enough to travel, for I would dearly love to show you the house in the country. The property there is quite extensive, and Rosecroft is far grander than this house. It's so peaceful there. Oh, Aidan, when Elizabeth is all set right again, you *must* invite her out for a visit!"

Aidan was eyeing Lainey. She looked all innocence, but he knew better. When his sister was up to something, her eyes took on an exceptionally bright sparkle, as they did now. The question was, what devious plot was running through her mind?

"Of course, you must join us sometime, Elizabeth." Lainey had put him in a bad position by making that demand of him. How could he know if he would ever even see Elizabeth again after she left his home? But Lainey seemed not to notice as she prattled on.

"I usually head out of London before the season draws to a close, and stay the remainder of the summer there, much to my brother's chagrin. He'd rather I stay in London for the entire season to find a husband, but I can't see why I need one. Why do I want to spend my days entertaining fops who are looking at me more for my money than who I am inside?"

"Lainey!"

"What? It's true, and you know it," Lainey admonished, turning to her brother. "You don't like the frivolous, simpering ladies any more than I like the ridiculous men. Isn't that the reason you're still a bachelor?"

For the first time since Elizabeth had known him, she witnessed Aidan flush. "It's less important for me to find a wife than it is for you to find a husband," he said pointedly.

"Nonsense. You need an heir. Besides, you'll take care of me, won't you?"

"And what if something happens to me?"

Lainey sighed dramatically. "All right, then. I'll get married. Just not yet," she added.

Aidan smiled at Elizabeth, who had been watching the exchange with great amusement. "Sometimes, I think I wouldn't have minded being an only child," he said dryly.

Lainey gasped and shot out of her chair. "You take that back, big brother! You'd be lost without me, and you can't deny it!" She flung her arms about his neck and peppered his cheek with kisses until he laughed and gave in.

"All right, all right! I take it back, just please stop assaulting me!" They were both laughing now, and Elizabeth sat transfixed as Aidan's rich laughter rolled across the table. "Do you see what I put up with?" he asked her. "You women are trouble, the lot of you," he chuckled, disentangling himself from Lainey.

"Pish, posh. We're the excitement in your lives." Lainey pushed a stray wisp of hair away from her forehead. "Now see what you've done. I have to fix my hair because you're such a brute." Aidan was about to protest that she had started it, but she cut him off. "I'll go fetch that bonnet for you, Elizabeth." She blew a kiss to Aidan and was out the door in a heartbeat.

"Good heavens, but that girl is a free spirit." Aidan shook his head in amusement, picking up the fork Lainey had caused him to drop. Elizabeth glanced out the door after her.

"I adore her," she stated simply.

Aidan looked up. "I do, too," he said, winking at Elizabeth.

idan offered Elizabeth his arm as they made their way to the stable. She seemed to be growing accustomed to having him physically close. He watched as the floral-kissed breeze played with wisps of her hair and she turned her face to the sun. She closed her eyes and trusted him to lead the way. Aidan's lips curved in a wry smile. At least she trusted him that much.

She was assisted onto Lainey's gray mare as the stable boy assured her she was a gentle creature and wouldn't give Elizabeth any trouble. He handed her the reins and turned away, and Elizabeth leaned forward to whisper in the mare's ear. "When I'm all better, I promise I'll come and take you out for a proper ride before I leave London," she whispered.

Aidan rode up next to her, a combination of amusement and surprise on his face. "You know how to ride?"

"Goodness, can't a girl and a horse have a private conversation?" She reached down and patted the mare's neck. "Yes, I know how to ride. At least, I did when I was younger. As I said, it's been many years since I've been on a horse." A far away look came into her eyes for a moment, then she blinked and it was gone. "So what's her name?"

"Sally."

"Sally?" Elizabeth made a little choking noise that sounded suspiciously like a snort.

Aidan led the way out of the stable on his magnificent black stallion. "Yes. What's wrong with Sally?"

"It's just…an unusual name for a horse."

"My sister named her. She was seven."

"Ah." Silence fell between them as Aidan led the way out of the stables. "And your stallion?"

Aidan let out a pained sigh. "Simon."

"*Simon?*" Elizabeth was incredulous. Aidan rolled his eyes, and Elizabeth could contain her merriment no longer. She laughed so hard she had to hold her side. "Ow! Oh, Lord Ashby, don't make me laugh like that! It hurts!" She did her best to regain control, but little fits of giggles still slipped out between deep breaths.

Aidan shot her a dirty look. "Are you through?"

Elizabeth hiccupped. "Not quite."

"You're making fun of me."

"Maybe a little," Elizabeth said, hiding her smile behind her hand. "I mean really. Simon? That hardly befits a huge black stallion."

"Again, Lainey. Need I say more?"

"Good heavens, it's a good thing you didn't have any younger siblings. She may have insisted on Lightning or Pudge for them!"

She was rewarded with a bark of laughter. "I think my mother would have put her foot down." He smiled warmly at her. "Shall we?"

They spent the next quarter hour meandering toward the park and chatting comfortably. Their talk turned to family as the pond came into view. Lainey had been right. The tiny park was nearly deserted. Aidan helped Elizabeth off of her horse, tied the reins, and tucked her arm in the crook of his elbow once again as he led her toward the water's edge.

"If I may be so bold, why is Lainey so set against marriage?" Elizabeth asked.

"She's not. But she had her heart broken a few years ago, so she's very cautious. She wants to take her time and find love that will last her a lifetime."

"Do you not wish to have the same thing for yourself?"

"No." There was not a hint of hesitation in his response. "No, I do not. I'm looking for intelligence. Practicality. Humor. Someone who will make me a good partner."

"You don't believe in love, then?"

Aidan stopped and looked down at her with a sad smile. "On the contrary. I believe in all-consuming love. I just want no part of it."

Elizabeth brows furrowed. "I don't understand."

Aidan sighed. "My father…loved my mother with every fiber of his being. It was like she was an extension of who he was." He resumed their slow pace around the edge of the pond, surveying the area with a distant look in his eyes as he spoke. "I still remember what it was like to see his face light up when she entered the room. When I was seventeen, she contracted scarlet fever. I watched my father cry and pray over her bed every day. When she died, she took his soul with her." Aidan paused, fighting the tightness in his throat. His voice was rough with emotion when he continued. "Her death completely destroyed him. I watched him go from a vibrant, happy man to an empty shell that just existed for Lainey's sake and mine. The light in his eyes had been completely snuffed out. Gone were the father and man I had once known. He never recovered from her death. He held on for four years, drifting from day to day, a ghost of who he once was, a shadow in the house. I truly believe the despair of life without her is what took him in the end. Once he knew I could take care of myself...he simply let go." He turned haunted eyes to Elizabeth. "I don't ever want to love someone like that. I fear I would never survive it."

Elizabeth studied him for a long moment, then said simply, "What a waste."

"How do you mean?" Aidan asked, surprised by her comment.

"Because you have so much love to give."

Aidan halted abruptly and turned to face her. "And how do you know that?"

"It shows in everything you do," she replied softly. "In how you treat your friends, your family...in how you've treated me." She moved a step closer and rested her hand on his forearm. "There are some who would have simply paid for my treatment, but most would have walked away, because a poor woman isn't worth the effort. But you...you have taken me into your own home and given me everything I needed to get well, not because you had to, but because you felt it was right. And you bothered to get to know me. Do you have any idea what that has meant to me?" She blinked rapidly, and Aidan detected the sheen of tears in her eyes. "There are few who would have done as you did. That is the mark of a kind and loving man, and it is a shame to hide such a good heart simply because you are afraid of what might happen. We will all face loss sooner or later, and while it's true a few never recover, you are not that man. You are strong and resilient, and you will allow the love of your family and friends to get you through. Your father chose to turn his back on that. But don't blame love for his death. Love can be such a wonderful thing if you are lucky enough to find it."

Aidan simply stared at her, rooted to his spot. He did not trust himself to speak past the lump in his throat. Her words had touched him very deeply, in a place only she seemed able to find. Somewhere deep inside, there was suddenly light where there had only been darkness, like the sun peeking through the shutters at dawn. He leaned closer, searching her face. "How do you do that?"

"Do what, my lord?"

"See right into my soul and lay me bare."

The breeze caught a strand of her hair, dancing it around, casting a spell on Aidan. He reached out to tuck it behind her ear, and in that moment, he knew he was a man undone. "Elizabeth, I...forgive me." Without another thought, he leaned forward and kissed her.

Her lips were as soft as the words she spoke from them. Despite her squeak of surprise, she didn't pull away. Lilac permeated the air, intoxicating him, and his heart began to race. It was a gentle embrace, but nothing he had ever experienced before was as tantalizing as this innocent kiss. He moved his mouth over hers, and felt her soften in his arms. Desire roared to life inside him, and he barely managed to restrain himself from crushing her to him in a decidedly less-innocent kiss. It was a tempting thought. Instead, he pulled back from her, his breath coming in short bursts, shocked to discover that he was trembling. Could such a simple kiss do that to a man?

Aidan looked down at her in confusion. He couldn't imagine what had made him lose control and kiss her, but now that he had, he burned to do it again. In fact, he wanted nothing more at that moment than to wrap his arms around her and kiss her senseless. Somehow, over the past month, she had utterly bewitched him.

Elizabeth was staring up at him with bewildered eyes, her lips parted in shock. Aidan managed to find his voice. "Forgive me, Elizabeth. I...I wasn't thinking," he stammered.

Elizabeth just blinked at him, her mouth still open. She

stood frozen for a moment, then blinked again, snapped her mouth shut, and moved past him. She was heading back to where they had come from, and at a much faster pace.

"Elizabeth—"

"It's all right." She waved a hand at him in dismissal, but she didn't look back. He finally regained the feeling in his legs and chased after her. He caught up to her easily and blocked her path.

"No, it's not. Clearly I've upset you."

"I'm fine." She pivoted on her heel and marched back to the edge of the pond. She was obviously not fine. He gave her a moment alone before joining her at the water's edge.

"Elizabeth." She turned to him, a look in her eyes he couldn't discern. "Really, I do beg your pardon. It was inappropriate of me to press my advantage. But honestly, I think I've wanted to do that for quite some time." That darned stray wisp of hair danced about in the breeze, taunting him. He grasped her shoulders. "Do forgive me," he implored. He could feel her trembling. So the kiss had rattled her, too. Good.

"My lord, I—"

"Aidan. My name is Aidan."

"I know that."

"Let me hear you say it. Please," he added softly.

Her eyes were huge in her face. "Aidan," she whispered.

A thrill raced down his spine. Yes, she intoxicated him.

"Aidan," she repeated, stronger now. "I beg you. Do not get attached to me. I must leave very soon and return to my life and you must return to yours."

"You cannot think I am just going to let you disappear… to just go back to living as you were."

"You must."

"Why must I?"

"I…I cannot tell you." She moved past him, but he caught her by the elbow.

"Tell me. *Please,*" he beseeched. "Tell me how to help you." She regarded him for so long that he thought she might acquiesce. But she blinked back the tears that were forming in her eyes and shook her head.

"You are a good man, Aidan Lockwood." And she walked away.

CHAPTER 17

*E*lizabeth was awake.

Again.

It seemed she'd hardly slept in the two days since her outing with Aidan. She had barely seen him because he'd been terribly busy with work—the season would officially start in less than a week—but she had not stopped thinking about him. About that kiss.

She hadn't even realized how much she'd wanted it until he'd kissed her. She had sworn she would never let another man touch her, but yet, here she was, trying to stifle the yearning to be in his arms.

But it didn't matter whether she yearned or not. She could never have him. She really couldn't even be associated with him after she left. Their worlds were too different, her past too tarnished. Her heart was breaking at the prospect of leaving the only home she'd known in years.

But she knew it was time to go. She was well enough. There was no reason to stay, and the longer she stayed, the more she risked bringing shame and danger to this family. She couldn't find Betsy without getting out of the house, and she couldn't very well ask Aidan to bring her to St. Giles. She had a quest to complete. Her parents were out there somewhere, and she *would* find them. She hadn't endured eight years of poverty, near starvation, and salacious men to give up now.

Elizabeth tossed the covers off in a huff. She was clearly not going to sleep any time soon, so she might as well get a book from the library.

AIDAN STOOD in his study pouring himself a brandy. It had been a long day. A promised shipment of silks hadn't arrived, resulting in many unhappy shopkeepers. With only one week to go before the official start of the season, he and Gavin had spent the day smoothing ruffled feathers and tamping down panic that shops wouldn't be able to fill their gown orders. He'd left the house very early this morning and arrived home well after dark—everyone had already retired for the evening. He hadn't seen Elizabeth all day.

But he hadn't stopped thinking about her for a minute. That's what bothered him, he thought, sipping his drink. It seemed that she was everywhere, no matter what he did to push her from his mind. She had definitely gotten under his skin. And he certainly hadn't been prepared for what he'd felt when he'd kissed her. It had been such a chaste kiss, yet it had shaken him to his very core.

Aidan leaned back on the velvet sofa and closed his eyes, listening to the soothing crackle of the fire and letting the brandy relax him. He lay there pondering his situation for some time, the toastiness of the fire seeping into his weary body.

IT WAS in this vulnerable position that Elizabeth found him when she happened past the study on her way to the library. The house was dark and quiet, except for the glow coming from Aidan's study. What business could he possibly be conducting at one o'clock in the morning? She couldn't resist tiptoeing to the door to peek in. She had no idea what she would do once she got there—she had no excuse for disturbing him. But she couldn't stop her traitorous heart from beating a little faster at the thought of seeing him.

She expected to find him sitting at his desk, scrawling something in the ledger or poring over invoices, but instead she saw him lying on the couch, his eyes closed and looking completely at peace. She couldn't tell if he was asleep or simply resting.

"Aidan?" she said softly. When she received no reply, she crept into the room. She knew she shouldn't be in his study without his permission, but she couldn't help herself. She stopped in front of the couch and whispered again. "Aidan?"

Still nothing. He was sound asleep. She wondered why he was here and not in his bedchamber. What had kept him from changing for bed? He was still in his trousers and white linen shirt, minus the ascot, the top portion of his shirt gaping open at the neck, revealing smooth skin with dark hair sprinkled across it. Elizabeth couldn't help but stare; the man was maddeningly attractive. The firelight bathed his features in a soft golden glow that only added to his mysterious air. A lock of dark hair had fallen across his forehead, and before she knew what she was doing, Elizabeth reached out to put it back in its place.

She was shocked at how soft his hair was. She had a sudden urge to run her fingers through it. He was much less intimidating when he was sleeping, which empowered Elizabeth to be bold. She lightly touched his hair at his temple while she studied his face. She noticed the line on his cheek where he had split it open on the cobblestones. She was sorry it had scarred his perfect face, yet somehow, it made him even more attractive. Why was it that every imperfection made men more attractive, yet women were expected to be flawless? It was hardly fair.

She continued her perusal, and decided she definitely liked what she saw. Even in his relaxed state, she could see that he had well-formed muscles under his shirt. She wondered what he did to keep his body in such fine condition.

One of his hands was draped across his stomach, the other lying face up by his side. Elizabeth knelt down and examined it. She knew his palm was smooth and warm, and that its touch could send tingles down her spine. She wondered if men had the same reaction to a simple caress. She bent closer to study the lines in his palm. The pleasing aroma of sandalwood and brandy tickled her nose.

She ached to thread her fingers through his, to feel that reassuring strength surround her. She had sworn off men years ago, but somehow…somehow he was different. He made her want to believe that he was all he appeared to be. She wanted to trust him. But could she? Could she go against everything she had learned and actually trust a man? No, she couldn't. At least, not until she figured out if Gavin really had anything to do with her family's death…she *knew* his was the voice she'd heard that awful night so long ago, but he seemed so genuine and gentle…did Gavin really have it in him to murder a family? And why hadn't he recognized her? Was he waiting for the right moment to make himself known to her? The pieces of the puzzle just didn't quite fit, and she couldn't risk telling Aidan the truth until she knew for sure if she was mistaken.

Elizabeth absently reached out one finger and softly

traced a line in Aidan's palm. She marveled at how his hands were always warm.

"Keep doing that and I can't be held responsible for my actions."

Elizabeth cried out and shot to her feet, losing her balance. She stumbled backwards toward the fireplace. Aidan was on his feet in an instant, making a grab for her, but she stepped on the hem of her robe and landed with a thud at the edge of the hearth. Aidan reached for her, and she cringed. She squeezed her eyes shut and turned her head, waiting for the explosion of pain across her jaw.

Only it never came.

She cracked open one eye and peeked fearfully at Aidan. He was still standing over her, his hand outstretched, palm up, completely frozen in place. She opened both eyes and registered the look of horror on his face, and she belatedly realized that he had only been trying to prevent her from getting hurt. Guilt flooded her, and looked away.

"You thought I was going to strike you," he said quietly. His wounded expression was a dagger to her heart.

Elizabeth hated herself, hated that her past experiences had made her jump to that conclusion. "I am trespassing in your private study. I entered without your permission."

"You didn't even protect yourself," he said incredulously, still frozen. "You just waited for it."

Elizabeth squirmed under his gaze. "It happened a lot," she finally admitted. "It ended faster if I didn't fight back."

Aidan looked ill. "I'm sorry I frightened you."

"I disturbed you," she replied quietly, staring at the floor.

"You weren't disturbing me. I was rather enjoying it." He let his hand fall to his side. "Are you hurt?"

"No," she replied softly, turning liquid eyes to him. "But you are."

Aidan sighed and moved to sit beside her. "Whatever you

have suffered in your past will shape your future, Elizabeth. I cannot fault you for your fears. I can only hope that I can somehow help allay them."

He covered her hand with his, offering her reassurance with his touch. Elizabeth's heart ached. The image of his hurt-filled eyes burned in her mind, the look of horror on his face when he realized what she had thought of him for just a moment. How could she have even thought…

"I'm sorry, Aidan," she whispered. "It was just a reaction. I didn't mean to offend you."

"I know." His eyes burned into hers, and she wasn't sure if it was the heat of the fire or the heat of his gaze that was causing the flood of warmth coursing through her body. "I promise you, Elizabeth," he said softly, reaching out to lay his palm against her cheek. "When my hand touches your face, it will always be like this." He moved his fingers to brush just under her earlobe, feathering his thumb back and forth across her cheek. It was enough to make her weep. A single tear slid out from underneath her lashes and wended its way down her cheek.

"Oh, Elizabeth. Please don't cry. I can't bear it." He wiped the tear away and tucked his knuckle under her chin, forcing her to look at him. "Tell me why you're crying."

Elizabeth shrugged, blinking back the other tears that threatened to come. "I don't know," she choked out against the tightness in her throat.

"Do you think I'm angry with you?"

"No. Maybe. I don't know. It's just that I…I upset you. I didn't mean to hurt your feelings."

"I know that." He tucked the ever-present stray wisp of hair behind her ear. "You don't have it in you."

Elizabeth allowed herself to bask in his caress. For the first time since they'd met, there was not a molecule in her body that wanted to shrink away from him. She searched his face, the glow from the fire highlighting the tiny golden flecks in his eyes, eyes that held nothing but compassion. She knew now that she had been an absolute fool. He had proven himself time and time again, but she had stubbornly refused to acknowledge that she could trust him not to hurt her. The only thing this man wanted to do was help her get back on her feet. She sighed inwardly. *When had she become such a coward?*

She again found the scar that she had accidentally given him, and she tentatively reached out to touch it. "I'm sorry I did that to you."

"I'm not," Aidan said, his voice husky. "The alternative would have been much worse."

She ran her finger along the scar, and Aidan closed his eyes, leaning into her soft caress.

"Elizabeth?"

"What?"

But he didn't answer her. Never opening his eyes, he tipped forward until his lips found her neck. He brushed them up to her earlobe, eliciting a small gasp. "Elizabeth," he whispered, dragging his lips across her jaw now, dropping kisses onto her sensitive skin.

Elizabeth was delirious. She knew she should make some sort of objection, but the power of speech had completely deserted her. Every inch of her skin tingled, her breath shallow. She was sure he could hear her heart pounding in her ears, because it was deafening her. Never before had she known a touch so gentle, nor so tantalizing. It frightened her beyond comprehension.

Aidan continued his path along her jaw until he reached her chin, and moved upward from there. He hesitated only a moment before touching his lips to hers.

Elizabeth threw caution to the wind and kissed him back.

She leaned into him, reveling in his touch. His lips were like velvet, caressing her with their softness. He nipped her lower lip and she gasped, giving him the opportunity to deepen the kiss. He thrust his hand into her hair and settled his mouth more firmly on hers, his tongue gently teasing hers. Elizabeth had never been kissed like this, ever, and her body hummed. Even the first time Aidan had kissed her, it had been far less seductive. This was full of longing and desire, something Elizabeth had never known. It both thrilled and alarmed her, and it occurred to her that if she were to die at this very moment, she would leave this world happier than she'd ever been.

That was it. Aidan made her happy. It was a feeling she could barely remember. Heavens, she could hardly think at all with his fingers tangling in her hair like that, his mouth teasing hers so intimately. Elizabeth drifted on a sea of bliss, her body numb to everything but his touch. Her mind wandered, and for just a moment, she let herself wonder what it would be like to give in completely, heart and body.

But just for a moment. The reality was, her past would remain unchanged, and Aidan would never be able to accept it. She couldn't be what he needed, in any way, no matter what her heart wanted. With a muffled sound, she broke the embrace and pushed him gently away.

"Aidan, we can't do this. I can't do this."

Aidan pulled back. "What's wrong?"

"I...I just can't. I'm so sorry." She scrambled to her feet, and Aidan followed. He caught her by the hand before she fled the room.

"What are you so afraid of, Elizabeth?"

She turned and looked at him, and for the first time, the absolute truth sprang to her lips. "Of liking you too much."

Aidan's expression softened. "I hardly think that's a bad thing."

She snorted. "You say that now, but you don't know..." She sighed. "You just don't know."

Aidan gave her hand a tug and pulled her into him, his free hand slipping about her waist to rest on the small of her back. "I want to know, Elizabeth. I want to know all about you."

Elizabeth stared up at him, very aware of how close his body was to hers. All of a sudden, she wanted to know what it was like to be held in his arms, protected from all of her fears, to rest her head on his shoulder and breathe in the very essence of him...to know she had a home. But it was useless to long for things that would never be. She gave him a small smile, full of regret.

"Aidan, you are the most wonderful man I have ever known. You have been so kind to me, and when I am gone from your life, I want you to remember me for who I am, not who I was. You and Lainey are the only friends I have. I cannot bear to lose you."

"You are not going to lose me, Elizabeth. There is nothing you could tell me that would change my good opinion of you."

"I wish I could believe that."

"Can you not see how I've come to care for you?"

"Aidan, don't. You can't. You'll only wind up hurt, and I'll not be the one to hurt you." She slipped her hand from his and stepped back, out of the circle of his arms. "Please try to understand. If indeed you care about me as you say you do, you'll let this go." She turned to leave the room, but Aidan's voice stopped her at the door.

"Elizabeth."

She froze, unable to face him.

"You will never be gone from my life."

Elizabeth's throat constricted. "Yes, Aidan. I will. Good night."

CHAPTER 18

idan was gone by the time Elizabeth managed to rouse herself the next morning, for which she was extremely grateful. She had lain awake all night after she had fled from the study, the memory of Aidan's kisses burning in her mind. It had been years since she'd allowed a man to touch her at all, much less kiss her. But none had ever touched her like that. She'd felt no fear, either, and that alarmed her because she knew it meant she was dangerously close to losing her heart to a man she could never have. But she couldn't seem to gather the courage to walk away.

She was just finishing her breakfast with Lainey when she heard the front door open, followed by the sound of Aidan's voice. She sighed inwardly. So she hadn't avoided facing him after all.

Moments later, he appeared in the doorway. "Good morning, ladies."

Elizabeth didn't want to look up, didn't want to see the hunger that she knew would be in his eyes. She mentally steeled herself and glanced up at him, and when she did, her breath caught. He had obviously been out riding, his hair tousled from the wind and his cheeks flushed. He had never looked more handsome. "Good morning, my lord." She broke off a too-large piece of toast and stuffed it in her mouth, studying her plate with astonishing scrutiny.

Lainey didn't say a word. She simply looked back and forth between her brother, who couldn't take his eyes off of Elizabeth, and Elizabeth, who couldn't meet his gaze. It was clear something had happened between them, and from the look of things, it had been quite powerful.

"The shipment of silks that was supposed to be here yesterday has arrived. I have to go down to the warehouse in a couple of hours to sort things out. I apologize for skipping out on breakfast, but I needed a good ride."

Elizabeth's fork clattered to her plate. *Surely that had been more innocent than it sounded.*

"We understand, brother dearest." Lainey chuckled when Aidan's gaze snapped to his sister, seemingly surprised to see her sitting there. Clearly, he had not even noticed her when he came in. "Perhaps you could take Elizabeth with you. The exercise would do her good."

"No!" Elizabeth's eyes widened in alarm. Both Aidan and Lainey regarded her curiously. "Er…I mean, I'm sure your brother is much too busy to drag me about with him."

"Nonsense. It's about time you got out of the house. And on the arm of one of London's finest." Lainey's eyes were dancing.

The last place Elizabeth wanted to be was out in a crowd. Too many prying eyes, too vulnerable. And she could hear the gossip already.

"What is the earl doing parading about with the likes of her?"

"She's clearly up and about. Doesn't she know she's overstayed her welcome?"

"I bet the earl is enjoying his little bit on the side."

Surely Aidan would realize the scandal that could be brought upon the family.

But Aidan, the blasted man, agreed with Lainey.

"I could show you my ship, if you like. It shouldn't take too long, and I should enjoy the company."

And just like that, Elizabeth was trapped again. She couldn't think of a shareable reason why she could refuse, so she reluctantly accepted.

She prayed that no one would recognize her.

ELIZABETH WAS VERY aware of the curious glances people were sending her way. She knew tongues were wagging all around them, but Aidan didn't seem to notice. He was far too intent on his company. She'd hoped they would take the carriage all the way to the dock, but Aidan had opted to stroll for awhile. Occasionally they would stop to say hello to someone he knew, and he introduced her simply by name, and then moved on. They were deep into a conversation about Aidan's business when someone called out his name.

"Ashby!"

Aidan's head snapped up to see his friend, William Everett, and his new wife heading toward them. He broke into a wide grin.

"About time you came back, Everett," he chided. "I was beginning to think we'd lost you permanently."

"We've only just returned." Will shook hands with his friend. "I was going to call on you this afternoon. Thank you for saving me the trouble."

"Good to have you home. Welcome back, Mrs. Everett. I see married life is agreeing quite well with you."

Louisa smiled. "Thank you, Lord Ashby," she replied, offering her hand.

Aidan kissed it, then indicated the woman standing next to him. "Mr. and Mrs. William Everett, may I present to you Miss Elizabeth Townsend. Miss Townsend, Mr. and Mrs. Everett."

"I'm pleased to make your acquaintance," Elizabeth said, inclining her head.

"The pleasure is ours, Miss Townsend," Louisa replied, bowing slightly. Will, however, was openly staring at Elizabeth.

"Good Lord, Ash. Could this be who I think it is?"

Elizabeth shifted uncomfortably under his scrutiny. Aidan glanced down at her and back to Will. "Forgive me," he replied. "I forgot she was unconscious the last time you saw her."

A friendly smile spread across Will's face, and he bowed gallantly. "Miss Townsend, it is indeed an honor to meet you. And might I say I'm quite happy to see you are much improved since the last time I saw you."

Realization dawned on Elizabeth. "You were there that night. I remember you now. You were the one who distracted Lord Ashby so I could slip away," she teased.

Will let out a shout of laughter. "I see you didn't get very far," he noted, looking pointedly at her arm still linked through Aidan's. "How fortunate for all of us."

"Oh, good heavens, my lord," she said, turning to Aidan. "Are all of your friends this charming?"

"Not all," he chuckled. "Will just tends to lay it on thick."

"Now see here, Ash—"

"It's all right, darling," Louisa chimed in, patting his arm. "It worked on me and that's all that matters." She was a petite brunette with a gentle manner and soft brown eyes. Elizabeth liked her immediately. "How very brave of you, Miss Townsend, to throw yourself in harm's way for a complete stranger," she continued. "We left for our honeymoon before we had much news of you. I imagine you've had quite a difficult recovery."

"Lord Ashby has taken very good care of me and I am quite on the mend now," Elizabeth assured her.

"I'm sure he has," Will agreed, shooting Aidan a knowing look. "Well, we simply must do something to celebrate your remarkable recovery and say thank you for saving my friend's life. What do you think, Mrs. Everett?"

"I think a dinner party in her honor would be a lovely idea!"

"Oh, thank you, but you really needn't bother," Elizabeth said hastily. "I'd hate to see you go to all that trouble just for me."

"It's no trouble at all, Miss Townsend," Will insisted. "It would be a good opportunity to catch up with all the friends we've missed terribly, and allow us to get to know you better. Besides," he added, slipping his arm about Louisa's waist, "it will give my wife the chance to be hostess in her new home."

Louisa beamed up at him, and Elizabeth felt her heart twist. How could she refuse when Louisa was obviously dying to host her first party? She sent a pleading glance to Aidan.

"It would be a nice way to make some new friends, Miss Townsend," Aidan said pointedly.

I don't want new friends! she wanted to scream. *I can't get attached to this life!*

"She has two new ones already," Louisa smiled. "Any friend of Lord Ashby's is a friend of ours."

"You really are too kind, Mr. and Mrs. Everett," Elizabeth smiled. How was is that she was constantly being cornered into things? "Thank you for your gracious invitation. It sounds marvelous."

"Capital!" Will clapped his hands together. "Consider it done. Shall we say two nights hence? And now, if you'll forgive us, we must be on our way. So very nice to have met you at last, Miss Townsend. I look forward to getting to know you better." He sketched a brief bow to her and nodded to Aidan. "Ash."

"Good day to you both," he replied, tipping his hat to Louisa. As soon as they had gone, Elizabeth dug her fingers into Aidan's arm in panic.

"Aidan, I've never been to a dinner party," she hissed. "I'm going to make a fool of myself!"

"I won't let that happen. The rules are quite simple, really. Conversation, dinner, more conversation, sometimes dancing."

"But I don't know how to conduct myself with these people!"

"Just be your beguiling self and you will be a hit, I promise."

Elizabeth shook her head. "This is a terrible idea. Perhaps I will become ill before Thursday."

Aidan laughed. "You will do no such thing. Lainey will tell you all you need to know. Come, Miss Townsend," he said, continuing their path down the street. "I'd like to show you what it is I do all day."

"Oh, very well," she sighed.

"If it's not too much trouble," he teased.

Her face flushed pink. "I don't mean to be churlish."

Aidan smiled tenderly at her. "I know."

They walked on in companionable silence, but she couldn't shake the feeling that she was being watched. She glanced furtively around, but saw nothing unusual. But it was the same tingling she'd felt the night she'd been out in the orchard watching her home burn.

She tightened her grip on Aidan's arm. As long as she was with him, she was safe.

That in itself was a startling realization.

AIDAN HAD RETURNED her to his home and left her at the door to go to an appointment. Tibbs let her in and took her—well, really, Lainey's—bonnet.

"This came for you while you were out, Miss," he said, handing her a sealed note.

"For me? Are you sure?"

"Yes, Miss. The lad was quite clear."

"Thank you, Tibbs." She turned the letter over in her hand as she wandered toward the drawing room. There was nothing on the outside. Who could know to send something here? She had met a few of Lainey's friends at tea last week, but it seemed unlikely that they would send her anything.

Then she knew. Betsy must have found her! At last, some news! She tore the seal and eagerly unfolded the note.

She gasped and fell against the wall, covering her mouth with her hand. It was not from Betsy.

She recovered herself and marched back out to Tibbs. "Who delivered this note?" she demanded.

"A messenger boy, Miss."

"Did he say anything?"

"Just to be sure you got the message."

She'd gotten the message, all right. Loud and clear.

I know who you are.

CHAPTER 19

*L*ater that evening, Gavin sprawled in a chair with a drink in his hand as he watched Aidan pace the study. Aidan was a man not easily rattled by anything—he had remarkable control over his temper, and rarely unleashed it. He was level headed and the person you'd want around during an emergency. Gavin had known him his entire life, and had seen him through most everything, but never, not once in his life, had he ever seen the man pace.

"Do you want to tell me what's got you so upset?" he asked, sipping his brandy.

Aidan stopped short. "I beg your pardon?"

"I've never seen you pace before." He paused. "Ever," he added for emphasis.

"I'm pacing?" Aidan asked, surprised.

"What is it, my friend? Everything has been worked out at Lockwood Imports, so I know it's not that. What's bothering you so?"

Aidan sighed and shoved his hand through his hair. "I came home this afternoon to find Elizabeth had packed everything and was preparing to leave. She looked as though she'd been crying."

"She left?"

"No. I reminded her of her promise to attend the dinner party on Thursday…the one that's being given in her honor. It took a bit of cajoling from both Lainey and me, but she capitulated. But she's not happy about it."

"Seems such an odd shift. Did something happen?"

"I don't know. She refused to talk. Something must have prompted this because she's behaving like a long-tailed cat in a room full of rockers."

"And Lainey knows nothing?"

Aidan shook his head. "She's as lost as I." He perched on the edge of his desk and regarded his brandy. "Funny, but I don't want her to go," he admitted.

Gavin studied his friend. He knew—*knew*—what that admission meant, even if Aidan couldn't accept it yet. "You like her."

"Well of course I like her, don't be ridiculous."

"That's not what I meant."

He looked at Gavin and sighed. "I kissed her, Gav. Last night. And maybe one other time," he added.

Gavin leaned back with a self-satisfied smile on his face. "*That's* what I meant." He shrugged off Aidan's scathing look. "Exactly how does one 'maybe' kiss someone?"

Aidan glared at him. "You're not going to make this easy, are you?"

"Hell, no," Gavin grinned. "So tell me about it. What happened?"

Aidan hesitated. Once he voiced his thoughts, there was no turning back. He sighed and began recounting the events of the past few days, right up until the moment when he had found himself leaning toward Elizabeth by the fire, inexplicably drawn in by the scent of lilacs and the taste of desire. "I don't know what happened to me…no woman has ever had power over me like that. I couldn't help myself. One minute I was lost in her eyes and the next I was…" He shrugged and spread his hands.

"Lost in her lips?" Gavin supplied helpfully.

"If you're going to poke fun at me, then I am not going to bother to confide in you!" Aidan snapped.

"All right, all right," Gavin said, throwing his hands up in surrender. "My apologies. But can you blame me, Aidan? This is the first time in our lives that you have ever come to me about a woman. Usually it's the other way around. I have to tease you just a little."

Aidan changed his expression from murderous to merely annoyed.

Gavin grinned. He could push every button Aidan owned. "So did she kiss you back?"

His expression softened. "Oh, yes." Aidan sighed again. "But then she pushed me away. Said she's afraid of liking me too much, and that she doesn't want to hurt me."

"Hurt you?"

"Yes. She said she couldn't bear to lose me because of her past…she wants to let it be so I can remember her just as she is."

"Deuced odd. What could she possibly be hiding that would make you not want to speak to her again?"

"I haven't any idea, and it's been bothering me for weeks." He rubbed his chin. "She's terrified of men—"

"Obviously, given her reaction to me."

Aidan grinned. "Nursing a little wounded pride, my friend? Not used to women ducking into the nearest doorway to avoid you?"

"She was terrified of you when you two met," Gavin pointed out.

"True. But she's not afraid of Tibbs. It seems to be more on the level of men in positions of authority. Do you think it might be possible that she worked for someone who… mistreated her? I've known a few men who have taken, shall we say, certain liberties, with the females in their employ. Do you think it possible that she ran away to break free from an abhorrent situation?"

"That would explain why she hasn't been forthcoming with information about her past. She doesn't want to be found. But we've all heard stories like that before. Is she really that naive to think she'd lose your good opinion because she's not innocent?"

"It does sound ridiculous, but who knows what's going on in her head?"

"She's well-educated, Aidan. She hasn't been a servant *all* her life. How do you explain that?"

"I can't. That's the missing piece of the puzzle, I'm sure of it." He shoved off his desk and moved to look out at the darkened street. "If I could just get her to trust me…if she'd tell me the truth, maybe I could help her. I can't bear the thought of her going back to…well, to the way I found her."

"Agreed. But what are we to do if she won't let us help?"

A knock sounded at the door. "Enter," Aidan called.

Mary slipped in and bobbed a curtsy. "Beggin' your pardon, my lord, I've no wish to disturb you, but…"

"What is it, Mary? Is Miss Townsend unwell?"

"No, my lord…well, not exactly." She wrung her hands. "Miss Townsend told me not to tell anyone, and I'm good at keeping secrets, but I thought you should know…"

"Go on, Mary. Please tell me what's wrong."

"I think Miss Townsend might be in danger."

The two men exchanged glances. "What makes you say that?" Aidan asked.

"She has a friend who's gone missing. Someone who was

supposed to meet her the night of your accident. Miss Townsend asked me to inquire about her at the markets when I went out, but no one has heard from her." Mary shifted nervously from foot to foot. "And then I found this." She handed Aidan a folded note.

"*I know who you are.*" He scowled at the note. "What the devil?"

Gavin took it from him. "Well, this would explain her sudden desire to leave."

"Mary, I'll need her friend's name."

"Betsy Clarke, my lord."

"Thank you, Mary. You did the right thing in telling me. But let's keep this conversation between, us, shall we? No need to upset Miss Townsend further."

"I agree, sir. Thank you. Good night."

"Good night."

She left and Aidan turned to Gavin. "Well. This is an interesting turn of events."

"I should say so. What are you going to do?"

"I think it's time to pay a visit to my old friend, Blake."

"The inquiry agent?"

"The very same. We need to find Betsy Clarke as soon as possible. If Elizabeth believes her friend is in danger, then I believe that means Elizabeth is, too. If we can find Betsy, perhaps we can help Elizabeth."

"She is going to be furious with you for interfering, you know."

"I know. And I don't care. She can be angry at me all she likes, so long as she's safe."

"Well then, here's to hoping Blake can find a missing person." He swallowed the last of his brandy and stood to go. "I'll see you tomorrow." He paused at the door and turned back to Aidan. "You do realize you are falling in love with her, don't you?"

Aidan looked steadily back at him but said nothing. Gavin nodded once and left.

Aidan closed his eyes and heaved a heavy sigh.

"Damn."

CHAPTER 20

They arrived at the Everetts' precisely fifteen minutes after seven o'clock. The Everett home was beautiful, and much larger than most townhouses. It had been built long before the others had moved in, and therefore was spacious and had a lovely plot of land in the back, perfect for afternoon teas outside. Louisa had yet to put her stamp on the house, as she'd only had a week, but it was tastefully decorated and surprisingly cozy inside.

They were shown upstairs to the drawing room, where Louisa rushed forth to welcome them. "Forgive me for not meeting you at the door myself. Miss Hastings had just arrived and I was escorting her. Ladies, you look splendid!"

Lainey was wearing a dinner gown of deep green trimmed at the cuffs and neckline with delicate blonde lace, while Elizabeth was heart-stopping in sapphire blue that matched her eyes exactly and black jet beading that complemented her dark hair and ivory skin. If Louisa recognized the gown as Lainey's, she said nothing. Instead, she turned to acknowledge the ladies' escorts. "How nice to see you, Mr. Mayfield. So glad you could join us."

"I thank you for the invitation, Mrs. Everett. Congratulations on your recent marriage. I'm sorry I could not attend," Gavin smiled, giving her a polite bow.

"We did miss you…though there was enough excitement to keep us distracted," she added wryly, glancing at Aidan as he bowed over her hand.

"You look radiant this evening, Mrs. Everett," Aidan purred. "I've always liked burgundy on brunettes."

"You've always liked brunettes," she teased.

He grinned and acquiesced, sending a sideways glance at Elizabeth. "Can you blame me?"

Elizabeth blushed furiously and looked away.

"Come now, Aidan. Stop being such a flirt," Lainey admonished. She sighed and turned to Elizabeth. "It's going to be a long night. I'm afraid I can already feel the charm beginning to ooze."

"Oh, hush, my dear!" Aidan capitulated, laughing. "Gavin, please keep your companion under control!"

"She's *your* sister!"

They all laughed and Louisa excused herself to greet more guests. Aidan took Elizabeth by the arm and led her off to introduce her to some of his friends. He left Lainey and Gavin on their own to mingle, more so to spare Elizabeth than anything else. She was incredibly nervous, most inexplicably every time Gavin went near her. She steadfastly avoided him every time he was in the same room, and though Gavin had made every attempt at conversing with her, she practically fled every time he approached. She insisted nothing was wrong and that Gavin was a perfectly nice gentleman, yet she avoided him as if he were diseased.

He introduced Elizabeth around the room, then showed her over to a small group standing by the window. They greeted Anne Hastings, Lainey's best friend whom Elizabeth had met at tea, and then a young man with red hair and an amiable face turned to address Aidan.

"Ashby! Good to see you, my friend."

"You as well," Aidan returned, shaking hands. "Miss Elizabeth Townsend, may I present to you Donovan MacKavoy? Mr. MacKavoy, Miss Townsend."

"A pleasure to meet you, Miss Townsend."

Elizabeth was standing frozen, staring at Donovan with her mouth hanging open slightly. It was almost as if she'd seen a ghost. Aidan touched her elbow.

"Elizabeth, is everything all right?"

Elizabeth shook her head and snapped to her senses. "Forgive me, sir. The pleasure is mine. I just wasn't expecting...MacKavoy, did you say?"

"Yes, that's right."

"Are you, by chance, any relation to Daniel MacKavoy?"

"Yes, ma'am. He was my grandfather. Did you know him?"

"No. He was an old friend of my father's. He was the reason I came to London in the first place, but he had passed on before I arrived."

Aidan tried to hide his surprise...to discover that her family had known Daniel MacKavoy was startling. Even more shocking was the fact that she had offered the information without any hesitation. If Donovan was taken aback, he didn't show it.

"I'm sorry you didn't get the chance to meet him. He was a wonderful man. Did you have business with him?"

"I'm not really sure. I know that sounds strange, but I was young at the time and didn't know the whole story. Apparently my father was planning to bring my mother and me to visit him, but they were killed before he had the chance. So I arrived by myself, but I was refused at the door. I believe perhaps he had just passed on and the butler couldn't imagine what business a child would have had with him anyway."

"Ah, that would have been Winston. Stuffy old bird, mean as the day is long. I was terrified of him as a child and never happier than when he retired. I'm sorry for your loss, Miss Townsend, and your great misfortune. You must have been very young, indeed."

Elizabeth was spared having to answer because dinner was announced just then. William approached Elizabeth and offered her his arm.

"Miss Townsend, as the guest of honor this evening, may I escort you down to dinner?"

Elizabeth smiled and slipped her arm through William's, while Aidan paired with Louisa. His mind was reeling. Her family knew the MacKavoys? Had her parents been killed in an accident? And why would she come to London on her own instead of turning to family? It didn't make sense.

And the fact that she had just blithely offered up information to Donovan that he'd been begging for since he met her really stuck in his craw. Could it be that she no longer felt she needed to hide her past because she was leaving tomorrow?

Aidan's chest tightened at the very thought.

THE DINING ROOM was comfortably sized to seat twelve, and Elizabeth had never seen such a fancy table in her life. It was covered with an ivory damask tablecloth, in the center of which sat a glorious crystal work of art in the form of a pair of swans, and crystal candle holders that held beeswax candles. Huge bowls of fresh flowers marched their way down the center of the table so that everyone had something pretty to look at while they ate. The china place settings practically glowed in the candlelight and were flanked by more utensils than Elizabeth knew what to do with, plus a bill of fare to the left of every place. It was quite a pleasing effect overall, and Elizabeth could hardly believe that this had been done on her account. She was seated on William's right, with Marcus Walker, Viscount Thorpe, next to her. Across from her was Louisa, next to Aidan, then Anne and Gavin. Next to Lord Thorpe sat Lainey, then Donovan. Anne's brother, Maxwell, completed the party.

They were seated, and a silent footman brought out the soup. Conversation began to flow as easily as the wine, and before long it turned to the night Elizabeth had saved Aidan's life.

"Do tell us, Miss Townsend," Anne said, "How did you ever find the courage to rush in front of a speeding carriage?" She, of course, already knew the story, but she wanted everyone to hear it.

"Yes, how did you manage to knock our boys off their feet?" Donovan grinned.

Elizabeth blushed and glanced at Aidan. "I don't think I was very courageous, Miss Hastings. I wasn't even thinking, I just reacted. And I'm sure desperation had everything to do with my strength, Mr. MacKavoy."

"Well, I for one, am very grateful to you," he returned. "You can't imagine what a scene it was when I came out of the club. I've never felt so helpless in my life."

Until that moment, Elizabeth hadn't realized that she had probably caused quite a ruckus. There had been few people about when the accident had happened, but obviously, she had no idea what had happened after she was knocked unconscious. "I gather I attracted some attention," Elizabeth said wryly.

"That would be a bit of an understatement," he agreed.

"Oh, dear," was all Elizabeth could think of to say. She

was horribly embarrassed at the thought of all those people gawking at her lying on the cobblestones. She was even more embarrassed that she had caused such a scene for Aidan.

"Don't worry, Miss Townsend," Anne reassured her. "You are viewed as quite the heroine. As a matter of fact, several of my friends were quite jealous to learn that I would be dining with you this evening."

"Really?" Elizabeth was doubtful.

"See, sweetheart?" Aidan said, grinning. "People are clamoring to meet you. Imagine that."

Elizabeth's heart caught in her throat. She glanced around the table to see if anyone had noticed the term of endearment Aidan had let slip. William Everett raised his eyebrow at Elizabeth and hid his amused smile behind his wineglass. Further down the table, Donovan snickered. Clearly, it had not been missed. Thankfully, Louisa was there to set things right.

"I'm sure Miss Townsend will tell us all the details you wish after dinner. Shame on you, Mr. MacKavoy, for putting her on the spot like that," she admonished good-naturedly. "Let the poor girl enjoy her dinner."

Elizabeth shot Louisa a grateful look, and dinner continued with the conversation turning to a different vein. Before Elizabeth knew it, an hour had passed and dessert was on the table in front of her. She could scarcely believe the chocolate confection before her, and it tasted as heavenly as it looked. She was enjoying herself immensely, so much so that when Louisa suggested that the ladies should retire to the drawing room to allow the gentleman to enjoy a glass of port, she went without even a backward glance at Aidan.

As soon as the women were gone, all eyes turned to Aidan. His gaze shifted suspiciously from one man to another. "What?" he said flatly. He didn't like the way they were looking at him.

"She's quite charming," Donovan said, casually leaning back in his chair and pinning Aidan with a pointed look.

"I'd have to agree," Maxwell Hastings chimed in. "Though I'm not sure what surprises me more—the fact that she's such a delight, or the fact that you are so obviously delighted *by* her."

"What the devil is that supposed to mean?" Aidan demanded. He was met with amused glances and silence. He turned and shot a dark look at Gavin. "What nonsense have you been spreading about?"

"Me? Aidan, you haven't taken your eyes off of her all evening! What are we supposed to think?"

"Yes, Ash. He's not the one who called her *'sweetheart'.*" Will was grinning from ear to ear. He swirled his port and pretended to study it while he voiced his next thoughts. "Correct me if I'm wrong, but I do believe that on the eve of my wedding, you stated quite clearly—in front of all those currently present, I might add—that if we could find you a woman who had a sharp mind and a sharper wit, you would marry her on the spot."

"I don't remember saying that."

"I remember it." Donovan grinned. "And I believe Miss Townsend qualifies."

Aidan was incredulous. "You must be joking."

"I'm afraid not, my friend," Will said. "We're just trying to help you out."

Aidan snorted. "This is absurd."

"Why?" Maxwell Hastings said. "She's a lovely girl. She's smart, funny, and…refreshing. I'd say she suits you quite well."

Will leaned forward. "There's a lightness to you now that we haven't seen in years. She's obviously the reason."

Aidan stared at his friends. "Have you all lost your minds?"

"Oh, come now, Ashby," Donvan scolded. "You can't really believe she wasn't at some point a well-bred lady. Her manners are impeccable and so is her speech. She's not fooling anyone, least of all you, I'm sure. She must have come from somewhere."

"I haven't been able to find out a thing about her," he admitted grudgingly. "Elizabeth Townsend apparently does not exist. The first clue I've gotten about her past was what she told *you* tonight."

Donovan raised his brows in mock surprise. "Do I hear a note of jealousy in your voice?"

Aidan set his glass down a little too forcefully, and Donovan burst out laughing. It was so rare to be able to tease Aidan about women that they were all taking great advantage of the situation, and he was very well aware of it. He growled at them, causing more outbursts of laughter. He gave Gavin the full brunt of his stare.

"Don't look at me, Aidan. It's obvious you're besotted with her."

"I'm not—damn you, Mayfield!" Aidan never got flustered, and he was beyond frustrated that he couldn't seem to put a coherent sentence together at the moment. "Miss Townsend is a lovely girl, and yes, I enjoy her company quite a bit. I have no intention, however, of marrying her. I do have a certain obligation to uphold a decent reputation, and the *ton*, I'm afraid, would not take that news very well." He left out the real reason he couldn't marry her. But William called his bluff.

"You've never given a damn what society thinks. They can all go hang for all you care." He leaned forward and studied his friend's face. "Why don't you tell us the real reason you don't want to marry her?"

"Because he doesn't want to love his wife," Donovan supplied.

"Too late," Gavin mumbled under his breath. Aidan shot him a withering glance, and then downed the rest of his port.

"Gentlemen, I think we've deprived the ladies of our presence long enough," he suggested, rising.

Maxwell chuckled. "Coward."

"That'll be enough out of you, Hastings," Aidan threatened.

"Darn," he pouted. "And I was having so much fun."

Aidan rolled his eyes and strode out of the room, the peals of laughter following him all the way up the stairs.

CHAPTER 21

*a*idan knew by the way the chatter stopped instantly when he appeared in the doorway that the ladies had been having a similar conversation. All four of them looked his way, wearing identical innocent expressions. *Heaven and earth.* Why had he thought a dinner party was a good idea?

"Ladies," he nodded. "I trust you are enjoying yourselves." They giggled, and he realized that that was probably an understatement. In his experience, there were few topics women enjoyed more than the topic of men—more accurately, how stupid they could be. "Miss Hastings," he said smoothly. "Will you be giving us the pleasure of your music this evening?"

Elizabeth drew in her breath. "Oh, you must! I dearly love music."

"I second that," Anne's brother added as the rest of the men filed into the room.

"Well then, how could I disappoint? You don't mind, Mrs. Everett?"

"It would give me great pleasure, dearest." She turned to Elizabeth. "Anne is quite an accomplished player."

"Too bad I can't sing a note!" Anne laughed, sitting down at the piano and beginning to pluck a beautiful melody from the keys. Elizabeth sat with rapt attention. Anne's playing was obviously a natural talent. The music brought tears to Elizabeth's eyes, and a brief silence fell when she was finished.

"Glorious as always, Anne," Aidan said, leading the applause.

"Why thank you, my lord." She turned to Louisa. "I see the carpets have been rolled back, Mrs. Everett. Perhaps you'd care for something a little livelier?"

"I believe we would, indeed." Louisa smiled.

And the dancing began.

ELIZABETH HAD NEVER HAD SO much fun in her life. She hardly knew what she was doing on the dance floor, but it didn't matter. Aidan was a good teacher and an accomplished dancer, and he had her twirling about and laughing as if she'd danced all her life.

After a particularly uproarious polka, she excused herself to the balcony to cool down and get some air.

"Miss Townsend?"

Elizabeth jumped and whirled around to find herself face to face with the very person who terrorized her every moment. She hadn't noticed him in the shadows. She schooled her face into what she hoped was a serene smile as she inclined her head slightly. "Mr. Mayfield."

He took a few slow steps toward her and she willed herself not to flee. He seemed to notice her discomfort, however, and remained where he was. "You seem to be going to great lengths to avoid me. Might I be so bold as to ask why?"

"Don't be silly, Mr. Mayfield," she laughed, a little too loud. "I am not trying to avoid you."

"And yet every time I am anywhere in the same room with you, you disappear. I try to engage you in conversation, and you give me the most stilted answers and then find the quickest possible way of making your exit. You can barely look me in the eye—you are always looking about to see if someone else is nearby, as you are doing right now."

Elizabeth's gaze flew to his face. She *had* just been looking over his shoulder to see if anyone knew they were out there. She felt herself blush at being caught.

"Aidan has told me of your fear of men, and living as you have, I can certainly understand," Gavin continued, his voice soft. "But what I don't understand is your particular aversion to *me*. I must know, what is it about me that frightens you so?"

He was looking at her so intently. She looked into his eyes —really looked into them for the first time, and she was caught off guard by what she saw in them. Confusion. Hurt.

And genuine concern.

Could she have made a mistake? He truly didn't seem to recognize her at all. If anything, he had been nothing but kind to her since they had met. But that voice. She would never forget that voice. No, she couldn't be mistaken. He had to have been there that night.

Yet…here he was, standing before her trying to make sense out of her strange behavior. And looking so anxious that it actually made her weaken a little. "My apologies, Mr. Mayfield. I fear I've behaved rather oddly with you. It was not intentional."

He leaned closer to her, searching her eyes. "Are you sure about that?"

She shifted, decidedly uncomfortable. Gavin shook his head. "I am quite sure we have never met, so I can't think of what I could have done to upset you so. I had hoped we could be friends, but alas..." He trailed off. "Good evening, Miss Townsend."

He turned to walk away, and before she could stop the words from tumbling out of her mouth, Elizabeth heard herself asking him to wait. She was trembling all over, but something in her made her want to give him some sort of explanation. She must be losing her mind. "You have done nothing since we met other than be kind to me, Mr. Mayfield. It's just that you...you remind me of someone."

"Oh?" He waited for her to continue.

"A bad someone...in my life."

"I see." Gavin came toward her, but Elizabeth didn't move. There was a room full of people just beyond those doors and all she had to do was scream, she told herself.

"So I look like someone you'd rather forget, is that it?"

"No...no, not exactly."

Gavin raised his eyebrows. "Miss Townsend, I must admit, you have me a bit baffled. How do I remind you of this person who wronged you?"

"You—you sound like him. I never actually saw his face. I only overheard him. But his voice is burned in my memory."

"What on earth did this person say that upset you so?" Gavin said, perplexed.

"I...I heard him give an order to have someone killed." There, she'd said it. Now he would know she was the girl he'd been searching for.

But instead of reaching for her as she'd expected, he recoiled in surprise. "Good Lord, Miss Townsend. You can't be serious."

"It's true."

"And you think *I'm* that man? Miss Townsend, I assure

you, I have never given such an order in my life. You simply must be mistaken."

"I can't be. I will never forget that voice. It's haunted me ever since." True, it had been eight years since she'd heard it, but it was ingrained in her memory.

"Miss Townsend, do forgive me, but I can't possibly be who you think I am. I am a peaceful man. I don't even *know* anyone who has taken someone else's life except—" He broke off, sudden realization hitting him. "*Oh, dear God.*" He went deathly pale and turned to place his hands on the balustrade for support, his body appearing to collapse in on itself.

"Mr. Mayfield, are you all right? You don't look well."

"Miss Townsend," he said, his voice tight with remorse. "I am truly sorry for anything that my brother has done to you."

CHAPTER 22

$\mathcal{E}$lizabeth blinked. "I beg your pardon?"

Gavin turned to her. "I have an identical twin." He let that sink in a moment before continuing. "His name is Garrett, and he is in prison now for the life he has led. The only things we share are how we look and how we sound. Apart from that, we could not be more different."

Elizabeth stared at him, his words slowly sinking in. An identical twin? That would certainly explain a lot. She eyed him skeptically. "How do I know you are telling the truth?"

"You may ask anyone here. When you have a suspected murderer for a brother, it's hard to keep that a secret." Gavin's face wore an expression of absolute disgust.

Elizabeth slowly digested this information. Never in her wildest imagination would she have thought...she was horribly embarrassed by the way she'd been behaving. "I'm sorry, Mr. Mayfield, for treating you as I did."

"Nonsense," he assured her. "How were you to know?"

Elizabeth took in his kind features and warm personality and thought she should have known from the start, but fear had clouded her usual good judgment. "May I ask, sir…how did Garrett become so…so unlike you?"

Gavin gave her a rueful smile. "As twins, we were born too early, and I'm afraid Garrett did not do well at first. My parents weren't sure he was going to live. He was very sickly as a child and not allowed to do much of anything. Instead, he watched me flourish and play with my friends while he was forced to let his childhood pass him by.

"As we grew older, he discovered that the more trouble he got into, the more attention he got. He was jealous of everything I had accomplished in my life, and he grew tired of seeing my parents dote on me. He did everything he could think of to gain their attention the wrong way. By the time my parents realized what he had become, it was too late. His heart had grown hard out of jealousy and anger that he could not have the same life I did.

"When he was about fifteen, he got mixed up with some… unsavory characters, shall we say. Father tried everything to get Garrett away from them and back on track in school, but the harder he tried, the more Garrett rebelled. It wasn't long before Garrett left school and home, and began his despicable life in earnest. Lying, cheating, stealing…and we thought that was the worst of it. But at some point he turned to violence. There were rumors…things no parent should ever hear. My mother used to sit in her drawing room at night, holding his picture and crying when she thought no one could hear her. But I could, and I vowed that if I ever found him, I would make him pay for everything he'd put our family through, brother or not." Gavin turned away and looked out over the gardens and into the night, his hands flexing at his sides, betraying his anger.

Surely no one could make up a story such as that. Elizabeth was hesitant to ask, but there was one thing she needed to know. "How…how did he finally get sent to prison?"

Gavin was silent for a moment. He leaned on the balustrade again, lost in thought as the memories assaulted him. The gossip and the whispers, the way he'd had to fight to dispel the rumors and keep his position in society, then the death of a childhood friend, possibly at the hands of Garrett, and ultimately, that of his mother, her spirit finally broken. He'd hunted his brother like a madman, and when they had at last come face to face…he shuddered as a chill went down his spine. That night would haunt him for the rest of his life. He sighed. "I will spare you the details, but suffice to say that I had hunted him down, and when I finally caught up to him…he shot me."

Elizabeth gasped. "How could your own brother do such a thing?"

"As I said, Miss Townsend," Gavin replied, his voice full of steel. "We are brothers by blood only."

Elizabeth struggled to grasp this information. She had always wanted siblings. Her childhood friends all had them, and they all got along quite well. They fought, of course, but Elizabeth had grown up surrounded by people who thought family was everything, and that the bond between siblings was sacred. It was difficult for her to imagine hating one's own sibling—*twin*, no less—so much as to try to kill him. It was unthinkable. She was desperately sorry for Gavin to have suffered such pain.

"So you see, Miss Townsend, you and I have a bit in common. We have both lost ones we love." He smiled sadly at her. "I know it is not quite the same thing, but it is a loss just the same. And I am deeply sorry for whatever he has done to you to make you so afraid. But you needn't fear anymore. I suspect he will spend the rest of his days in prison."

Elizabeth wasn't sure she could allow herself to hope that that was true, because if it was…

It meant that she was finally free.

No more hiding. No more running. No more looking over her shoulder every time a man approached. She could stop sleeping with a knife under her pillow. She could hold down a real job, find a cheap rent somewhere, and finally begin a life. A real one. She could make friends and put down roots in the city. At long last, she could conduct a proper search for her parents, and maybe, just maybe, Aidan would help her.

Hope bloomed in her chest at the thought of not having to leave her new friends.

But then she remembered the note. If the man who'd been chasing her all these years hadn't sent it, then who did? She may be out of mortal danger, but there was still the problem of the past she'd run from. Someone knew about it, and until she figured out who it was and what they wanted, she couldn't continue her relationship with the Lockwoods. There was too high a risk someone would tell Aidan the truth, and she couldn't bear his censure. The loss of his admiration would destroy her. So, she still had to leave.

It was a crushing realization.

"Miss Townsend, are you all right? You look a little dazed."

"I…I was just thinking. And dreaming. You have no idea —" she stopped, her throat closing off with tears. "I seem to have been blessed with two angels in my life, Mr. Mayfield," she said, blinking rapidly. "One who saved my life, and one who set me free to enjoy it. Thank you."

Gavin studied her face for a moment, watching the play of the emotions travel across it. His eyes narrowed. "Good Lord, Miss Townsend," he said softly. "What has he done to you?" There was a beat of silence, and then he shook his head. "Never mind. I do not wish to know. Let this be the last time we speak of my brother."

"Agreed."

He smiled kindly at her. "Does this mean we are to be friends?"

"If you can forgive me."

"There is nothing to forgive, Miss Townsend."

"Then perhaps we may start over, and I promise, I will not avoid you this time!"

Gavin chuckled. "You do seem to be adept at that."

"I've spent years in hiding," Elizabeth admitted. "It sort of comes naturally." Elizabeth hesitated and bit her lip. "Mr. Mayfield, perhaps, if it's not too much to ask...perhaps we can keep this conversation between us?"

Gavin looked down at her, his disappointment written in his features. "Talk to him, Elizabeth," he urged, squeezing her shoulders gently. "He cares a great deal for you."

"Mr. Mayfield..." She trailed off. There was so much more to the story, so much she couldn't reveal. It was a risk she was not willing to take.

"I won't say a word," Gavin promised. "But you need to know that you can trust Aidan with the truth, no matter what it is. He is a good man, Miss Townsend. He won't let anything happen to you."

Elizabeth studied him a moment, then nodded. Just then, the balcony doors opened.

"There you are," Lainey said, stepping out into the night air. "Eliza, Aidan is looking for you. What on earth have you been talking about for so long? Wait." Her eyes narrowed suspiciously. "You two are *talking*."

"Yes. I've been apologizing for being a complete arse," Elizabeth explained.

"Eliza!"

Gavin laughed and offered his arm to Elizabeth. "Let's just say we've worked out our differences and we've decided to start over. As friends." He grinned at Elizabeth. "Shall we return to your party, Miss Townsend?"

"Gladly," she smiled, linking her arm with his. Her heart was practically soaring as Gavin offered his other arm to Lainey and escorted both ladies back inside.

CHAPTER 23

$\mathcal{A}$idan lay awake, thinking of Elizabeth.

She'd gone out to the balcony the Elizabeth he knew, and returned—on the arm of Gavin Mayfield—a different woman. She'd laughed, chatted, and danced gaily… it had been rather like watching a butterfly emerge from its cocoon. She hadn't even glanced furtively about when they waited for the carriage. She seemed…relaxed.

And she'd reminded him she'd be leaving tomorrow.

He should be happy that she was ready to be on her own. That had been the plan all along, hadn't it? She was only supposed to stay long enough to recover.

So why was he so restless? She was right, of course. She was well healed, and there was no real reason for her to stay. He was well aware of the rumors that were circulating through the *ton*. It was probably best she leave.

But he really, *really* didn't want her to.

He had become a different man since Elizabeth had arrived. He smiled more. He laughed more. She'd filled his quiet life with sound.

It hit him then. The house had been so empty before Elizabeth arrived, filling it with her musical laughter. She had taught him how to laugh at himself, how to appreciate little things like the scent of the earth after a rain or the simple pleasure of a conversation, and how to sometimes let go of the persona everyone expected of an earl and show the man who lay underneath.

Elizabeth had brought him to life.

He couldn't imagine going back to his life the way it was before she came. He needed her. She was a breath of fresh air, a balance that he couldn't seem to find on his own. He could think of only one way to keep her with him, but he wasn't sure it was a good option.

Aidan shook his head. Marrying Elizabeth was a preposterous idea. She deserved no less than someone who could love her fiercely with no reservations. He was not that man.

With a loud sigh, he flung off the covers and pulled on the trousers he'd removed a mere hour before. Pulling a loose shirt over his head, he went out on the balcony.

The cool air kissed his skin and ruffled his hair, the breeze bringing the aroma of blooming lilacs with it. He closed his eyes and inhaled deeply. The breeze seemed to whisper...*Elizabeth.*

"Damn it all to hell," he swore softly.

He was just about to turn around and return to his chambers when he saw her. She was at the opposite end of the balcony, standing by the railing, bathed in moonlight. In the white nightgown she wore, she looked like a spirit conjured up from his imagination. Her alluring tresses hung loose down her back, the flowing gown swirling about her legs in the breeze. He was transfixed for a moment, watching her gaze up at the stars. Desire swelled up in him, taking him by surprise. He so badly wanted to feel her body beneath his hands, to taste her tempting skin, and simply hold her in his arms all night.

He smiled to himself. Yes, she had definitely bewitched him.

She seemed to sense his presence, because she turned and met his eyes. Their gazes locked for a moment, then she gave him a little wave. He took that as an invitation and sauntered over to her.

"You couldn't sleep, either?"

Her voice sounded so sultry, a sound to which his traitorous body instantly responded. "Forgive me," he said quietly. "I don't mean to intrude." He was acutely aware of his current state of undress. His shirt gaped open at the neck, his feet were bare, his hair rumpled from tossing and turning in bed.

She was not wearing much more. Aidan knew even being out here with her could prove dangerous. She was far too tempting to him when she was completely covered, let alone just wearing a nightgown that left her arms enticingly bare. He needed to excuse himself and return to bed.

"You're not intruding," she said, smiling at him. "I was just admiring the stars. Aren't they amazing? Like tiny little diamonds sparkling in the sky. They're absolutely spellbinding, don't you think?"

He'd hardly given them a thought in years. "I couldn't agree more. I shall take my leave of you and let you enjoy them in peace." He turned to go, but her voice stopped him.

"They have stories, don't they?" she asked quietly. "The stars, I mean. Each constellation has a story behind it, right?"

"Yes," Aidan agreed. "Each has roots in mythology."

"Can you show me a constellation?" she asked, still staring up at the sky.

Damn. Did she know what trouble she was inviting? "Elizabeth, I really should—"

She put her finger to her lips and beckoned to him with her other hand. "Tell me a story," she said softly.

Aidan sighed. She was trusting him to behave himself, but he didn't know if he could. He gave in, however, and padded over to join her at the railing. They stood in silence for a moment, taking in the view side by side, and Aidan saw the stars through Elizabeth's eyes. It was like he was seeing them for the first time.

"What's your favorite constellation?" Elizabeth asked, her voice a caress in the darkness.

"Hmm…that's a tough one," Aidan replied. "They all have such good stories. But personally, I like that of Cassiopeia. It's said that she was so vain that she bragged that she and her daughter were more beautiful than any other. This angered the sea nymphs, so Neptune sent a sea monster to ravage her village. After consulting an oracle, Cassiopeia and her husband were told the only way to stop the monster was to sacrifice their daughter, Andromeda, to it. She was rescued, however, by Perseus, and they were married and lived happily together for many years. Cassiopeia's punishment for her vanity was to be placed in a chair in the heavens, sometimes hanging upside down as a warning to others."

Elizabeth laughed. "That sounds like a fitting punishment. Where is she?"

"Well, she's not visible this time of year. But there's another one," he said, moving behind her and putting his hands on her shoulders, turning her slightly to the right. "Do you see that cluster of stars over there?"

"No, where?"

"Right there," he said, reaching around her and pointing. Her head turned slightly to follow his aim, and her hair tickled his cheek.

"I see them now," she whispered, a hint of excitement in her voice.

"That's Corona Borealis, the crown that was awarded to Ariadne for her loyalty to Theseus when he was sent to be sacrificed to the minotaur," he said softly, returning his hand to her shoulder, his body smoldering at being so close to her. He caught the floral fragrance of her hair, and he wanted to just bury his face in the cascade of curls and inhale deeply. He was in very dangerous territory now. He had to leave before he did something incredibly stupid.

But he simply couldn't force himself to move.

"So vanity is punished and loyalty rewarded," Elizabeth said, interrupting his thoughts. "It doesn't seem society has quite learned that lesson, does it?"

Aidan chuckled softly. "Some of us have. Others need a little more time." He kissed her on the temple, then rested his cheek there and sighed, pulling her ever so slightly against him.

She leaned on him for a few moments, then turned to face him. His hands fluttered away from her briefly, then came to land again on her shoulders in a light caress. He slowly slid his hands down her arms to her elbows, reveling in the softness of her skin, continuing on down to slip his hands in hers. He bent his head closer to her and peered at her in the moonlight.

"Don't go."

Elizabeth drew back in surprise. "I beg your pardon?"

"Don't leave me. Not just yet. Please. I…I enjoy your company," he floundered, not used to being in the position of so desperately wanting something that he was actually willing to beg for it. He didn't simply want her. He *needed* her.

Elizabeth smiled sadly. "I have to go, Aidan. You and I both know that."

"Just one more day." He squeezed her hand. "Please."

"Aidan, I—"

"Come to the ball with me Saturday," he blurt out.

"What?"

"There's a ball hosted by the Duke and Duchess of Adden-dale on Saturday. It's the start of the season. Surely Lainey must have mentioned it to you."

"Well, yes, but—"

"Come with me. Us."

"Have you lost your mind?"

"Possibly." He pressed a kiss to the back of her hand. "It's just two days away. Just two. And then I'll let you go, I promise."

Her eyes were suspiciously bright. "Aidan, you don't know what you ask."

"Two more days. I just can't...I can't let you go just yet." He stared at her for a moment, searching her eyes. Then he asked the question before he could stop himself, for he wasn't really sure he wanted to know the answer. "Do you not care for me, Elizabeth?"

"Of course I care for you!" she exclaimed. "You must know that. I care for you very much." She hadn't noticed that in her earnestness, she had rested her hand on his chest, her fingers just touching the bare skin at his throat. The instant she realized it, she moved to yank it back, but Aidan was too quick for her. He caught her hand with his own and flattened it against his chest.

"It's all right to touch me," he whispered huskily. She hesitated, but then she gave his chest a tentative caress. It sent shock waves through his body, which leapt to attention with alarming fierceness. Never had he wanted a woman so desperately as he wanted this one right now.

He slowly drew her into his arms. When she didn't resist, he leaned forward and kissed her forehead, her nose, and finally, each cheek. He brought his hand up to lightly touch her face and rested his forehead against hers. "Kiss me, Eliza-beth," he whispered. "For the love of God, *please kiss me.*"

Heaven help him, she did. Her lips were velvety soft

against his, hesitant and sweet. He palmed her cheek, tilting her head and coaxing her lips apart. His tongue explored the sweetness of her mouth, softly at first, but then more demanding. A moan sounded deep in her throat, and he intensified the kiss. His hand made its way into her glorious mass of hair, and he marveled at its silkiness. He tightened his arm about her waist and drew her snug up against him, which was a terrible mistake. The feel of her luscious body with so little fabric between them fueled his flame of desire into a raging inferno in a matter of seconds, and it was all he could do to keep from yanking the fine lawn of her night-gown up around her thighs and burying himself in her right on the balcony. His hand wandered to one of her delicious breasts and he cupped it. Elizabeth immediately stiffened in his arms.

Damn. He broke the kiss, realizing he'd gone to far. *What was wrong with him?* He wasn't a randy twenty-year-old anymore. He should know how to behave himself. His breath came in heavy gasps, and he leaned his forehead forward to touch hers.

"Come to the ball with me."

"I...I don't have anything to wear."

"I'll take care of that," he said silkily, grazing her temple and her ear with his lips.

"You always take care of things, don't you?" she said breathlessly.

"Yes." He nuzzled her neck, inhaling her lilac perfume. He smiled to himself when she unconsciously tilted her head to allow him better access. "Say you'll come with me," he murmured, his lips enjoying her softness. "Please." He waited. So long, he thought she would refuse. But then she sighed in resignation.

"Yes. I'll come."

He said a silent prayer of thanks. He had her for two

more days. He would make the most of them. He forced himself to step back, then nodded at her.

"Good night, Elizabeth."

And he walked away.

WAIT. What had she just agreed to? *Damn the man!* It was hardly fair of him to extract promises from her by drugging her with kisses.

But then again, she had let him. Her willpower had taken a holiday the moment his lips had touched hers. His arms had been so warm around her, so gentle and reassuring. She'd felt...protected. What was it about this man that made her even consider...

No. She'd promised herself, no more men. She would not give herself again, even to Aidan.

Even if it broke her own heart.

CHAPTER 24

*A*idan sighed heavily, checking the clock on the foyer table. "By the time we get there, the ball will be over."

Tibbs waited by the door. "I believe it's called being fashionably late, my lord."

Aidan rolled his eyes at Tibbs's explanation of the obvious.

Lainey had not been pleased when Aidan first told her of his plans for this evening. She knew how cruel the *ton* could be to outsiders, especially those of ignoble origins.

"*The cats have claws, my dear, and they won't hesitate to use them,*" she said. "*I do not want to see Elizabeth hurt after all she's been through. You and Anne and I can only do so much to protect her.*"

"*I strongly suspect she can take care of herself,*" he replied. "*I want to do this for her.*"

"*For her?*" Lainey shot him an amused smile. "*I rather think it's for you.*"

"*And just what do you mean by that?*"

"You can't bring yourself to let her go. When are you going to admit that you're in love with her?"

"Don't be absurd. I'm not in love with her." But the denial sounded feeble even to his own ears. "And I promised I would let her go after the ball. I won't go back on my word."

Lainey took both of his hands in hers and kissed him on the cheek. "I love you, Aidan. But you are an idiot."

Aidan smiled at the memory. He did adore his sister, even when she was pointing out things he didn't want to acknowledge.

A slight rustling of silk sounded overhead, and Aidan turned to glance up the stairs.

His breath stole from his lungs with a soft *whoosh*.

He was quite sure that, just for a moment, his heart had actually stopped beating as his eyes took in the vision that was Elizabeth. She wore a pale blue silk gown that did amazing things to her eyes. The neckline was daringly low, showing off her lovely décolletage. Tissue silk in a matching shade of blue swept from the vee of her neckline to perch on the edge of her shoulders, and was captured there with cream-colored silk roses. Three rows of the tissue silk were swagged across the front, held with more cascades of roses, and brilliants winked out at him from their folds. Three huge loops of silk trailed down the back, and the whole ensemble ended in a froth of delicate ivory lace that trimmed the bottom edge of the skirt and the train. Her shining dark hair had been curled and swept up, a cascade of ringlets trailing down the back of her neck. In it were tucked the ivory roses Louisa had so thoughtfully sent over from her glasshouse for the occasion. Elizabeth was all creamy skin and wonderful curves, and Aidan couldn't take his eyes off of her.

As he stood there staring at her, the jewels on her gown and in her hair sparkling in the candlelight, he came to a startling conclusion.

His sister was right.

Despite his best intentions, he had gone and fallen in love. He wasn't entirely sure, but it might have happened the moment he had first laid eyes on her. He had looked into her eyes, and had seen his own soul reflected there. It had scared him to death, and he had done everything he could to ignore it.

But Elizabeth was perfect for him. She was gracious and kind, intelligent and witty, and she understood him in a way no other woman ever had. But it was more than that. It was the way he felt when he was with her. Like his own life had been waiting for him to discover it.

He knew in that instant that he couldn't let her go, promise or no promise. He had to find a way to convince her she belonged with him, no matter what her past.

She came to a stop in front of him, looking up at him with a shy smile that told him how unsure of herself she really was. "You're staring," she said softly.

"You're stunning," he countered, and he was rewarded with a charming blush.

"I might say the same for you," she replied, taking in the perfectly fitted trousers and tailcoat, set off with a snowy white shirt, waistcoat, and bow tie. "Richard is worth his weight in gold."

He chuckled. "I'll thank you not to tell him that." He drank her in with his eyes. "I daresay your dance card will be filled the moment we step through the door," he teased. "Perhaps I should fill my name in now while I still can."

"You won't be doing any dancing if we don't actually leave the house," came Lainey's voice from behind Elizabeth. Aidan blinked and tried to focus his eyes on his sister. He hadn't even noticed she was there.

"Lainey. You look—"

"Don't bother. I know you're not even seeing me right now." She grinned and kissed his cheek. "You are *such* an idiot."

Aidan grinned back. "I know. You look radiant, Lainey. Forgive my tardiness in my observation."

"You're forgiven. Are we ready?"

Aidan studied the two captivating women before him. "I think you forgot something."

Elizabeth glanced at Lainey, then down at her own gown, a miracle of a confection they'd pulled together with astonishing speed. When she looked back up to say nothing was missing, a gold pendant necklace was dangling from Aidan's hand.

Her Celtic knot. It had taken Lainey four days to convince Elizabeth to let Aidan take it to a jeweler to have it cleaned and restored, but now it seemed he had had other plans. He had also bought a chain to go with it so she could wear it properly.

He decided that tonight seemed the perfect night to do so. "May I?"

"Oh, Aidan," she breathed. She presented her back to him so he could put it on for her. The charm came to rest in the hollow of her throat, and she fingered it lovingly. "Aidan, you shouldn't have done this," she whispered, her eyes bright.

"It's a symbol of love," he said softly, meaning more than the knot itself. "You should keep it close to your heart."

Forgetting that there were people watching them, Elizabeth raised her hand and laid it on Aidan's cheek. "Thank you."

They looked into each other's eyes for a moment, and probably would have stayed there longer had Lainey not cleared her throat.

"We should be getting on our way. It's going to be a crush.

It's too bad Gavin won't be attending this evening," she mused, a faint pout on her lips.

"I don't think he feels the same way," Aidan said wryly. "But he's doing me a favor by following up on something for me this evening. He said he would make an appearance if he could. Shall we?"

He led the ladies out the door and handed them into the carriage, and they were off to the ball.

ELIZABETH HARDLY SAID a word on the drive over, and she tried not to panic as the carriage pulled up to the house. Mansion, actually. Elizabeth had never seen a residence so large in her life. She fixed her eyes on the gleaming set of about fifty marble steps that led up to the massive front door. Huge pillars graced the facade of the house, making for a two-story entrance that dwarfed the guests entering the house. A magnificent fountain gurgled nearby, and there were hundreds of spring flowers in bloom that perfumed the air. She was so awestruck that she didn't notice Aidan waiting for her with an outstretched hand.

"It's much easier to dance if you don't stay in the carriage," he teased. Elizabeth snapped to attention and blushed furiously.

"I'm sorry…it's just…a little more than I anticipated."

"Don't be nervous. You'll be fine." Aidan wrapped his hand around hers. "You look amazing," he said softly, a hint of encouragement in his voice. She smiled tentatively and allowed him to help her out of the carriage. A familiar voice called out to them the moment she set foot on the ground.

"Ashby! Didn't anyone ever tell you that it's not fair to keep all the ravishing women to yourself?"

Elizabeth turned to see Donovan MacKavoy striding toward them.

"Damned selfish of me, isn't it?" Aidan returned, grinning.

"Ladies, you are looking splendid this evening," Donovan said, kissing each one's hand in turn. "Lady Elaine, you are a vision as always. And Miss Townsend…well, well, well. Couldn't have gone a little easier on the men this evening, my dear?" She blushed furiously at his compliment, and he smiled and looked over the top of her head at Aidan. "Might I encourage you to share, Ash, and let me escort one of these fine ladies into the ballroom so I don't have to trail behind you looking pathetically alone?"

Aidan laughed and Lainey detached herself from his arm almost instantly. "I'd be happy to accompany you, Mr. MacK-avoy. Thank you." She took his offered arm and they preceded the other couple up the steps. Elizabeth's insides were quaking the entire journey. It seemed to take forever just to reach the front door, and then suddenly, it was swinging open and they were being ushered into the foyer.

Elizabeth tried not to be astonished. The pink marble floor gleamed with the reflection of the huge crystal chandelier that hung overhead. There was an elegant double staircase that curved in opposite directions up to the second floor, and crowds of ladies in fine gowns and men in their evening blacks swarmed up and down it. In between the staircases was a set of gilded French doors that led to the ballroom. They were standing open, and Elizabeth could hear the conversation and music that was coming from within. There were people milling all about, and those who knew Aidan looked in his direction and nodded a polite hello. They were, however, less politely assessing her. She tightened her grip on Aidan's arm.

"Just smile and nod, sweetheart," he whispered in her ear. "This is supposed to be a fun evening."

Elizabeth obeyed and plastered a smile on her face as they were lead into the ballroom and formally announced.

Conversation died around them immediately as their names rolled out over the crowd. Slowly, everyone turned to stare at the Earl of Ashby and the woman on his arm, blatant curiosity on their faces. *Mother in heaven*, Elizabeth thought.

This had most definitely been a terrible idea.

CHAPTER 25

*E*lizabeth stopped breathing. She was obviously the subject of interest tonight, and she desperately tried not to wither under the scrutiny of the fifty or so pairs of eyes that were trained on her. Thankfully, the music was still playing and the dancers were still dancing, though some were trying to take a peek at the couple even as they twirled around the floor. Nearby, however, was silence. Elizabeth forced a deep breath and bestowed her best smile on the crowd as Aidan protectively placed his hand over hers in the crook of his arm.

"Lord Ashby!" a sweet voice rang out. "So good of you to come."

The most attractive woman Elizabeth had ever seen stood before them in the receiving line. She was tall and thin, with hair that was stunningly white, the color and lustre of pearls. She had wise, blue eyes that crinkled at the corners, indicating she had spent a good deal of her life smiling. She offered her cheek to Aidan for a kiss, and there was an unmistakable elegance about her that told Elizabeth who she was before he spoke the words.

"Duchess." Aidan smiled, obliging her with a kiss. "You are lovely as ever. Thank you for hosting this little get together."

"Ah, you know how I love a good party. What better way to start off the season?" She turned her gaze to Elizabeth and bestowed upon her a brilliant smile.

"Your Grace, may I introduce Miss Elizabeth Townsend? Miss Townsend, please meet Isabella Whitmore, the Duchess of Addendale."

"Pleased to make your acquaintance, Your Grace," Elizabeth said, curtsying. Aidan had told her that the duchess and his mother had been best friends, and so she had known him since birth. She looked on him as one of her own.

"My dear Miss Townsend! May I take a moment to thank you for saving our beloved Lord Ashby's life? Such a brave woman you are!" the Duchess declared, at a volume that would ensure that everyone within earshot knew that Elizabeth Townsend was not only welcome in her home, but also had the Duchess in her corner. Conversation slowly began to return, and Elizabeth smiled gratefully as she began to breathe again.

"You are too kind, Your Grace. It was not so much an act of bravery as a reaction, but I thank you for your kind words."

"I am glad to see you are well healed after your trauma, and able to grace us with your presence this evening. You are a strong woman, indeed," she replied, the double meaning of her words clear. She squeezed Elizabeth's hand. "Allow me to introduce you to a few young ladies who can help you navigate the den of dragons this evening. Ladies!" she called, instantly commanding the attention of three nearby girls. They flocked to her side immediately. "May I present Miss Elizabeth Townsend? Miss Townsend, allow me to introduce Miss Lydia Blousson, Miss Anne Hastings, and Miss Ella

Beauregard. Ladies, this is Miss Townsend's very first ball. I trust you will help her enjoy herself."

"Yes, Your Grace, of course," Lydia bubbled.

Within seconds, Elizabeth was surrounded by the girls and separated from Aidan. The Duchess turned clear blue eyes to him.

"Oh, Aidan, she's lovely."

"MISS TOWNSEND, how wonderful to see you again," Anne Hastings said, smiling. "You look incredibly fetching tonight."

"Yes, you are certainly exquisite!" Lydia appeared ready to burst. "I was simply mad with jealously when I had heard Anne had already met you!" She had a mass of dark, curly hair and incredibly bright blue eyes. Her freckled face was round, her cheeks full, and Elizabeth suspected she appeared younger than she actually was, though Elizabeth would put her at about nineteen. "Tell us, Miss Townsend...or may I call you Elizabeth? What is it like to be a heroine?" Lydia practically shouted in her excitement.

"Lydia, do calm down," Anne scolded. "You're being rude."

"Oh, she's not," Elizabeth countered. "And please, do call me Elizabeth. I'm afraid I'm not as much a heroine as everyone makes me out to be. I saw the man who had just rescued me in need of some rescuing of his own, and I had to help. That's all."

Lydia's eyes grew huge. "He rescued you? I didn't hear that part of the story!"

"Lydia, please," Ella chimed in. Ella was taller than either of the other two, with mousy brown hair and huge brown eyes that reflected a genuine soul. "Give the girl a moment to breathe. Can't you see you're embarrassing her?"

"I'm sorry," Lydia gushed, not looking the least bit apologetic. "It's just that I've been dying to meet you, and here you are! You've been the talk of the town for two months now. I mean, you saved the Earl of Ashby from a runaway carriage and were almost killed yourself in the process. What a romantic story! And Lord Ashby, of all people. I mean, he's just so…so…" Lydia stopped, at a loss for words for the first time in her life.

"Handsome?" Anne supplied.

"Wonderful?" Ella sighed.

"Oh, he's the very thing a girl's dreams are made of!" Lydia blurted.

Elizabeth's hand went to her mouth. She had seen Aidan approaching, but couldn't stop Lydia's outburst in time. She was sure he'd heard every word.

"Pardon me, ladies," he said from behind Lydia. Her eyes went round as saucers and she flushed scarlet all the way up to her hairline when she heard Aidan's voice. She took a step sideways and disappeared behind Ella, who was struggling to keep a straight face. If Aidan knew that they had been talking about him, he didn't show it. Only Elizabeth caught the mirth in his eyes. "Miss Townsend, may I have the honor of a dance?" he said, bowing slightly and holding out his hand.

"I'd be delighted," she replied, placing her gloved hand in his. "If you'll excuse me," she said, nodding to the girls. "It was nice to meet you. I hope we can continue this conversation later in the evening."

Aidan led her out to the dance floor, leaving the girls to stare adoringly after him.

"Well, you must be quite pleased with yourself, my lord."

"I can't imagine what you mean," he answered her in a tone that belied his words.

"'The very thing a girl's dreams are made of!'" Elizabeth giggled. "Quite flattering words, are they not?"

Aidan's laughter rumbled through his chest. "I promise

not to let it go to my head," he said, sweeping her into his arms. He gazed down at her. "You are so beautiful," he said softly. "You know that, don't you?" She looked away, embarrassed. He grinned at her. "You have, however committed a serious faux pas."

She snapped her attention back to him. "I have? What have I done?"

"You've managed to outshine every woman here. Usually that's reserved for the hostess."

"Aidan…" Elizabeth's voice trailed off. He was making it very difficult for her to be strong and walk away from him tomorrow. She felt her resolve weakening with every kind word, every warm smile. She realized she had come to care very deeply for him, and she tried to put herself in his place. If he harbored a terrible secret, could she still care for him even after he told her the truth?

She didn't want to admit the answer, even to herself.

Because admitting the truth would put her heart on the line. And even though she was now free of the man who had dogged her for years, she still had a mission to complete. She'd return to her hometown, start asking questions. Someone must know what happened that night.

She glanced around the ballroom at all the glittering ladies and finely-dressed men. She should belong to this world, but she didn't. Not anymore. She couldn't ask Aidan to give this up. Love would not be enough to overcome being ostracized from society, which she knew would happen if her secret ever got out. No, she had to be strong and leave all this behind. She'd been on her own for years; so she would be again. Aidan would find someone suitable to marry and live a long happy life.

Without her.

Her throat unexpectedly closed off and she blinked back threatening tears.

"Elizabeth?"

She shook her head to clear her thoughts and brought Aidan's face into focus.

"The music has stopped," he said. "Are you well?"

She swallowed hard and nodded. Aidan rested her hand in the crook of his elbow and led her back toward Anne, who had been watching them dance with rapt attention. She was smiling.

It appeared that the Earl of Ashby was finally off the market.

"Are you enjoying your evening so far, Elizabeth?" Anne asked later, coming up behind her.

"Very much so," Elizabeth replied. "More than I thought I would." She had run into the Everetts, and Will had kindly asked her to dance. She hadn't truly expected to do much dancing since she was sure that no man in his right mind would want to be seen with her. And Lainey had introduced her to some more of her friends who had been very kind to her. And there was, of course, Lydia, whom Elizabeth had barely been able to shake loose all evening. She'd wanted to hear every romantic detail of the past eight weeks. Elizabeth thought her very sweet, and highly amusing.

"You were very brave to come here tonight, Miss Townsend. I do not know that I would have made the same choice."

"I'm not sure if it was bravery or stupidity," Elizabeth quipped. "But so far, it's been a peaceful evening."

Anne laughed, the sound like music. She glanced over Elizabeth's shoulder and her laughter died on her lips. "I'm afraid that's about to change."

Elizabeth turned to follow her gaze and saw Margaret Burnham and her herd striding toward them. "Oh dear," she sighed. "And I was enjoying myself so thoroughly."

Margaret Burnham was one of the dragons she had been warned about. Lainey put up with her only because her mother was a large part of Aidan's business. The Burnhams were incredibly wealthy, but not titled. Lainey was quite sure Mrs. Burnham requested her dressmakers use only silks imported by Lockwood Imports in order to secure Aidan's attentions for Margaret, but Aidan had only ever been civil to her, much to Mrs. Burnham's disappointment. Margaret was a classic beauty, with blonde hair, cornflower blue eyes, and a petite, turned-up nose, but her attractiveness ended there. She was hopelessly conceited, spoiled, and considered herself far superior to any other human being. She'd insisted on an introduction to Elizabeth, but as soon as it had been accomplished, Lainey had whisked Elizabeth away and managed to keep them separate all evening.

Until now. "Miss Townsend," Margaret trilled. "How good of you to join us this evening. I didn't get to speak with you at length earlier. Are you enjoying yourself?" Her overly bright tone indicated trouble to Elizabeth.

"Indeed I am, Miss Burnham," Elizabeth nodded, polite coolness in her voice. "Are you having a pleasant evening as well?"

"Quite so. There are many fine gentlemen here to partner with in a dance. I daresay my card is already half full." She tittered, artfully snapping open her fan and hiding coyly behind it.

"How lovely for you." Elizabeth smiled serenely. This woman made the hair on the back of her neck stand on end. "I'm sure Lord Ashby's name must be on it many times," she added innocently. Anne nudged Elizabeth with an elbow jab, but Elizabeth ignored her. She was going to have fun.

Margaret's eyes narrowed. "I know you do not under-stand the rules of society, so I will forgive that impertinence. You should know, however, that it is unseemly to dance more than three dances with a lady in an evening, even if one is courting the lady. "

"My apologies," Elizabeth said tightly. "Thank you for enlightening me. I suppose you are not in danger of being unseemly since I haven't yet seen you dance with the earl."

Anne began to fan herself furiously as Margaret's eyes narrowed further.

"I must admit, I was surprised to see you here," she said casually, snapping her fan shut. "Lord Ashby hardly ever escorts anyone to a ball, save for his sister. And his taste in women usually runs to high standards. But I suppose Lord Ashby felt he owed it to you after keeping you all to himself these past weeks." She smiled sweetly. Her words were carefully chosen to sound innocuous, but Elizabeth could hear the venom behind them. Elizabeth knew in an instant that Margaret Burnham wanted Aidan, and this conversation was being driven by nothing more than jealousy.

"It is I who owe him a great deal," she replied. "I cannot repay him for the kindness he has bestowed upon me."

"Indeed." Margaret raised one eyebrow. "I'm sure you can think of something. You must have learned all manner of talents living on the street as you do."

Stunned silence fell on the party surrounding the two women. Margaret's cronies were soaking in every word, waiting to see what happened next. This was *incredible* fodder for gossip.

Elizabeth drew in a deep breath to calm herself before she knocked out Margaret's perfect teeth. "You do not know anything about my life, Miss Burnham, no matter what you may think. You have no idea what circumstances have befallen me to land me in the position in which I now find myself."

"Well, we'd surely like to know, Miss Townsend," she said, indicating the two women standing next to her. "Do enlighten us."

"I don't particularly care to discuss it with anyone."

"Yes, of course. I'm being terribly nosey, aren't I?" Margaret laughed. "I'm just trying to get to know you better. After all, it's best not to have any secrets if you are going to try to parade yourself around as one of us."

Elizabeth paled. Did this woman know something she ought not? Was *she* the one who sent that note? Elizabeth took a steadying breath and pasted a smile on her face. "Believe me, Miss Burnham. I have no intention of that. I am not, nor, thankfully, will I ever be, one of you."

"Careful, darling," Margaret said evenly. "That sounded like a snub, and I daresay one would not want to offend me. It might make things difficult for one in society."

Elizabeth tilted her head, the breeze from Anne's over-worked fan stirring the curl at her temple. "Are you threatening me, Miss Burnham?"

"Not at all. I'm just giving you advice because I know you don't know all the rules of the game. It's rather magnanimous of me, don't you think? I do so like to help the underprivileged." She leaned slightly forward, a calculating glint in her eye. "Now tell me, Miss Townsend, woman to woman," she said in a voice that was just a little too loud, "I'm just dying to know. What's it like to warm the bed of London's most eligible bachelor?"

BY GOD, he was going to wring that woman's neck. Aidan had come to claim Elizabeth for a dance, but had stepped behind a potted fern when he'd heard his name enter the conversation. He'd wanted to see how Elizabeth handled herself, but this last statement from that vile woman was simply beyond the pale. He was about to step into the group of women to defend Elizabeth when her cool reply stopped him in his tracks.

"Jealous, are you?"

Aidan's eyes widened. He didn't want to get any rumors confirmed. But he held his position as he watched Elizabeth fold her arms across her chest, a decidedly disdainful look on her face.

"Poor Margaret," she crooned, pouting just slightly. " You've been trying for years to win the affections of his lordship, but you haven't been able to, have you? Don't fret, darling. As you said," she pointed out, leveling her gaze at Margaret, "he does have high standards."

Aidan nearly choked keeping his laughter at bay. He watched as Margaret puffed herself up like a peacock, her eyes fiery with indignation.

"You insolent wench! How dare you speak to me like that!"

"I speak only as I am spoken to, Miss Burnham," Elizabeth returned, "and I am only stating the truth. You *are* jealous. But not because you think I am warming his lordship's bed, which, I assure you, I most certainly am not." She uncrossed her arms and leaned in toward Margaret. "You're jealous because you know I warm his heart. Good evening." She turned on her heel to walk away, and slammed right into Aidan's great expanse of chest.

She bounced off of him and stumbled backward. "My lord," she mumbled, dropping a curtsy. Laughter tittered around her and she stared at the floor, her cheeks flaming.

"Miss Townsend," he returned, bowing his head slightly. "Ladies. Do forgive the intrusion, but our hosts have requested an audience with Miss Townsend."

Her gaze snapped up to meet his, her eyes wide with surprise.

He nodded to the group. "Ladies…Miss Burnham," he added, a wicked smile on his face. "Do forgive me for spoiling your…*fun,*" he said darkly. With that, he calmly led Elizabeth away.

"Did the Duke and Duchess really ask to see me?" she asked when they were out of earshot.

"No. But I would like to talk to them, and introduce you to their son…and it seemed you were in need of some rescuing."

"I suppose you heard that conversation," Elizabeth mumbled, her cheeks flaming.

"Every last word. And I think you were marvelous!" He grinned.

"Truly?"

He nodded. "Lainey will be so proud when I tell her of how you put that viper in her place."

"I do know how to make a scene, don't I?"

Aidan laughed heartily as they made their way around the edge of the ballroom. "Have I told you how resplendent you look tonight?"

"I think you did mention it, yes," she replied, blushing furiously.

"Ah. I see you've so affected me that I now forget myself." He whispered in her ear, "I can hardly remember who I was before I met you."

Elizabeth's heart stopped. "Surely you can't mean that."

"I've never meant anything more. You've completely changed me, Eliza. I don't think I can go back to my life the way it was."

"I'm afraid you must." Her conscience pricked at her. She had to tell him the truth. He'd been so kind for so long, and she'd done nothing but shut him out. He deserved to know everything. But could she risk his friendship? And Lainey's? He had promised to help her get back on her feet—would he be so angry with her that he would withdraw his support?

And what of her heart, which, if she were being honest, was all tangled up with his? He certainly couldn't marry her even if he wanted to, and it would hurt down to her soul when he did take a wife.

Still, she should tell him.

She would.

Just not tonight.

"Ah, Ashby, there you are," the duchess gushed.

"Duke, Duchess," he bowed. "My lord," he said, turning to their son. "May I introduce Miss Elizabeth Townsend? Miss Townsend, meet Henry Whitmore, Marquess of Cranston."

"I'm very pleased to meet you, my lord," Elizabeth smiled, dropping a curtsy.

"The pleasure is mine," he returned, taking her hand and kissing it. "Might I be so bold as to beg of you the next dance?"

Elizabeth gulped. "I—I'm not a very good dancer. I only know how to waltz a little." Dancing with men she knew was one thing, but the marquess? The musicians were queuing up a country dance. "I'm afraid I don't know this one."

"Fortunately, I do." He offered her his arm. "Let's go have some fun, shall we?"

"Ah…excuse us," she said, sending Aidan an alarmed look as the marquess settled her hand on his elbow.

Aidan grinned. "Good luck."

Her brows slammed down and she glared at him as Cranston led her off to the dance floor.

"Aidan, a word, if you please," Isabella intoned. He turned to find both her and her husband staring at him. He raised an eyebrow.

"Why do I feel an ambush coming on?" he asked warily.

"Don't be silly, dear. I just want to chat a bit."

"I tried to stop her," the duke chimed in, "but you know I have no real power over her. My lady gets what she wants," he chuckled.

"Nonsense, Edward," she scolded. "I wanted to ask about Elizabeth, that's all."

He eyed the duchess. "What about her?"

"I was wondering when you're planning to marry her."

Aidan's eyebrows shot up. "I beg your pardon?"

The Duke was laughing. "Sorry, my boy. I told her it was none of her business, but of course, to her, you are her business."

It couldn't have been more true. As far as the Duke and Duchess of Addendale were concerned, the only thing that prevented Aidan from being family was his surname.

"I see the way you look at her. As a matter of fact, you've hardly taken your eyes off of her all evening," Isabella said. "I've never seen someone so much in love."

"Except, of course, for me," Edward said, sliding his arm about her waist. Aidan just looked from one to the other and blinked. Isabella put up a hand the moment he opened his mouth to speak.

"Don't even try to deny it, my dear boy. You can't."

Aidan simply stared at her, and then a slow smile spread across his face and he began to laugh. "Good God, am I that transparent?"

"My dear. *Everyone* can see it." She patted his hand. "So

you are planning to marry her?"

Aidan hesitated. "If she'll have me. But she seems to believe that I won't be able to accept her past."

Isabella made a clucking sound. "Poor child. We *all* have a past. If you love her, it won't matter one whit."

Aidan sighed. "I didn't plan to fall in love with her…or anyone, for that matter. But she managed to break down my walls."

"A good woman has a way of doing that," the duke replied. "And you promised your father you would marry for love."

"I didn't mean it."

"Yes, my boy," Edward said quietly, "You did. And he would be so happy to know you've fulfilled his dying wish."

Aidan blinked back the sting of tears. He'd wanted to keep that promise so badly, but he'd been too scared. Now, it felt like everything in his life was finally falling into place, and his heart was lighter than it had been in nearly ten years.

He nodded. "I'm afraid it may cause a bit of a scandal. She's not exactly the match society expects of me."

"Aidan, my boy, if she makes you happy, marry her." He pulled his wife closer. "The Devil what the rest of the world thinks."

CHAPTER 27

*E*lizabeth was completely out of breath. Lord Cranston had proved an excellent dancer, and she had laughed her way through the spirited dance, partly because he was an amiable fellow, but mostly because she had no idea what she was doing. She'd ignored the disgusted looks from people who obviously thought her uncouth. How dare she enjoy herself so!

The marquess escorted her to the refreshment table and took his leave of her with a bow. She thanked him with a curtsy and turned to get a glass of punch. She was lost in thought as she turned away and accidentally bumped into someone, nearly spilling her punch. She looked up into Gavin's blue eyes.

"Mr. Mayfield! You deigned to join us after all!"

He looked down at her, his eyes taking her in slowly, from head to toe. A slow, odd smile spread across his face.

"I know, it's a bit of a change from when we first met, isn't it?" She laughed, patting her hair.

"I daresay."

"Thank you. Aidan told me you might be here this

evening, but I was beginning to lose hope."

"Yes, well…I'm afraid I was detained."

Elizabeth studied him for a moment. "You look tired tonight. Perhaps you shouldn't stay so very long."

"I don't intend to."

"But you must dance with Lainey at least once before you go. She was disappointed you deserted us this evening."

They were interrupted by the sudden appearance of Ella and a young, shy-looking blonde. "I hope I'm not disturbing you," Ella said to Elizabeth. "Melodie wanted to meet you, and this is the first chance I've had to catch up with you! You have turned out to be quite popular."

They all laughed, and Gavin looked over Elizabeth's shoulder and nodded to someone. He returned his attention to the group. "Don't let me interrupt your fun. I'm afraid I must take leave of you anyway if I'm to find Lainey in this crush." His smile lacked its usual affability, Elizabeth noted, as he gave a short bow to Elizabeth's friends. "Ladies." He inclined his head to Elizabeth. "Leighton." Then he was gone.

Elizabeth went absolutely still as the blood drained from her face. Either Gavin had discovered who she was or…or that wasn't Gavin. Elizabeth ran over the conversation in her mind, but nothing had seemed out of place except that he had lacked his characteristic enthusiasm. Had he not used the wrong name, she would never have known. Her chest constricted and darkness began closing in around her.

Garrett had found her.

"Miss Townsend? Are you well?" Ella asked, concerned by the pallor of Elizabeth's stricken countenance. "Why did Mr. Mayfield call you 'Leighton'?"

Elizabeth couldn't answer. She couldn't breathe, couldn't hear over the roaring in her ears. She shoved her glass of punch toward Ella with violently trembling hands, sloshing the sticky liquid over the side. She had to get out of there—

immediately. She turned frightened eyes to Ella. "I...I have to go."

With that, she turned on her heel and fled. Elizabeth pushed through the ballroom, heedless of the heads that were turning her way, their whispers falling on deaf ears. On the dance floor, Aidan caught a flash of movement out of the corner of his eye. It took him a moment to realize that it was Elizabeth running full tilt through the ballroom.

Anne saw her, too. "What on earth?"

"I don't know," Aidan replied, "But I'm afraid I'm going to have to cut our dance short."

"Of course," Anne said, already allowing him to lead her off the floor.

"My apologies, Miss Hastings," he said in a rush as soon as he'd gotten her off the dance floor. "Do forgive me." He took off after Elizabeth, not catching up with her until she was nearly at the bottom of the front steps.

"Elizabeth!"

She clearly hadn't heard him, for she kept running. He managed to get close enough to grab her elbow to try to get her attention, but it was a mistake. She whirled around just as he began to repeat her name, but the word never passed his lips because Elizabeth began to scream.

"No! Let go of me!" In a blind rage, she struck out and slapped Aidan hard across the face. She wrenched free of his grasp and began to run away before his voice finally registered in her brain.

"*Christ*, Elizabeth! What the hell—?" He rubbed his stinging cheek.

"Oh!" Elizabeth stopped, horrified. "Oh, Aidan! I'm so sorry! I thought...I...I—" She stopped, close to hysterics. Aidan gripped her shoulders.

"Elizabeth! What's happened? What's wrong?"

"I...I can't...oh, Aidan," she choked. "I have to leave. Now."

"Tell me what's going on. Did someone say something to upset you?"

"No, no," she wailed, desperate to get away. "Please take me home, Aidan. Take me home now. Please!" she cried. Great sobs wracked her body, and oxygen suddenly seemed at a premium. Aidan wrapped his arms around her and tried to calm her down. Behind her, Aidan's coachman appeared out of nowhere.

"Is everything all right, my lord?"

"The carriage, Jack. Now."

"Yes, my lord. Right away." Jack was gone in a flash, but it seemed like an eternity before he returned with the carriage. Elizabeth was trembling violently in his arms, and he worried she might faint. She was gasping for air, unable to calm herself. Aidan settled her into the carriage, and he nodded at Jack, implying to get them home as fast as possible. He climbed into the seat next to Elizabeth, and without a word, he pulled her into his arms and she melted into him. He asked her no questions. He just kept taking slow, deep breaths, encouraging her to match him, rubbing her back in languid circles. By the time they reached his front door thirty minutes later, she had regained her most of her composure. Aidan ushered her into his study.

"Are you going to tell me what happened?" Aidan asked.

Elizabeth looked down at the floor, deciding how best to begin. The silence stretched between them, but Aidan said nothing. Elizabeth sighed. "Garrett Mayfield was at the ball tonight," she finally said.

"What?" Aidan frowned. "That's impossible."

"No, Aidan, it's not. It was him." Elizabeth turned away and stared into the dying fire.

"Elizabeth, the man is in prison. He couldn't have been there."

She whirled around to face him. "I can't explain it, but he

was there! I spoke to him!" she cried.

"Are you…sure?"

Elizabeth threw her hands up in exasperation. "Yes, I'm sure! I thought it was Gavin at first, when we were talking. He was acting a little strange, but I didn't think anything of it. But then…when he left…he called me Leighton."

"Leighton? Who the devil is Leighton?"

Elizabeth sighed. "I am." She ignored the question in his eyes and forged ahead. "My name is Leighton Elizabeth Courtwright. Garrett Mayfield murdered my family and burned my house to the ground because he thought I was in it."

AIDAN STARED AT HER. Rather, he was staring at the pendant she wore around her neck. A memory flashed through his mind, and in an instant, the truth slapped him right in the face.

He knew exactly who she was.

He was so stunned all he could do was stand there with his mouth hanging open. How could he have been so stupid? It made perfect sense now, and he couldn't believe he hadn't seen it before.

The news of the crime against the Courtwright family had been so shocking that it had made it all the way to London's papers. Joshua Courtwright had owned one of the largest breweries in England, up in Derby. One summer's night, he and his wife had been kidnapped, his home burned to the ground. His young daughter had disappeared. It was thought she died in the fire, and after a few years, everyone had forgotten about her.

But he hadn't, and neither had Gavin.

And here she was, standing right in front of him, the

destitute girl who was actually heiress to her father's empire. He gaped at her, incredulous.

Elizabeth was apparently done waiting for Aidan to say something. She reached out and grabbed Aidan's lapels to get his attention. "Don't you see, Aidan? He knows I didn't die that night, and now he's going to come after me. I felt someone's eyes on me at the edge of the woods that night, and I knew I'd never be safe. I had the same feeling in town last week. Honestly, I've had it for years! I've spent the last eight of them running, hoping that he would never find me. And he shows up at a stupid *ball!* Somewhere I should never have been in the first place!" Her voice was getting shrill as panic set in again. "Now I've put you and Lainey in danger just by being here. I can't thank you enough for all you've done for me, but for your safety I must leave as quickly as possible."

She tried to get around him, but he reached out and grabbed her arm to stop her. "I'm afraid that won't be possible."

"Wh...why not?" she asked, a wary look on her face.

Aidan took a deep breath. "Because I'm in love with you and I have no intention of letting you go."

Elizabeth blinked. "I beg your pardon?"

"Marry me, Elizabeth. I'll keep you safe, I promise you that."

Elizabeth blinked again, confusion clouding her eyes. Clearly, that was not what she had expected him to say.

"I...oh, Aidan...I couldn't..."

"I can't possibly protect you if you are not under my roof. And I can't have you under my roof anymore unless you are my wife. Do you have any idea how you torture me, Elizabeth? You enchanted me the moment we met, and I've loved you ever since."

"Aidan, I can't marry you—"

"You cannot change your past, Elizabeth. What's done is

done. You have to let it go."

"You…you don't understand."

He pulled her close. "None of it matters, Elizabeth. I'll still love you no matter what you tell me. Please do me the honor of becoming my wife."

He kissed her then, and for a moment, he thought she would surrender. But then her hands were on his chest, pushing him away.

"I can't, Aidan! I'm sorry. I just can't!" She fled the room in tears.

Well. That hadn't exactly gone as he'd imagined. He stood in the study for a moment, his mind reeling, then strode to his desk and scrawled two hasty notes.

"Tibbs!" he bellowed, entering the foyer.

"Yes, my lord?"

"Get these to a messenger immediately," he said, handing him the notes. "Tell him to make haste. Then get word to Lainey that she is to go home with Anne Hastings this evening and remain there until further notice. Under no circumstances is she to return to this house—I will send Meg along with a trunk of clothing and an explanation. Post some men at every entrance to this house. Miss Townsend may be in grave danger."

"Danger, my lord?"

"Yes, Tibbs." He paused. "She's Joshua Courtwright's daughter."

It took him a moment, but then he placed the name. "The brewer's daughter?"

"Yes. And it appears Garrett has returned to finish the job he started years ago. Get that note on its way—we'll be preparing to leave at dawn." He started for the stairs. "And please have Mrs. Bartlett bring some tea with brandy for Miss Townsend." Aidan strode up the stairs. It was time to get the truth.

CHAPTER 28

$\mathcal{E}$lizabeth sat at the vanity, brushing her hair and staring blankly into the mirror. She would be on the run again. There was no way she could marry Aidan. She would have to tell him the horrifying truth, and then he wouldn't want her. And she couldn't bear the thought of putting him in danger, no matter how much he wanted to protect her. Garrett Mayfield was an evil man, and she wanted him nowhere near Aidan.

She set the brush down. She should leave tonight. Perhaps Aidan would let her borrow the carriage so she could leave London altogether.

There was a soft knock at the door. Mary had probably come back to see if she required any more help after Elizabeth had shooed her out so quickly after getting out of her gown. "Come in," Elizabeth called out, not bothering to look up when she heard the door open.

"I hope I'm not disturbing you," Aidan said quietly from the doorway.

"Oh!" Elizabeth whirled around at the sound of his voice. "Aidan. I…I thought you'd gone to bed."

"May I come in?"

Elizabeth hesitated, then nodded. His feet were bare, his tie, jacket, and waistcoat removed, and his shirt was untucked and hanging loosely about him. He looked far more relaxed than she felt, but no less dangerously handsome than he had looked earlier when he was fully dressed. Elizabeth clutched her hairbrush as she watched him cross the room. Instead of going to her, he crossed in front of the sofa and, leaning an arm on the mantel, poked the logs in the fire. A silence hung between them as Elizabeth stared at his back, waiting for him to speak. He sighed and returned the poker to its place.

"We need to talk." He turned to face her. "Or rather, you do."

Elizabeth tried not to shrink in her seat as he pinned her with his stare and stalked toward her. "I...I haven't finished dressing for bed," she stammered, suddenly unable to breathe. She returned to her brushing in a feeble attempt to reiterate her point. Aidan came to rest behind her and met her gaze in the mirror. Her hand stilled in mid stroke as Aidan's hand closed over hers.

"Let me do it."

Elizabeth's breath caught. She grudgingly let Aidan remove the brush from her hand, all the while not breaking his gaze. He must know she was coiled as tightly as a spring, ready to explode. When he pulled her hair back, his fingertips grazed her neck, sending chills down her spine. He turned his attention to the shining mass of waves and began to pull the brush through, being careful not to make eye contact with her again. "Why did Garrett murder your family?"

Her eyes filled with tears as she struggled for an answer. "I don't know," she replied in a strangled whisper. "But I think it had something to do with my father. I was only fourteen."

"What happened after you fled?"

Elizabeth bit her lip. She was trying to figure out how to tell Aidan the truth without telling him everything when he put his hands on her shoulders and bent down to meet her gaze in the mirror.

"Elizabeth, I know that you don't trust me, but I don't know why. I know that you are not from the streets of London, but I don't know anything about your background. And I know that you care for me, but yet you fled when I proposed marriage for reasons you won't disclose. You have repeatedly told me you want to find a way to repay me for all I have done for you." He paused, watching the combination of panic and pain on her face. He moved to her side and tipped her chin up to look at him. "Talk to me, Elizabeth. I want to know you. All of you. I know that you are frightened, but you must trust me. It's time to tell me who you are…or were. You owe me that much."

Her eyes were brimming with tears. She knew that he was right. He had done everything to earn her trust, and nothing to break it.

After a long pause, she nodded. He held out his hand to her. "Come sit by the fire," he commanded gently.

She took his hand and allowed him to lead her to the sofa, where she had just settled down when there was a knock at the door.

"Ah," Aidan said. "I took the liberty of ordering us some tea. Excuse me." He went to the door and mumbled something to Mrs. Bartlett, then he shut the door and brought the tea to her himself. He placed it on the table in front of her, then sat beside her as he poured each of them a cup. Handing it to her, he said, "Don't be surprised, but there's a liberal amount of brandy in it. I thought you could use it tonight. It will help you sleep." He expected some sort of protest, but there was none. Elizabeth simply took the cup and began sipping, evidently to postpone their conversation.

Aidan smiled. "You can drink as much of that as you want to to avoid talking to me for now, but I have to warn you, you'll wind up talking much more freely if you continue to down it like that."

Elizabeth looked startled, then huffed out a breath. "I fear you're right. Either way, I suppose I can't avoid this conversation any longer."

"I'm afraid not." He settled back on the sofa, facing her with one arm draped across the back and the other holding the cup of tea. "Perhaps you can start by telling me why you can't marry me," he prompted.

Elizabeth paled visibly. "It's...it's complicated. But I should think the reasons would be obvious."

"There are no obvious reasons that are acceptable to me," he stated flatly. "So perhaps you'd better go back to the beginning."

Elizabeth looked at him and gave a resigned nod, and then began to recount her story. She swiped at the tears that were coursing down her cheeks as she spoke, angry at herself for not being able to be stronger. She didn't dare look Aidan in the eye, so she stared vacantly down into the fire instead. "They set the house on fire," she began. "I took what I could with me, and fled the house, praying for God's forgiveness for leaving my parents. It was the hardest thing I've ever done, but I knew I couldn't do anything to help them. I decided to go to London to the family my father had mentioned hoping they would come for me...but of course, they never did."

"Daniel MacKavoy."

"Yes," Elizabeth said. "When I arrived on the doorstep, I was told the old man had died, and I was too frightened to realize I should have asked after other relatives. I was only fourteen, and the butler was very unfriendly," she added.

"You are very brave to have traveled to London alone," Aidan pointed out.

She shot him a rueful smile. "We'll see what you really think of me in a few minutes." She tried to pull herself together some before she continued. "I found a room in a hotel, and waited for my parents to collect me, but…" A knife lodged in her heart, and the tears began to fall again, but she paid them no heed this time. "I refused to believe they were dead, and I spent my days searching for them, all to no avail. Six months later, I was running out of money, so I looked for employment, but I had no experience and no references, so I had to take a job as a server at a tavern. It was there I met Betsy Clarke, the only friend I have in the world, and the reason I came back to London. She had written to me to tell me she might have a new clue as to what had happened to my parents. I was supposed to meet her that night of the accident, but I ran into Peter Smythe instead. You know the rest."

"Why didn't you ask me for help?"

"Because I would have had to tell you the truth about my past."

Aidan regarded her thoughtfully. If Gavin had had any success this evening, Betsy would be holed up in hotel by now. "Why had you left London?"

This was the question Elizabeth had hoped to never have to answer. She looked at Aidan, his eyes full of questions, his warm hand reassuring on hers, and she knew in her heart that if she could ever trust a man, it was the one sitting right in front of her. She took a deep breath.

"Because I killed a man."

CHAPTER 29

Aidan blinked. "You...what?" He tried to hide his surprise, but failed miserably. "Perhaps you'd better explain this in greater detail."

Elizabeth hesitated. She had spent years trying to push that man out of her memory...she hadn't so much as uttered his name since that night. She struggled to gain control of her emotions and find the strength to tell Aidan the secret she had been keeping for so long.

"His name was Vincent Marbury, Viscount Burke. He would come into the tavern at least once a week. He was handsome, well dressed...always left a good tip. He took an interest in me. At first, it was wonderful. He was charming and attentive, and I couldn't help but be swept off my feet. I was sixteen." She smiled ruefully. "After nearly two years on my own, it was heavenly to have someone in my life again. So, when he asked me to live with him, I agreed. I thought it was because he loved me," Elizabeth said sadly. "I was expecting to be living in grand style, but it was immediately clear that I'd taken up with an impoverished peer. It didn't take long for his true nature to show. He was abusive, he gambled, and he drank too much. Any money that came in went to his vices. About six months into our relationship, I shared the news that I was expecting. I stupidly thought he might be happy."

"You have a child?" Aidan made no effort to hide his shock this time.

Elizabeth's face crumpled. "No," she wailed. "Vincent was angry about it. He said he had no use for brats and why hadn't I been more careful. He beat me so badly I…I lost the baby."

"Oh, sweetheart," Aidan said softly, tears in his eyes. It was clear now why she had been so afraid of him, why she had refused to trust him even though he had shown her nothing but kindness. She had been there before and given her trust to a man whom she had thought had loved her, and she had paid dearly for it.

"That was when the visits from his friends started," Elizabeth said quietly. She looked away in shame. "Vincent seemed to have no more interest in keeping me to himself, and he said we needed the money so it was about time I earned my keep. He would invite his friends to my room and they would…pay him to let them…take liberties with me." She could barely get the words out, and her face was flaming with embarrassment.

If this man were still alive, Aidan would gladly strangle him himself. "He turned you into a doxy," he concluded, swearing bitterly.

Elizabeth tried to blink back the tears, but they fell unchecked. She turned to look at him and nodded. "And if I didn't comply, he would beat me."

"Elizabeth," Aidan breathed.

"Don't," she choked out. "Don't pity me. I can't bear it."

Aidan shook his head. "I wish you had told me this earlier. It would have explained so much."

"Aidan, how could I? If anyone found out…it's bad enough you took me in, but if anyone discovered I was a…a whore, and worse yet, a murderer, your family's reputation would be ruined forever. Lainey's chances of a good match would be gone, your business potentially destroyed. I couldn't let that happen. And—" she broke off, emotion closing her throat.

"What? What is it, Elizabeth?" But she couldn't speak, and then he knew. "You thought I wouldn't be able to look at you without disgust."

She hung her head in shame and nodded, a sob tearing from her throat. Aidan moved closer to her, taking her hands in his. "Elizabeth, look at me."

She shook her head, so he put his hand on her cheek and turned her face toward his, but she continued to stare at the floor.

"Look at me," Aidan urged, and she finally lifted her tear-filled eyes. "What happened to you wasn't your fault. Any of it. You didn't choose to sell yourself—you trusted someone you loved, and he manipulated you." He tucked a strand of hair behind her ear. "What disgusts me is the way that man treated you, not what you have done. I love you, Elizabeth. Your past is just that, and it is of no consequence to me."

She stared at him in disbelief. How could he shrug off what she had just told him? Was it possible that he truly cared for her that much? She sniffed in a decidedly unlady-like manner and continued her story. "I lived two more years of hell. I never conceived again." She gave him a small smile. "I suppose that was a blessing then, but now…I'd always thought I'd have children, but I don't think it's possible. He ruined me in so many ways," she whispered. She'd lived a lifetime of regret in those two years. "I hated my life. I hated myself. And I hated him. One night while he was out, I took out the portrait of my parents that I had carried with me all those years. I kept it hidden because it was the only thing I had left of them, and I knew he would take it from me. It was what got me through my darkest days, and there were many of them. It always restored my soul to look into my parents' eyes." She looked wistfully into the fire and sighed. "What I wouldn't give to have that picture now."

"He took it from you?"

"Not exactly. He came home unexpectedly and caught me looking at it. I shoved it behind my back, but he could tell I was hiding something. When I refused to show it to him, he grabbed my hair and threw me into the table, and of course, it slipped out of my hand. He snatched it up and started screaming at me, wanting to know who the people were and why I had been hiding it from him. He'd been drinking heavily, so he was worse than usual, and things got out of control pretty quickly. The rest of it happened so fast I'm surprised I can remember it. But I do," she said, a haunted look coming into her eyes. "Every last moment.

"He threw the frame into the fire. I screamed and tried to get to it, but he knocked me back. It was gone before I could do anything about it. I watched as the only precious thing left in my life disappeared into the flames, taking the rest of me with it. And all at once, every horrifying moment, every beating I had taken, every last thing I had lost came rushing at me in a torrent of anger and bitterness. And in that moment I decided that I couldn't take it anymore. Not one more slap, not one more perverse encounter…I swore that no man would ever touch me again, and I picked up the knife that was on the table. When he lunged at me, much to his surprise, I stood my ground. He lost his footing and pitched forward, and when he fell back, the knife was in his stomach. He just lay there, gasping, and I panicked. I grabbed any money I could find and ran out the door. I never looked back." She fell silent for a moment, reliving the memory of seeing Vincent lying by the hearth, bleeding profusely and making horrible gurgling sounds. She had fled the flat, and London, and had never returned for fear of prosecution. "Do you see now why I couldn't tell you?" Elizabeth stared down into the fire. "I couldn't risk it." She turned to face Aidan. "You were so kind to me. I felt safe here…after all I'd been through, I felt safe for the first time in years. I can't tell you what that's like. And there you were, ignoring everything society says you should do, and calling me a friend. How could I admit to you that you were harboring a murderer and a prostitute in your own home?"

"Elizabeth, you are not a murderer. You did not intend to kill him, it was an accident."

"Accident or not, he wouldn't be dead if it weren't for me."

"I think it's pretty fair to say he deserved what befell him after all he did to you."

"How can you sit there and defend me? I took a man's life! A peer's, at that! Do you know what they do to paupers who attack members of the aristocracy?"

"Elizabeth, he tripped. Because he was drinking. Because he was about to attack you. How do you know that it wouldn't have been the time he finally killed *you?*" Aidan touched her elbow. "You can't keep blaming yourself. Lord Burke got what he deserved. He was a vicious man who never thought twice about hurting you…or your baby. Does it mean nothing to you that he killed your child?"

Elizabeth closed her eyes. She had tried for so long to put that out of her mind, because she couldn't handle the anger that came with the thought.

"Don't torture yourself, Elizabeth. Even if you had wanted to save him, there was nothing you could have done."

Elizabeth gazed at him. Even after all she had told him, he was still sitting with her, his hand on her arm, looking at her with love in his eyes. There was nothing left he didn't know about her now, and he was still looking at her like that. She should have known he was too good a man to turn his back on her. But others wouldn't be so kind, and it didn't change the fact that she wouldn't be able to give Aidan the heirs he needed to continue his family's name. She couldn't let him sacrifice so much just for her.

She sighed and stood to poke at the fire. "Do you see now why I can't marry you?"

Aidan blinked. "No."

"What?" Disbelief colored her shock.

"Elizabeth, I told you before. Your past matters not to me. You lived your life as you had to in order to survive. No one can blame you for that. What matters to me is who you are now, and what you mean to me."

"But Aidan, you'd be resigning yourself to a life without… I mean, I can't perform…I—" She flushed at what she was about to say, but Aidan interrupted.

"I am sure we can change that, Elizabeth. It will take time, but I would hope that as you learn to trust me, the physical aspect of our relationship will blossom as well."

"I…I don't know…"

"Do you find kissing me unbearable?" he asked with a smile, coming up behind her and resting his hands on her shoulders. "Because you seemed to enjoy it at least a little bit."

Elizabeth flushed. He had a point. Hadn't she just the other night practically given herself to him on the balcony? But still…

"Aidan, I don't know if I can bear you children. You need heirs to continue your title," she pointed out, turning to face him.

"Elizabeth, my father would come back from the grave to throttle me if I ever chose my title over love. It's simply not the most important thing. Besides, the estate itself is not entailed. It will go to Lainey and her children if I have none."

"You deserve a house full of children. Don't you want children?" she cried desperately.

"I didn't want any of this, remember?" He tucked her hair behind her ear. "I wasn't supposed to wake up each morning with your name on my lips, or lie awake at night wondering why you're not beside me. It wasn't supposed to hurt when you told me you were leaving. I'm not supposed to be jealous when I see you dancing with other men. I didn't want any of it. My life was perfectly ordered until you…came barreling into it. I didn't want to care about you, didn't want to know what it was like to have my heart beat faster when you walk into the room or have my breath stolen away when I look into your eyes. I didn't want to want you, I didn't want to need you…I didn't want to love you, Elizabeth." He reached out and touched her cheek. "But I do. I love you with my body and soul. And it's the most wonderful feeling I've ever known. Can you look me in the eye and deny you feel the same?"

Elizabeth shifted uncomfortably. She regarded Aidan for a moment, willing herself to be able to lie, but no matter what her logical mind said, she couldn't convince herself that she did not love him.

"I cannot," she said softly. "But I—"

"Stop," Aidan said, holding up his hand. "You've had an emotional evening, and I do not want an answer from you tonight. I just want you to think about it." He gave her shoulders a gentle squeeze and peered intently at her. "Elizabeth, I cannot erase what has been done to you, nor can I fix the conflict of emotions within you. But I can promise you that I will spend the rest of my life helping you put this behind you so that you can live in peace at last. I want to replace all your bad experiences with good ones so you never again have anything to fear." He touched her cheek. "Starting tonight."

"Tonight?" she said, startled. "What do you mean?"

"I mean, it's late and you need to get some rest before we leave, so I am going to lie down with you—dressed as I am," he pointed out when he saw her eyes widen with alarm, "and I am going to hold you. So, you can sleep, you can cry, you can lie awake for the next few hours because you're afraid, but whatever you choose, I am going to hold you in my arms all night as you begin to learn to trust me."

Elizabeth was torn between fear and longing. She didn't know what kind of memories this would stir, or if she was prepared to deal with them. But at the same time, the thought of Aidan's comforting presence surrounding her all night appealed to her immensely at the moment. She didn't want to be alone tonight. "Where are we going?"

Aidan pursed his lips. "I'm afraid I can't tell you that or you won't want to go."

"What? Why?" she asked, a note of panic in her voice.

"Don't worry, I promise you'll be safe." She looked doubtful, and he sighed. "Elizabeth, I am begging you to trust me. For once, just please trust me."

She didn't move, but stared hard into his eyes, and saw everything she needed to see. "I trust you," she said softly.

He regarded her for a moment, and then held out his hand. "Come lie down with me."

She took his hand and allowed him to lead her to the bed, where he settled himself down on the coverlet. He grabbed a nearby blanket and waited for Elizabeth to join him. She hesitated, then crawled onto the bed beside him. He said not a word as he pulled her into his arms and tossed the blanket over them. She rested one arm on his chest and settled her head against his shoulder, soaking in the warmth and solidness of his body. Aidan closed his eyes and began to absently stroke her forearm. The fire crackled in the fireplace as it died down, and many minutes had passed when Aidan heard the change in Elizabeth's breathing. He tightened his arm around her and pressed a kiss into her hair.

"Sweetheart. Don't be afraid to cry. You're allowed."

She didn't respond, but her whole body tensed, and Aidan wasn't surprised when he heard the first whimpers emanating from her. It was all so overwhelming for her to confront her demons, expose her secrets, and come face to face with the man who had murdered her family all in one night. He encircled her with his other arm and pulled her even closer as her crying began in earnest.

"It's all right, my love. I promise you, from now on, everything will be all right."

He comforted her the best he could until she had finally cried herself to sleep. He, however, didn't close his eyes for the rest of the night.

CHAPTER 30

The first rays of dawn were streaking across the sky when Aidan gave Elizabeth a little nudge. "Time to wake up, love," he murmured, rolling her over. She inhaled deeply as she began to stir. He smiled down at her as her eyes fluttered open and focused in on his face. She was momentarily startled, and he chuckled. "Forgot I was here, did you?"

She nodded, then smiled shyly. It was a little odd waking up with him beside her, but somehow…somehow she felt as though this was exactly where she was supposed to be. He was still here. She had told him every horrible detail of her life, and he was still here, and looking so…so…tired. "You didn't sleep much, did you?"

Aidan shook his head. "Did you sleep well?"

Elizabeth blinked. "Yes," she said, a little surprised. "I haven't slept that well in years."

"It feels good to let go of all your darkest secrets, does it not?"

Elizabeth realized in that moment exactly how she felt. She felt wonderful, the enormous weight she'd been carrying around for years finally lifted from her shoulders. She stared into Aidan's eyes for a moment, so grateful for everything he had been to her. "Thank you, Aidan," she said softly.

He smiled. "You're welcome." He brushed her cheek with his fingertips. "So was it as horrible as you imagined?"

"Was what horrible?"

"Spending the night next to me, of course," he said with a grin.

"Oh, Aidan," she giggled. "Honestly."

"What? I should know if I'm an ogre or not, shouldn't I?"

Elizabeth grinned. "How would I know? I was sound asleep!"

Aidan chuckled. "Wench," he chided, kissing her temple. "I hate to rush you, but we have a long day ahead of us and must be on our way soon. Mary will be in soon to help you pack a few things."

"Are you still insisting on not telling me where we are going?"

"I'll tell you once we're underway, I promise." He pulled himself upright and swung his feet to the floor. "Come on, then. Up and about. I want to catch the early train."

"Goodness! That's not much time."

"My point exactly." There was a brief knock at the door before Mary dragged herself in. It really *was* early. Elizabeth blushed furiously at having been caught with Aidan in her bedchamber, but Mary didn't seem surprised at all. Rather, Elizabeth wasn't entirely sure Mary's eyes were actually open.

"Mornin', my lord. Miss Elizabeth," she yawned. "We'd best get you on your feet. We've not much time to get you dressed and packed."

Elizabeth looked at Aidan, but he just winked at her and left the room. Mary picked a travel costume out of the wardrobe while Elizabeth pulled her hair into a chignon. She was dressed, packed, fed, and in the foyer in under an hour.

Aidan was already outside giving last minute instructions to Tibbs. Mrs. Bartlett handed off Elizabeth's small bag to the footman and squeezed her hand reassuringly.

"Have a safe trip, my dear."

"Thank you, Mrs. Bartlett. I would rest a little easier if I knew where I was going."

The housekeeper smiled. "His Lordship told me you might ask that."

"You're not going to tell me, are you?"

She chuckled. "No, Miss, I'm not."

Elizabeth sighed. "Sometimes I think you are too devoted to your master, Mrs. Bartlett," she laughed.

"I'm just as devoted to you, Miss Elizabeth. Now off you go. Don't keep his lordship waiting."

Elizabeth walked down the steps to the waiting carriage, and Aidan handed her inside, followed by a very sleepy Mary. The morning dawned gray and cool, and Elizabeth hoped it wasn't going to rain.

"Let me just give a few instructions, then we'll be off. Gavin will be meeting us at the train station."

"Gavin is coming with us?"

"Yes, and don't panic. I assure you, it is Gavin." He closed the door and went back into the house, leaving a footman guarding the carriage. Elizabeth waited nervously for what seemed like an eternity, then Aidan yanked open the door and climbed inside. Though shaved and in fresh clothing, he still looked exhausted. Elizabeth felt a little guilty that she had slept so well, albeit only for a few hours.

The carriage jolted, and they were on their way. Aidan leaned his head back and closed his eyes. He was silent for so long that Elizabeth was sure he was asleep, until he unexpectedly spoke and nearly startled her off the seat.

"I suppose you'd like to know where we are headed." He opened his eyes and pinned her with a questioning gaze.

"That would be nice." She fidgeted with her gloves. Aidan leaned forward and put his elbows on his knees, steeling himself for her reaction.

"We're going to Colonel Mayfield's estate."

"Colonel Mayfield?" she gasped. "Garrett's *father?*"

"One and the same."

"Have you lost your mind?" she cried. "That's the first place he'll look for me!"

"That's what I'm hoping."

"*What?*" she shrieked. "Aidan, he'll kill me!"

That got Mary's attention. She was wide awake now and taking in every word.

"He's not going to kill you, I won't let him. I promised to protect you and that's exactly what I'm going to do. But I have to get rid of him once and for all to do it, and in order to do that, I have to draw him out of hiding."

"By using me as bait?" she snapped.

Aidan sighed. "Where you go, he will follow, and when he shows up, we'll be ready for him."

"Aidan, you're not…you're not going to kill him, are you?" she said, horrified.

"Not if I don't have to. But if it comes down to him or you…" He took her hand and kissed it. "I think you know which one of you I'm going to choose."

"Aidan, you can't," she whispered, her eyes filling with tears. "I can't let you murder someone to protect me!"

"Elizabeth, killing Garrett is not my intention, but I will do what must be done to ensure your safety. For heaven's sake, take a deep breath and try to think rationally. Colonel Mayfield is a well-respected man with many of his former comrades who have stayed on with him to protect his family from his own son. All he has to do is ask, and many more men will arrive at his doorstep to help him protect you. It's the best place I can think of to end this nightmare. You'll be safe, we'll capture Garrett and send him back to prison where he belongs, and you and I can start living our lives...together."

"But what if...oh, Aidan, what if he sneaks in and finds me when I'm alone? He'll take me away and—"

"You're not going to be alone. Anywhere. I will have your bed chamber door guarded while you sleep and you will be accompanied wherever you go." He sighed, squeezing her hand. "I know you're scared, but I promise you, everything will be all right. You'll see. You just have to trust me."

Elizabeth sat in worried silence, her mind racing. People were going to be put in danger, and it was all her fault. If only she had been able to confirm Betsy's message before the carriage had hit her, she might have been able to find Garrett before he'd found her. Good Lord. Everything was such a mess.

But if Aidan was right and they were able to send Garrett to prison for good, her life could have a peace and happiness that she hadn't known since she was a child. If she could just get through this, things would get better.

She understood why Aidan hadn't told her of his plans earlier. She would have run in the opposite direction. She was frightened out of her mind, both for herself and everyone involved. She just prayed that it would all be over soon.

CHAPTER 31

They had made it to the train station without incident, and had travelled along in silence. Elizabeth had never seen Gavin so stony-faced. When they hired a carriage and team for the remainder of the trip, he played coachman, a pistol resting by his side on the seat. Inside, all was quiet as Mary sat dozing in the corner. It had already been a long day.

Elizabeth could bear the silence no longer. "Aidan," she said quietly, so as not to wake Mary. "Why did you save me?"

Aidan knit his brow. "I did what any decent man would do."

"No." Elizabeth shifted in her seat. "I mean before the accident. Why did you cross the street to defend a gutter rat you shouldn't have even spared a glance?"

Aidan leaned forward. "Elizabeth, what's wrong?"

"Nothing. I just…sometimes I wonder why you fight so hard for me."

"Because I love you. I've loved you from the first. And to answer your question, I saw someone who needed my help. Smythe is a weasel of a man, and no woman is deserving of his attentions. Besides" he grinned, "I'd do anything to best him. It was an opportunity I couldn't resist."

Elizabeth stared at him, unsmiling. Aidan sighed. "Elizabeth, I can't explain what propelled me across the street. I saw a young woman in a difficult situation, and that's all that mattered to me. You must know me well enough by now to know that I believe in basic human kindness." He reached out and took her hand. "No matter what choice was made by either one of us that night, I believe neither of us really had a hand in what brought us together. I think someone knew I needed you and gave you a push in my direction."

"Really? I thought I pushed you," she teased.

Aidan smiled, his brown eyes dancing with light. "It was a figure of speech. I'm a firm believer in fate, Elizabeth, and I am sure that you and I were meant to cross paths. And I am ever so grateful."

The road underneath them smoothed out, and Aidan glanced out the window. "We're here."

Elizabeth twisted her hands in her lap.

"Don't fret, Elizabeth. You will love his parents," Aidan said. "I know you will."

"Do they know—"

"I couldn't explain the whole story in the note I sent, but yes, they know your situation. They will accept you just as you are."

In only a few moments, the carriage door swung open and Elizabeth froze. Not only was she was completely intruding on total strangers, she was about to tell them about all the hideous things their son had done, and possibly get him killed. What kind of first impression could that possibly leave?

"Elizabeth?" Gavin was standing with his hand outstretched, waiting to assist her. She hesitated before taking his hand and alighting from the carriage. She was stiff from the long ride, and it felt good to get moving again. Mary tumbled out next, followed by Aidan. He placed Elizabeth's hand in the crook of his elbow, covering it protectively with his own as he escorted her to the door. Elizabeth squeezed Aidan's arm.

"Perhaps we'd best not mention that fact that I was a light-skirt," she whispered. "That might reflect poorly on me." She gave him a nervous smile.

"Duly noted." Aidan patted her hand. At least she was attempting humor. "Ah. Here we are."

They were greeted by an enthusiastic butler, who was obviously fond of Aidan and hadn't seen him in quite some time, and then shown into the parlor where Colonel Mayfield awaited them.

He stood with his back to the door, arms clasped behind him. His broad shoulders and ramrod straight stance seemed to fill the room, and before he even turned around, Elizabeth could feel the air of authority he had about him.

"Lord Ashby, Mr. Mayfield, and Miss Elizabeth Townsend to see you, sir," the butler said. Colonel Mayfield turned toward them, a welcoming smile on his face.

"Aidan, my dear boy! Come in, come in. It's been a long time."

"Yes, sir, it has. My apologies for the sudden intrusion."

"Nonsense," he said, shaking Aidan's hand. "You're family, and welcome anytime." He smiled at Gavin. "Hello, son," he said fondly, embracing him. He turned to Elizabeth, tenderness coming into his eyes. He was a handsome man of about sixty, with pale blue eyes, an endearing smile, and a full head of silver hair that only added to his air of distinction. He gave her a small smile. "And this must be the young lady you mentioned in your note," he said softly.

"Yes. Colonel George Mayfield, may I present Miss Elizabeth Townsend?"

"Pleased to meet you, sir," she said, curtsying.

"The pleasure is mine, Miss Townsend," he returned, kissing her hand. He was looking at her so intently that it made Elizabeth shift uncomfortably. He studied her a moment more before saying, "My apologies, Miss Townsend. It is my understanding that my other son is responsible for your unfortunate hardship. My deepest regrets for the pain he has caused you."

Elizabeth's mouth dropped open slightly in surprise. "You do not need to apologize to me, sir. You are not responsible for what Garrett has done. And you have raised a very fine son in Gavin, indeed. I am honored he has chosen to befriend me."

The Colonel nodded. "Both lovely and gracious. You are a true delight, Miss Townsend. Now," he said, clapping his hands together. "You must be famished after your trip. May I offer you some tea?"

"That would be lovely, thank you."

He turned to ring for the tea when a voice from the doorway stopped him.

"Gavin, Aidan!" Mrs. Mayfield bubbled. "What a surprise! George told me to expect visitors, but he didn't tell me it was you."

Aidan's head snapped toward the Colonel. "You didn't tell her?" Aidan asked him under his breath.

"I couldn't risk it," he returned quietly.

"How lovely to see you!" Mrs. Mayfield continued, coming into the room. "Your visits are far too infr—" She broke off as her gaze took in Elizabeth standing at Aidan's side.

Beside him, Elizabeth had gone deathly pale and her fingers dug into his arm. He felt her begin to tremble as she turned to look up at him, her eyes brimming with tears. "Ai—Aidan?"

A pang of guilt stabbed through him as he stared down into her sapphire eyes. Eyes that he was now mentally kicking himself for not recognizing earlier. "Do not misunderstand, Elizabeth. I didn't know who you were until last night." He touched her cheek. "You know, you really look nothing like your mother."

CHAPTER 32

*E*lizabeth's gaze shot back to the freckled, willowy redhead that she would recognize anywhere. Kate Mayfield was staring back at her, her face completely drained of color. Her vivid blue eyes looked Elizabeth slowly up and down, finally coming to rest on the pendant Elizabeth wore around her neck.

A Celtic knot that exactly matched the pendant that Kate wore around her own neck.

"Leighton?" she whispered. "My God, is it you? Is it really you?"

Elizabeth shoved herself away from Aidan and stumbled toward her mother. "It's me, Mama, it's me!"

Kate held out her arms and Elizabeth launched herself into them, sobbing. Kate clung to her. "Oh, my child, my dear child! Oh dear God, at last, at last!" Kate held her daughter tightly as they collapsed to the floor, overwhelmed with joy and tears.

Aidan was not a man very often moved to tears, but the emotional scene unfolding before him was too much. He felt a hand on his shoulder, and he turned to find Colonel Mayfield looking at him with misty eyes. "Thank you, my boy. You have no idea what you've done."

"I didn't do anything," Aidan said softly, blinking against the sting in his eyes. "She found me." It was the most wonderful sight he had ever seen. Elizabeth was finally home.

SOMETIME LATER, the two women were seated on the settee, still sniffling and almost afraid to take their eyes off of one another, lest one should disappear again. Tea had been brought for everyone, and they sat gathered around, listening to Kate recount the story of her family's demise. The men had offered the women privacy, but Elizabeth had insisted they stay. Aidan had waited a long time to find out who she was. She wanted him to hear the story as much as she wanted to hear it.

"Mama, what did Papa do that was so terrible?"

"He didn't really do anything. He was just in the wrong place at the wrong time." Kate sighed, placing her teacup back in its saucer. "He happened to witness a murder."

Elizabeth gasped. "Garrett?"

Kate nodded. "Your father was at the brewery late one night, long after everyone had gone home. He was working upstairs in his office when he heard shouting on the floor, so he went to investigate. Garrett was there, along with Martin, your father's foreman. They were having a fierce argument, about what, I don't know. But it ended with Garrett striking Martin with a piece of pipe and killing him. Right in front of your father's eyes. Your father was terrified and tried to leave quietly, but in his haste, he knocked over a shovel on his way out. He didn't think Garrett had seen him, but Garrett knew that someone had seen *him,* and he must have noticed the lamp burning in your father's office and put two and two together."

Elizabeth shook her head. Her father had been a most elegant dancer, but when it came to the every day, he'd been a clumsy oaf. If he hadn't knocked a blasted shovel over on his way out, he would still be here, and she wouldn't have lived a lifetime of hell. It seemed like such a tiny moment, yet it had defined the rest of her life.

"Garrett was sweet on one of your father's workers, a young lady named Sarah, whom your father liked very much. Sarah and Garrett had a rocky relationship according to everyone who knew them. Garrett was known for his violent temper, and they often had great rows.

"After witnessing the extent of Garrett's temper, your father was worried for Sarah's safety, and went to her the next day to tell her what he'd seen. He gave her money and begged her to leave Garrett while she had the chance. His big heart is what sealed his fate." She paused a moment, risking a glance at Gavin, who sat with his lips pressed in a thin line, his jaw clenched. She took a deep breath and continued.

"This next bit was told to me by Garrett himself. Apparently, when he arrived home that evening, Sarah confronted him and insisted he turn himself in. He obviously disagreed, and a terrible fight ensued. Frightened, Sarah told him she was leaving him and fled the house. Unfortunately, it was already dark, and Sarah was not an experienced horse-woman. She tried to jump a downed tree, but failed, and the horse threw her. Both she and her unborn child were killed."

Elizabeth gasped. "Oh, Gavin..." She turned to him, realizing he had lost not only a brother, but a niece or nephew as well.

Gavin made no response other than blinking, a muscle in his jaw twitching, so Kate continued. "Garrett absolutely lost his mind. He gathered up some of his cohorts and they broke into our house later that night."

Elizabeth reached out her hand and squeezed her mother's. "Tell me what happened before you came upstairs."

Kate drew an unsteady breath. "They came from all directions. I don't know how many there were. They grabbed your father and me, and demanded to know where your room was. When I refused to tell them, they dragged me upstairs and took your father out the door. I nearly collapsed from relief when I saw you weren't there."

"I woke up when you screamed. I hid in the tunnel…until they set the fire." Elizabeth paused. "Mama, what happened to the servants?"

"Being Sunday, many of them were off for the day, thankfully. But as for the rest, honestly, I don't know. There was so much going on…it was chaos. Some of them tried to come to our rescue, only to be beaten back. I fear some of them must have died in the fire, but I don't know for sure. I've always told myself they all got out safely."

Elizabeth nodded. It would be what Elizabeth chose to believe as well. "What happened after he took you?"

Kate hesitated, rearranging her skirt. "Well, ah…Garrett kept at us for days, demanding to know where you were. He…was brutal. To both of us. I…I don't know what made him snap in the end, but he decided he wasn't simply going to kill your father, he wanted to torture him, to make him suffer as he had. I really think the man wasn't right in the head. He couldn't have been, to have to lived as he did…to do what he did." She looked apologetically at her husband and stepson. George nodded to her. Gavin was about to hear the part of the story he had never heard before.

"What did he do, mama?" Elizabeth whispered in horror.

Kate squeezed her eyes shut and the words came out in a rush. "He violated me while your father was forced to watch. Garrett told him that he was taking his wife, as your father had taken his own love. And then Garrett shot him."

Gavin bolted off of the divan with an indecipherable expletive, raking his hands through his hair as he stumbled to the fireplace. He grasped the mantel like a lifeline, collapsing over it with a shattered moan, sucking in great gulps of air. George joined him, draping his arm around his son while Gavin absorbed the shock.

Aidan was still as a statue, but Elizabeth couldn't hold back her tears anymore. She wept for her mother, humiliated and beaten; she wept for her father, whose good intentions had cost him everything. She even wept for Sarah and her unborn child. Sarah, who had done nothing but chosen to love the wrong man. It took some time, but eventually Gavin returned to his seat having regained most of his composure, and Elizabeth was able to stem the flow of tears.

"I'm so sorry, mama," Elizabeth said softly, hugging her. "However did you land here?"

"Gavin found me." She smiled wryly. "Imagine my surprise when I saw them both in that field, standing together. I thought I was hallucinating."

"Your mother had been beaten within an inch of her life," Gavin interjected. "Kate, had I known..."

"Don't, dearest. You didn't need to know. I only told you now because my daughter deserves to know what happened. I'm so sorry to hurt you like this."

Gavin nodded, swallowing hard. He took a steadying breath before turning to Elizabeth. "I'd been tracking Garrett for a few months, determined to bring him to justice. He was reportedly responsible for the murder of my good friend, and I still blamed him for my mother's death. When I finally found Garrett, your mother was with him, clinging to life, but your father was already gone. As Kate said earlier, my brother had no intention of being turned in, and he fought hard, shooting me in an effort to flee. But eventually, my men sent his men fleeing, and he was captured and turned over to the authorities. Both your mother and I were brought here, and my father nursed her back to health."

"The rest, as they say, is history," George said. "Your mother had me wrapped around her finger in no time at all."

"I see it runs in the family," Aidan said dryly.

"I still can't believe she found her way to you," Kate said, shaking her head. It was nearly inconceivable that Elizabeth had stumbled upon one of the few people who could reunite her with her mother, but yet, miraculously, here she was. "Sweetheart, what happened to you? Where have you been all these years?"

Elizabeth looked at Aidan. There were certain aspects of her past that she wanted to remain buried—there was no reason for her mother to know the extent of the horrors Elizabeth had suffered. The expression on his face told her that he would not utter a word to anyone else, least of all her mother.

So, Elizabeth began her story with how she'd escaped that night, how she'd arrived in London hoping against hope that her parents had escaped as well and would turn up there, and how she'd supported herself and changed her name, leaving out the part about being forced into prostitution and the murder of the man who was supposed to take care of her. She told her mother that she ran away because he became abusive, told her of her life in Kent, and how she had returned to London to find out at last what had become of her parents. She spoke of how Aidan had rescued her on the street, and diligently cared for her these past months, despite the secrets that she kept from him. She told her how she had thought Gavin was the man who'd killed her family (here, she sent Gavin an apologetic glance), and the bone-chilling moment at the ball when she'd come face to face with Garrett, thinking he was Gavin. She spoke for nearly an hour, her mother holding her hand the entire time, their tea grown cold in its cups. When she was finished, her mother looked at her for a long moment, her eyes bright with tears. The silence stretched between them as Kate processed everything Elizabeth had told her. Kate gave her hand a tight squeeze.

"You are so strong, and brave, and beautiful," she choked out. "And so very much like your father," she whispered.

Elizabeth whimpered, and her mother patted her hand, rising. She moved to the back window and stared out unseeingly at the garden beyond. Elizabeth exchanged glances with the others, not sure of what to do.

It was Aidan who rose and went to her. "Mrs. Mayfield, I—"

Without taking her eyes from the window, she reached out her hand and grabbed him by the lapel. "My dear boy," she managed, her voice thick with tears. Her grip tightened, her knuckles turning white as she shook him a little. "Thank you." Her whole body tensed. "Thank you, thank you, thank —" The last word caught on a sob, and every bit of fear, every bit of worry, and every bit of sadness she'd felt over the past eight years, absolutely everything she had ever kept at bay to maintain her own sanity, bubbled to the surface. She visibly shook with the effort of keeping it in, but Aidan drew her into his arms.

"You're welcome."

She gave in then, and her body convulsed with sobs. The anguish that came howling out of her was chilling.

Elizabeth put her hand to her mouth, and Gavin moved to sit beside her. He slid his arm protectively around her.

"She'll be just fine, Elizabeth. She's kept it all inside for eight years…she needs this."

Elizabeth only nodded, then laid her head on his shoulder. She knew all too well what it was like to need to cry until there were no tears left.

CHAPTER 33

It was some hours later before everyone had settled down. Elizabeth had sat in shock at the dinner table while Aidan prompted her to eat. She could scarcely believe this was all real. Her mother was alive, and after all those years of searching, she was sitting across from her daughter at the dinner table as if it were an everyday occurrence. It was all too much to comprehend.

Aidan had finally shooed Elizabeth off to bed, knowing that she was exhausted even if she didn't. He was worn out emotionally himself. The reunion he had witnessed had been overwhelming, and the very real danger of Garrett's arrival into their lives still had him on edge. He was a threat to all of them.

He was in the drawing room, staring into the fire and swirling a glass of Madeira, when Kate caught up with him.

"Aidan?"

He turned at the soft question, taking in the slightly dazed expression on Kate's face. He understood. He couldn't quite believe it, either. "I thought you'd gone to bed," he said, rising.

"I wanted to talk to you first. May I?" she asked, indicating the chair next to the one Aidan had just been sitting in. He waited until she was seated, and then joined her.

"My dear boy." She stopped, attempting to voice what was in her heart. "You have been a godsend to this family from the very start, and today is no exception. You have always taken my best interests to heart, even when I was but a stranger to you. You did your best to help, as you always do. And now I find that you have cared for my daughter and kept her safe these past months until we could be reunited. No, let me finish," she said, holding up a hand when Aidan began to protest. "I know what you are about to say, and you are wrong. You went above and beyond your duty in the care of my daughter, and for that you have my deepest gratitude. I am only sorry she so stubbornly hid her identity from you. Otherwise, we may have found each other sooner. Even so, I thought this was a day that would never come." Tears sprang to her eyes, and Aidan sat quietly, waiting for her to continue.

"Eight years. Eight years I wondered and hoped and prayed, but never did I truly believe I would ever see her again. How can I even begin to thank you for bringing my daughter back to me?" She swiped at the tears that had begun to fall, and Aidan reached into his pocket and handed her a handkerchief.

"No thanks are necessary, Mrs. Mayfield. Yours and Elizabeth's happiness are all that I require."

Kate sniffed and gave him a watery smile. "How very like you to say that." She paused and dabbed her eyes. "I have been saved more times in my life than I think is fair for one person, my dear. First, by Leighton's father, who married me and saved me from starvation when the famine struck Ireland, then by Gavin when he came charging into that field and rescued me from his brother, and then once more by

George, who saved me from death itself. And now, you. You have saved me from a lifetime of pain, and of wondering what happened to my little girl. I do not know what I have done to deserve such men in my life, but I am eternally grateful for each one of them."

Aidan squeezed her hand. "I think you have done nothing but prove your worthiness by showing strength and perseverance through all you have suffered. Perhaps now you will know nothing but a lifetime of peace."

"Indeed I shall, thanks to you." She released his hand and dug into the hidden pocket in her skirt. "I have something I wanted to give you," she said, withdrawing a small, gold frame and handing it to him.

"What is this?" he asked, taking it from her. He glanced down at the portrait and a little girl with dark curls and stunning eyes stared back at him. A slow smile spread across his face.

"It's Leighton when she was three. I snatched it off the table just before Garrett dragged me out the door. I don't know why he let me keep it, but he did. It's all I've had of her all these years."

"I cannot possibly accept this."

"Why not? You've brought me the real thing. I thought she might enjoy having a bit of her past."

"Then why not give it to her?"

Kate smiled, her eyes dancing. "I'd rather hoped the two of you could share it."

"Ah." Aidan chuckled, grasping her meaning. "In that case, I think you should know I've asked her to marry me. With your permission, of course."

Kate clasped her hands together, joy washing over her features. "Oh, Aidan, nothing would make me happier. You know I've come to think of you as a son. There is no one I would rather see her wed than you." She smiled tenderly at him. "You love her very much, don't you?"

Aidan took a sip of his Madeira and then looked her straight in the eye. "More than I ever knew was possible."

Kate positively beamed. "When will you be married?"

"Ah…she hasn't exactly accepted yet. She's still thinking about it."

"Thinking? What on earth is there to think about?"

"It's complicated." Aidan hesitated. "She's had a tough life these past years."

Kate regarded him a moment, pain glinting in her eyes. "She didn't leave that man though he tortured her, did she?"

Aidan studied her, debating about how much to tell her without revealing the information he had silently promised Elizabeth he never would. But he also knew that a mother's instincts were very strong when it came to her children, and he saw no point in denying what she already knew. "No," he said quietly. "She did not."

Kate sat back in her chair and closed her eyes, and a silence fell between them. "Thank you for being honest," she finally said. "I gather there are things she must overcome before she gives herself over to another man."

Aidan nodded. "A few still remain."

"I see." Kate stood, and Aidan followed suit. She took both his hands in hers and looked him square in the eye. "Does she love you?"

Aidan hesitated. "Dear God, I hope so."

Kate smiled and patted his cheek. "She does. Have faith, my dear. She'll come around. There is nothing on earth so powerful as love. It can overcome just about anything."

"I'm beginning to see that," Aidan said, a faint smile touching his lips. His father would be so proud to hear him say that.

Kate grinned. "Welcome to the family."

Aidan laughed as she drew him into a tight hug. She clung to him for a moment, the emotion of the day taking hold of her once again. "Incidentally," she whispered in his ear, "I love you, too."

Aidan closed his eyes briefly, not trusting himself to speak. Kate disentangled herself from his arms and looked up at him with suspiciously bright eyes, then she rested her hand on his cheek and gave him a small smile before turning away.

Aidan stared after her for a few moments before sinking back down into the velvet chair. He unconsciously began to twirl his glass of Madeira once again as he gazed into the fire.

Garrett was out there. That, he knew. It was just a matter of when he would strike. Aidan knew he had made the right decision in coming here, but would the colonel's friends be enough to protect both Elizabeth and her mother? And would this be the time Garrett decided to attack his own family as well? He had shot Gavin once. Aidan knew he would do it again, and he'd kill Gavin this time if he were given the chance.

Aidan got to his feet and tossed back the rest of his wine. He wasn't going to let that happen. He would not let his family be torn apart again.

Even if he had to sacrifice everything to protect them.

CHAPTER 34

Elizabeth's heart was pounding as she stood outside Aidan's door. Her hand was frozen in place, just about to knock, but then she had thought better of it. If she never knocked, he would never know she had been there. She knew he was awake. The firelight flickered under the door and she could hear him moving about. It wasn't too late to turn around and go back to her room.

But she knocked. It was a huge thing she was about to do, but it was the only solution she could see.

"Come in."

Somehow she'd hoped he hadn't heard her. She closed her eyes and took a tremulous breath, but she couldn't force herself to grasp the doorknob. She had turned to stone in the dark hallway. She was contemplating running, but suddenly the door flew open and he was there, staring down at her with surprise.

"Elizabeth! Is something wrong?"

He wasn't wearing a shirt. Heaven help her, he wasn't wearing a shirt. She had caught him getting undressed for bed. She stared, transfixed, at the wide expanse of muscled chest before her. Her mouth opened, but no sound came out. She couldn't for the life of her remember why she was standing there.

"Elizabeth?"

She snapped her eyes up to find him gazing at her with concern. She managed to find her voice despite the fact that her mouth had turned to dust. "May I…may I come in?"

Aidan lifted an eyebrow and hesitated for several heartbeats before stepping back and opening the door wider. Elizabeth slipped past him without so much as a glance.

"To what do I owe the pleasure of this visit?" He hadn't moved.

"Close the door," she commanded.

Aidan looked surprised, but did as he was told. "Elizabeth, is anything amiss?"

"No. I…just needed to talk to you." She fell silent. Aidan waited, but no more information seemed to be coming forth.

"I'm listening," he prompted. Elizabeth said nothing, but came forward and rested her palms against his chest. He drew in a sharp breath and the muscles under his skin jumped at her touch. She sighed and let her forehead fall against his chest. He gripped her by the shoulders. "Sweetheart, what is it?" He tried to get her to look at him, but her head remained stubbornly where it was. She was quiet for a few moments more, then,

"Thank you."

He did pull her away from him then. "I beg your pardon?"

"Thank you," she repeated. "I can't begin to find words to express the gratitude that's in my heart for all you have done for me."

"I thought we agreed we weren't going to talk about this anymore."

"My mother, Aidan. You brought me to my mother. I've spent the last eight years believing she was dead. And just like magic, you conjured her up for me. How did you know?"

"I wasn't certain," he admitted. "That's why I didn't want to tell you the real reason we were coming here. I would never have forgiven myself if I had gotten your hopes up and it turned out not to be true. Honestly, we'd despaired of ever finding you and had just about given up the search. But after the ball, when you mentioned Garrett's name, and the circumstances of your family's demise, I put two and two together. I only recognized the pendant in that instant."

"So you truly didn't know until last night?"

"No. Why?"

"Is that why you proposed? Because it turns out I come from a respectable family?"

"No," he said sternly. "I want to marry you because I love you. Who you are or who I thought you were doesn't make a bit of difference to me. Either way, there's simply no way I can let you walk out of my life."

"And you still want to marry me, even though I have told you of my, er, intimacy issues?"

"I've never wanted anything more."

Elizabeth sighed and took a small step back.

"I can't in good conscience marry you without knowing… that is, I'd like to…" she trailed off, embarrassment at what she was trying to say clogging her throat. She'd done it a hundred times, but never talked about it. But she didn't have to say anything more.

"You want to have sex."

Elizabeth colored at his frankness, but nodded. "I have to know if I can do this, Aidan. I can't punish you for the rest of your life if I can't."

"Meaning you won't marry me."

"That's right."

"And if you can?"

Elizabeth swallowed hard. This man could make her every dream come true, yet she was still hesitant, terrified that it would all turn out to be a cruel hoax. "Let's see how things progress tonight," she said simply.

Aidan regarded her for a moment, then reached out and gently pulled her into his arms and ran his hands reassuringly over her back, tucking her head under his chin.

Elizabeth's skin tingled. Even from the very first time Aidan had touched her hand, she had always felt a tinge of excitement in spite of herself. She realized now that deep down, she had always felt safe with him, even if her stubborn mind wouldn't allow her to admit it. She sighed inwardly and resigned herself to begin the task at hand.

ONE MOMENT she was in his arms, and the next, she'd dropped to her knees in front of him. She tugged at the button on his trousers, and it took Aidan a second to realize what was happening. He swiftly moved to cover her hand with his.

"Elizabeth, what are you doing?"

She blinked up at him. "Pleasuring you."

"Ah…"

"Is that wrong? I thought men liked being pleasured by a woman's mouth."

Oh, dear God. A strangled noise Aidan hadn't known he could physically make sounded somewhere in his throat, and he hauled her to her feet. "Er…they do. I mean, I do. No! I mean, it's…it's just…there's just so much more…Christ, Elizabeth," he swore, raking a hand through his hair. He put his other hand on his hip and stepped away from her to catch his breath. The image of Elizabeth sucking on him was more than he could take at the moment.

"We haven't even started and already I've displeased you," Elizabeth said softly, looking down at the floor.

"What? No," Aidan quickly assured her. "I just…I want to make this right for you. This is supposed to be an enjoyable experience, not some duty you need to perform. We don't even have to do this."

"Yes, we do. Don't you see, Aidan?"

He sighed. "I see that you are one damn stubborn female." He watched her knit her fingers together and untangle them again. Damn. He had to set this right. "Elizabeth, what has sex been like for you?"

"I'm sorry?" She looked slightly alarmed and more than a little embarrassed.

"Forgive me for being so indelicate. I just want to know what your experience has been so I can make it better for you. There's a lot a stake here." He didn't mention the fact that once her mother found out he'd slept with her daughter, Elizabeth would be forced to marry him no matter what. She wasn't alone in her decision making anymore, but that thought hadn't seemed to occur to her. Aidan wasn't above taking advantage of that fact. "You can tell me, Elizabeth. You need to talk about this if you are ever going to get past it."

She stared at him for a moment before sinking onto the ottoman. Aidan moved behind her and gently began to undo her braid, his fingers occasionally brushing over her skin. When her hair was loose, he began pulling his fingers through it, playing with it until she seemed almost hypnotized by the motion. He swept it aside and gently kissed the nape of her neck, eliciting a gasp.

"What was it like?" he murmured in her ear, nipping her lobe. This time he was rewarded by a small squeak.

"Painful," she replied, closing her eyes and leaning just a little into him.

He stopped. "Painful? You mean, the first time."

"No, every time."

This bothered him. "Elizabeth, it's not supposed to be painful." He sat on the ottoman behind her, settling her into the vee of his legs and wrapping his arms protectively around her. "What did Vincent do to you?" he asked, subtly untying the belt on her robe.

She squirmed against him. He clenched his teeth at the thrilling sensation of her bottom rubbing innocently against his groin.

"Well…most of the time he was drunk. The others that came to see me weren't, but they weren't any different, really. All were demanding and treated me like…well, like the whore that I was." She stiffened in Aidan's arms. "Vincent liked me to pleasure him with my mouth first, like I was about to do with you. That was how it always started."

When she paused, Aidan drew his hands up and down her arms in an effort to soothe her. It was also, he admitted, partly to contain his hands from wandering to the other parts of her he so desperately wanted to touch. He rested his chin in the crook of her neck. "Then what happened?"

"Ah…when he'd had enough of that, he'd make me take off my clothes and get on my hands and knees and…ah, erhm… I'm sure you get the idea." Her hands fluttered nervously, her discomfort on display.

"And that was it?" he pressed. "What of your pleasure?"

Elizabeth snorted. "Women aren't supposed to get pleasure from sex."

"Dear God, who told you *that*?"

"Everyone knows that. Don't be ridiculous."

"Oh, Elizabeth," he chuckled, standing up and taking her with him. He spun her around to face him. "You might as well be a virgin with all that you know."

Elizabeth moved away from him and crossed her arms. "I never received any complaints," she snapped. His eyebrows shot up to his hairline. He stared at her, mouth agape, and thoroughly enjoyed the moment she realized what she'd said. They both burst out laughing.

"I'm sure you haven't," Aidan said gently, still chuckling. "But do you have any idea why the act of intercourse was painful for you?"

Her cheeks flushed and she shrugged.

"You weren't ready to receive him, Elizabeth. There are certain responses your body has to stimulation, but because you never received any, you weren't…you know what? Never mind. I'll let you figure it out for yourself. You are sure you want to do this?"

She nodded.

"Fine then. But tonight is about pleasuring *you,* Elizabeth, not me." He stalked toward her and slipped her robe from her shoulders. "I promise you, I won't hurt you," he murmured, snaking his arm about her waist and bending to kiss her bared shoulder. "You may do whatever you like to me," he said, trailing his lips up her neck. "You may do nothing at all." He was nibbling her earlobe again. "Whatever the case may be, you will understand that women do, indeed, derive pleasure from sex. I will make sure of that."

CHAPTER 35

*E*lizabeth was trembling so badly she could hardly stand. That statement, so full of promise, also filled her with a sense of dread. She wanted to marry him with all of her heart. Could she fake her way through this enough to fool him into believing she didn't despise it? He was not like the other men she had been with; he knew his way around women. She could tell that just by the way he was torturing her with his mouth.

Already, this was like nothing she had ever known. She breathed in deeply, inhaling the intoxicating mix of sandalwood and maleness that she'd come to know so well. The very scent that could send her senses reeling. His hands were warm and reassuring as they moved across her back in a slow, thorough possession.

He dragged his lips along her jawline, setting her ablaze everywhere they touched her. He moved down, dropping light kisses on the swell of her breast, then nudged the fabric aside so he could flick his tongue over her nipple. She gasped at the sensation, and instinctively put her hands on his shoulders, holding onto him. He placed his hands over hers and slid them down his chest and around his waist. He wanted her to hold him, she realized…because she'd never done it before.

His arms went around her, pulling her toward him, and he claimed her mouth in a deep kiss. He sighed when she tightened her arms about him and she unconsciously molded her body to his. It was the most wonderful feeling.

"I've wanted this for so long, my love," he whispered against her mouth, his voice husky with desire. "Tell me what feels good. Tell me what scares you. Tell me what you want me to do," he said, nibbling once again on her earlobe. "I want to show you what it's like to make love to someone, to feel real desire. I want you to want me as much as I want you."

Elizabeth couldn't answer. His hands were everywhere, scalding her skin wherever he touched. He massaged her breast and ran his thumb over her nipple while he traced the edge of her ear with his tongue, making her weak at the knees. She slung her arms about his neck in an act of self preservation.

"I'm afraid to want you," she whispered. "I've spent years trying to put this act out of my memory…what if…"

"No more." Aidan pulled back from her and stared at her intently. "This is not going to be like the other times. I promise I am not going to hurt you, and if you want me to stop, I will stop. I know this must be difficult for you, but you have to put your memories aside for the moment and allow some new ones to form. Have I yet done anything you haven't liked?"

She had to admit that he hadn't. Something new stirred inside her every time he touched her. "I just don't want to lose you."

He took her face in his hands. "You are not going to lose

me. Not over this. Not ever. Please don't be afraid. Put your trust in me."

She nodded, letting the comfort of his nearness soak into her. She gazed up into his eyes, those warm, soulful eyes that made her want to melt, and she saw reflected in them exactly what he had been telling her all along. He loved her. Without a doubt, this man loved her.

And she would do whatever it took to make him happy. It was a small price to pay for love, something she never thought she would have. She curled her fingers into the hair at the nape of his neck and tugged him gently down toward her. Aidan complied without hesitation.

He hauled her against him and kissed her as though she were a treat to be devoured, his tongue delving into her mouth, a hand thrust into her hair. The last of Elizabeth's defenses crumbled, and in their place, a maelstrom of desire swept over her. She responded with equal passion, her hands traveling over him of their own accord.

He whisked her off her feet and deposited her gently on the bed, sinking down beside her. He ran his hand slowly down her side and over her hip, caressing her thigh. He pulled up the fabric of her nightgown so he could touch her bare skin.

Elizabeth lost herself in the ecstasy of his touch. Her skin was tingling, her body humming a tune she didn't recognize as she kissed him with reckless abandon, which only seemed to fuel his passion more. He nibbled and licked and kissed all the sensitive spots she hadn't known she possessed, eliciting moans from her that she couldn't seem to keep inside.

Aidan slid her nightgown up to her waist, then paused. "May I?"

She hesitated only a moment before nodding, and he drew it over her head, leaving her completely naked under his potent gaze. She looked everywhere but at him. He smiled down at her.

"Don't you dare be embarrassed, my sweet. You're the most delicious thing I've ever seen."

Elizabeth flushed at his compliment. He stood up, unbuttoning his trousers. "Let's make things even, shall we?"

In seconds, he was every bit as naked as she was. She sucked in a breath. She had seen many naked men before, but never one quite so…exquisite. The firelight bathed him in a golden glow, accenting the hills and valleys of his well-formed chest. She tried not to look lower—honestly, she did—but she couldn't resist taking a gander, and when she did, her mouth went dry. Even *that* was impressive.

"Do you like what you see?" He grinned at her frank perusal and returned to the bed, stalking her on his hands and knees like a panther stalks its prey. Elizabeth nodded, unable to speak. The anticipation of his body on hers was both frightening and exciting, and the feel of his warm skin on hers did not disappoint. He dropped a kiss at the hollow of her throat, then rolled them both on their sides, propped his head up on his hand, and gazed down at her. His eyes were so dark they were almost black.

"Touch me, Elizabeth," he whispered. "I want to feel your hands on me."

She hesitated, then reached out a tentative hand and brushed her fingers over his chest. He closed his eyes on a sigh. Emboldened, she flattened her palm against his skin, marveling at how soft it was, like silk over steel. He caressed her hip, and she was fascinated by the play of muscles in his arms under her touch. The more she touched him, the more the humming in her own body increased. Her hand drifted down his side and over his hip, her breathing ticking up a pace. Finally, she wrapped her hands around his cock and squeezed, giving him an experimental stroke. His sharp intake of breath startled her, but Aidan flexed his fingers on her backside and groaned. She smiled to herself, feeling for the first time in her life as though she was the powerful one in bed.

She liked that.

Another few strokes and Aidan closed his hand over hers, stilling her movements. "Christ, Elizabeth," he swore. "You'll do me in in no time at all if you keep touching me like that."

Elizabeth smiled, pleased to know she had that effect on him. He pulled her into his arms and kissed her deeply, returning her to her back. "Someday soon I would love to continue that," he assured her, "but tonight is about you and your pleasure." He trailed his hand down her thigh while he nuzzled her neck. "Open for me, my love," he whispered, applying light pressure against the inside of her leg. She complied, and he palmed her silky skin. "God, you are so soft. I will never tire of touching you." His hand moved in seductive circles as he made his way to the thatch of curls at the apex of her thighs. He brushed his fingers lightly over her most sensitive parts and she gasped. "May I?" he asked huskily.

"Oh, yes," she breathed. Her body was strung taught as a bow string, and when he dipped a finger briefly into her and withdrew to stroke her aching flesh, she thought she was going to explode. A strange pressure began to build inside her, starting low and slowly unfurling throughout her body. Her breath came faster and she began to tremble, Aidan's slow strokes torturing her and pleasing her at the same time. Elizabeth was completely out of her senses. Her heart was pounding, she couldn't think…she could barely breathe. "Aidan, stop!" she cried out in desperation. "Something's wrong!"

His hand stilled instantly. "What is it?"

"I…I don't know. I feel…strange."

Aidan chuckled. "Like you're going to fly apart at the seams?" Elizabeth nodded, and a wide grin spread over Aidan's face. His fingers resumed their task. "Perfect." He quickened his pace, and her whole body tensed. "Don't fight it, let it wash over you…I promise you are safe," he said softly. "Come for me, Elizabeth. Come for me."

"What do you me-ohhhhh." The strangled question barely made it out of her throat. Every muscle she possessed tensed and she clawed at the sheets. A throaty cry ripped through her as her body exploded with overwhelming sensation. It completely took her breath away, and it was several heart-beats before she could gasp for air again. Her legs quivered while she lay there, panting. Aidan was staring down at her, his eyes smoldering, but she lacked the strength to speak, so she closed her eyes and concentrated on just breathing.

WATCHING Elizabeth climax was the most erotic thing Aidan had ever seen, and he nearly spent himself right then. He wanted her with a fierceness that surprised him, and he prayed that she would be able to get past her anxiety, because he would never get enough of making love to her. Her eyes fluttered open and she looked up at him, bewildered.

"That's never happened before."

"That's because you haven't been doing it right. Any of it," he added. "Did you enjoy that?" he asked, slinging his thigh over hers and dipping his head to suckle a breast.

"I think you know I did," she replied, a teasing note to her voice.

He kissed her and settled himself between her thighs. Their bodies fit together as if they had always been meant for each other. "Then I think I would like to continue, my love. I'm afraid I can't wait much longer," he said against her lips.

"I'm ready," she said, squeezing her eyes shut and wrinkling her nose. Aidan took one look at her face and burst out laughing.

"You're hardly encouraging me."

Elizabeth cracked open an eye and giggled. "I'm a little nervous."

"I see." Aidan smoothed the hair at her temples. "You've trusted me enough to come this far. Don't give up on me yet." He kissed her again, and positioned himself against her slick warmth, hovering just at the edge. "I love you, Eliza," he whispered, pressing into her channel just a little and withdrawing. She tensed, but only for a moment. "I need you, Elizabeth," he continued, entering her further this time, and she heaved a breathy sigh. No sign of pain on her face, only contentment. "And oh dear God, I need you to love me." He buried himself deep inside her with a groan. Her body welcomed him easily, and it was glorious. He definitely was not going to last long, but he didn't care. He moved slowly at first, allowing her to adjust to him, and soon, her body seemed to be responding of its own free will. He kissed her deeply, reverently, and she moved her hips to meet his, tucking her foot around the back of his knee. Her kisses grew more fervent as he continued to stroke in and out of her, and she clung more tightly to him. He moved faster. Her body tightened around him, her cries of ecstasy increasing his ardor.

"Yes, my love, yes," he urged. She dug her nails into his back and let out a cry.

It was too much for him. With one last thrust, he drove into her. A guttural moan tore from him as he poured himself into her, reaching a powerful climax that left him shaking and gasping for breath. He collapsed on her, burying his face in her neck.

"Mother in heaven," he mumbled.

Elizabeth was silent. Aidan waited to regain his breath, then pulled back to look at her. Tears leaked from the corners of her eyes. "Sweetheart, what is it?"

Elizabeth could hardly speak. "I just…I never knew…" she whispered, her hands flailing as she groped for words. She shook her head. "I never knew it could be like this."

Aidan gave her a small smile. "I didn't, either. I've never quite been so out of my mind with need," he admitted. "You do this to me, Elizabeth. Only you."

He rolled to her side, cradling her to his chest and idly stroking her hair. He pressed a kiss to her forehead and sighed. "Thank you, Elizabeth."

She frowned. "For what?"

He tightened his arms about her. "For caring enough to come here tonight. For wanting to try." He kissed her forehead again. "For saving me…in every possible way."

CHAPTER 36

*E*lizabeth stood gazing out the window. Twilight was settling in, bathing the manicured lawns and gardens in a pinkish hue. Though there were four other people in the room with her, the only sound was that of the ticking clock. Garrett was out there—she could feel his presence. And all she could do was stand here and wait. Wait to see what he had planned this time, wait to see what harm he would do, wait to see if he would be successful. Elizabeth was tired of waiting.

"Aidan," she said, turning from the window. "I'd like to go for a turn in the garden."

"Absolutely not," her mother answered, looking up from her needlework. "I'll not have you out in the dark. It's dangerous."

"I am hoping it will be."

Kate let her needlework fall to her lap. "What do you mean by that?"

"I mean I am hoping to draw him out and end this."

Aidan straightened, placing his brandy on the mantel. His sharp gaze bored into her. "Are you sure about this?"

"What? No, she is not sure," Kate protested. "Have you all lost your minds?"

"Mama," Elizabeth said, coming to sit beside her and taking her hands in hers. "I have been running for eight years. I am tired of hiding. I want to end this so our family can live in peace once and for all. The longer we wait for this confrontation, the better Garrett will be able to plan. He's already here; I know he is. Right now, you and I are two sitting ducks in this same room together. Perhaps if we separate, we can disrupt his plan, catch him off guard. I won't sit here just waiting to be slaughtered."

"He doesn't want to kill you," Kate said quietly. "He wants to take you."

Gavin sat up straight. "Elizabeth, this is too dangerous. I've already lost my brother. I won't give up my sister, too."

Elizabeth's head swiveled in Gavin's direction. She hadn't even realized until that moment that they were siblings now. Her eyes misted over. "I'm not going anywhere, Gavin. But this must end. I cannot think of another way we might outsmart him."

A heavy silence fell in the room as seconds ticked by. The Colonel sighed. "I'm afraid she's right."

"No! No, George! You can't let her do this!" her mother cried.

"Colonel, how many men do you have patrolling the grounds and house?" Aidan said.

"A dozen outside. Half a dozen in the house."

"And I am armed as well, as is Gavin. We'll take Griggs with us," Aidan returned, nodding at the man standing guard by the door. "Gavin, your pistol is loaded?"

Gavin rose from his chair. "Aidan, are you sure about this?"

"I am open to other suggestions. You know your brother better than anyone."

Gavin hesitated. "Watch yourself, Aidan. He will surprise you."

Aidan nodded, and stepped toward Elizabeth. "Shall we go, my dear? I believe we have an important matter to discuss," he said pointedly. They had hardly exchanged a word all day.

"No!" Kate clawed at her daughter's hands. "Please don't go!"

"I have to, Mama."

"I will protect her. She will come back to you, I promise."

"You can't make me that promise, my boy." Kate looked from Aidan to Elizabeth and back again. Elizabeth watched the tears course down her mother's face, and her heart twisted.

"I love you, Mama."

Kate turned a watery gaze back to Elizabeth, and she could see the moment Kate conceded defeat. "I love you, too, my dear." she hugged her fiercely, then turned to Aidan. "You bring her back to me, do you hear? If I lose her again, I am dead no matter what happens."

"I will keep her safe," he vowed. He nodded to the guard to precede them, then he left with Elizabeth on his arm.

ONCE THEY WERE in the garden, Griggs set off down the path, scouting the darkness, leaving Aidan and Elizabeth alone at the center where all four paths converged. Benson was also out here somewhere, and neither would be more than a hundred yards away. The white stone that surrounded them would aid in signaling anyone's arrival. Aidan looked adoringly down at Elizabeth in the rapidly fading light. The moon was beginning to rise on the horizon, making a magical mix of gold and silver dance over her features. His heart swelled with the love he felt for her, and he brought her hand to his lips for a soft kiss. "Elizabeth, a few days ago, I asked you a question which you have yet to answer." He caressed her cheek, smiling. "I'm afraid I surprised us both that evening, and did a very poor job of proposing. Not very proper, indeed."

"Well, of course that's the real reason I haven't accepted you. A girl likes a proper proposal."

"Oh, is that the problem?" He laughed and pulled her close. "Elizabeth, tell me you love me."

"You must know how I feel."

He kissed her softly, finally understanding why his father couldn't live without his mother, but why it was worth it to love her so much in the first place. He pulled back from her and took both her hands in his.

"Elizabeth, my father was right. I now know why he begged me to marry for love. I was so afraid of love, but now that I have you in my life, I see how empty it was before you arrived, and I could never go back to that existence. Even if we are allowed only a short time together, loving you is a risk worth taking, and I can only hope that you feel the same. Miss Leighton Elizabeth Townsend Courtwright, will you do me the honor of becoming my wife?"

She opened her mouth to give her reply, but it was drowned out by a sudden explosion at the house. The orangery shattered into a million pieces, glass raining down amongst the flaming timbers. They froze in shock for just a moment, but then a movement in the shadows up the path caught Elizabeth's attention, and she glanced up in time to see a flash of light as it reflected off the barrel of a pistol.

"Garrett!" she gasped.

Aidan whirled around, at once shoving Elizabeth away from him with one hand and reaching for the pistol in his coat with his other. Elizabeth stumbled and fell to the ground, her palms scraping along the stone as another explosion rocked the house, nearly simultaneously with the shot that rang out. She curled into a ball until she realized it was not she who had been shot. She cracked her eyes open, and her heart went still.

Aidan was lying flat on his back on the ground a few feet away, blood staining the white stone.

"*Aidan!*"

Elizabeth struggled to find her footing, her legs getting tangled in her skirts. She landed in a heap next to him, near hysterical. "Aidan! Aidan! Can you hear me? Oh, God!" Blood was slowly spreading across his chest. She shook him, but he didn't move. Fear gripped her, and Elizabeth began to cry in earnest. "Aidan…don't you leave me, Aidan! Please don't leave me!" She ran her hands over his chest, trying to find a heartbeat. She touched his face, willing him to open his eyes. Panic threatened to overwhelm her, and she fought for control. "Aidan, please…please…" she sobbed, leaning down and resting her cheek against his.

"I'm all right. Go with him."

Elizabeth gasped and sat bolt upright. "Aidan?" Had he really whispered in her ear, or was her desperate mind playing tricks on her? She studied his face, but there was no indication that he had said anything at all. "Aidan?" she repeated, choking on her sobs. She felt a movement by his side, and he squeezed her knee—hard—with the hand that was covered by her skirts. He was trying to tell her something. Her gaze shifted to take in the entire scene, and her eyes traveled up his outstretched right hand, which still held the pistol, his finger still on the trigger. Instanly, she understood his plan.

Elizabeth was about to give the performance of her lifetime.

She shook Aidan as she worked herself into hysterics.

"Aidan!" she wailed, her cry echoing in the night. "No," she sobbed. "No!"

Footsteps crunched on the stone, and then he was there. Garrett stood over her, looking down with contempt at Aidan's lifeless form. Elizabeth caught her breath, because it was like she was looking straight at Gavin, except that his face was twisted into a sneer and his eyes were full of hate.

"Oh, now look what I've done," Garrett said, his voice dripping with feigned sympathy. "I've gone and killed him, haven't I?"

Elizabeth looked up at him, pure venom in her voice. "You," she spat. "Why are you doing this to me? Why have you taken everything I love?"

"Because your father took everything away from me," he returned viciously. "I made a promise to myself years ago and I intend on honoring it." He pointed the pistol at her. "Get up."

"Why don't you just shoot me here?"

"Oh no, I'm not going to kill you. Not yet. But I am going to make you wish you were dead." He reached down and yanked her on her feet. "Say goodbye to your love, Leighton. You belong to me now." He shoved her down the path.

"I belong to no one, least of all you."

"We'll see about that." He grabbed her by the elbow and yanked her around to face him. She stiffened when he touched her face. "You're going to belong to me in every way possible, just like your mother," he growled, squeezing her jaw. "It's too bad I had to kill your lover. I would have loved to have made him watch. Your father really enjoyed it." He grabbed the back of her neck and kissed her hard, and she did break then. She bit his lip and he stumbled back from her with an oath.

"Bitch! You'll pay for that!" He backhanded her hard enough to knock her off her feet, and as she went down, a second shot ripped through the night. Garrett hit the ground with a sickening thud. There was a short interlude of utter silence as Elizabeth peeked over her shoulder. She fought back a wave of nausea as she took in the grisly scene before her. The bullet had landed in the side of Garrett's skull, destroying part of his face, and spattering her gown with his blood. She retched as her stomach threatened to rebel. The injury was horrifying, the white stones now stained red. She raised a hand to press it to her mouth, belatedly realizing her hands were covered in blood, too.

Aidan's blood.

She whirled around to find him standing still as a statue ten yards away, feet planted firmly apart, staring down the barrel of a still-smoking pistol, his features as hard as granite. He didn't even notice her scramble to her feet.

"Aidan?" she said softly. He shifted his gaze and their eyes met, and all at once, the whole world began moving again. Elizabeth picked up her skirts and ran toward him, the pistol clattering to the ground as she landed in his arms. He let out a grunt when she nearly knocked him over with the force of her embrace. "Aidan, my God, Aidan," she cried. "Are you all right? What happened?" She stepped back, noticing the alarming amount of blood that was gathering on his shirt. "Why aren't you dead?" she asked in wonder.

"Because you got in the way, my darling."

"How? You pushed me to the ground. I wasn't anywhere near you."

He smiled broadly, reaching into his inside coat pocket and withdrawing the portrait of Elizabeth. "You mother gave this to me last night." He handed her the frame. The top was bent back. "I've had it in my pocket all evening, intending to give it to you. The bullet hit the edge of the frame, altering its course just enough so as to not hit me straight in the heart. Which is exactly where it would have landed had you not been there. So it would seem, dear Eliza, that you have saved my life yet again."

Elizabeth stared at the picture frame in astonishment. Aidan had come so close to dying. A few centimeters to his right and he would not have lived long enough to know when he hit the ground. The realization was almost too much to bear, and tears sprang to her eyes again. "I thought I'd lost you," she said softly.

He caressed her cheek. "You can't be rid of me that easily." He swayed on his feet. "But I do think, my love," he rasped, "perhaps you should get a doctor." He pitched forward onto her, but she couldn't hold his weight, and he slid to the ground, unconscious.

"Aidan!" she screamed. But he did not respond. "Aidan! Don't leave me! You made me love you, damn it! Don't you dare leave me!" She moved to stand, to run to find help, but Gavin was already there, sprinting toward her.

"Gavin, help me! He's bleeding so much," Elizabeth wailed, ripping material from the hem of her skirt and covering the wound, pressing hard. Aidan moaned. "He needs a doctor. Gavin, please get a doctor. Please don't let him die!"

"What happened?" he asked, kneeling beside Aidan and checking his pulse.

"Garrett came out of nowhere. We were distracted by the explosion—oh my God, is everyone alright? Is Mama—"

"She's fine. Everyone is fine. The explosions were meant to be diversions. Where is my brother?"

"Oh, Gavin, I'm sorry…"

Gavin followed her gaze down the path to the body lying crumpled on the stones. He looked back to Elizabeth. "He is dead?" She nodded. He bowed his head with a sigh and said a quick prayer under his breath. "We'll get to him later. We've got to get Aidan to the house before he bleeds to death. Help me with him, if you would."

It was a struggle, but between them they managed to get Aidan slung over Gavin's shoulders, and they made their way back to the house as quickly as possible, the light from the fire illuminating their way.

CHAPTER 37

It was chaos in the house. Servants and Colonel Mayfield's men rushed to and fro, and the Colonel himself stood in the center of it all, barking out orders. Several of his men were apparently missing, and the worst was feared. Someone was dispatched to fetch the doctor, and a brigade was set up to try to contain the fire in the orangery. Fortunately, much of the house was made of stone; as long as they could keep it from spreading, it would burn itself out. Gavin stumbled toward the stairs, exhausted from carrying Aidan all the way up from the gardens.

"Mallory! Help my son," the Colonel ordered. "Bring linens and hot water to whatever room they land in," he said to a passing servant. Elizabeth was ushered into the drawing room, crying and loudly protesting that she would not leave Aidan. Kate stopped the servant and added a cold compress and a basin of water to the list of things to be gathered.

Elizabeth was near hysterics. It took both Kate and George to force Elizabeth into the drawing room to sit. The colonel went to the sideboard and poured her a brandy.

"Mama, he's going to die and it's all my fault!"

"Try not to get overwrought, sweetheart. That's not going to help him."

The Colonel handed Elizabeth the brandy, wrapping her hands around the snifter. "Drink this. It will calm you. Davis!" he called, turning his attention back to the chaos.

A tall, wiry man appeared in the doorway. "Yes, sir?"

"What have you learned from the boy?" A young boy of about twelve had been captured after the first explosion. No one else had been caught.

"Not much, sir. He only knows what he was told to do."

"I figured as much. We'll deal with him later." He turned to his wife. "I am needed in the orangery. You'll be all right?"

"Go, George."

He nodded, and he and Davis dashed out the door without another word. The water and cloth arrived, and Kate took the compress to Elizabeth's face and wiped away her tears, and then began calmly washing the blood from her hands. "Tell me what happened."

"I'm not sure. One minute he was asking me to marry him and the next he was on the ground bleeding. All because I had some ridiculous notion—oh, this is all my fault!" Fresh tears sprang to her eyes, and her mother smoothed her hair as she pulled her into her arms.

"It is not your fault. Garrett would have found a way to get to you no matter what. We did everything we could to keep you safe, and he still managed to get through George's guards. The important thing is that he has been stopped."

She forced Elizabeth to sip some more brandy. There was a knock at the front door, and then the doctor barged through it before anyone could answer it. Gavin appeared out of nowhere and ushered the physician upstairs. Elizabeth flew to her feet as the ruckus passed by the drawing room. The only reason she didn't charge up the stairs after them is because her mother physically restrained her by grabbing both her arms and tugging her backwards into the room.

"Leighton Elizabeth, there is no way you are going up there. You can best help by staying out of the way and let the doctor do what he needs to do. Aidan is in good hands," she assured her, dragging her back to the sofa. She forced the brandy upon her once again. Grudgingly, Elizabeth took a sip.

"Mother," she choked out. "What if he dies?" She mentally berated herself for being so naive as to think they would triumph over Garrett without casualties. If she had just followed her plan and fled London, then Garett would have come after her and Aidan would have been safe.

But then her mother laid her hand on her cheek, and Elizabeth knew that if they hadn't come here, she would never have been reunited with her. Was that what the fate Aidan so strongly believed in had in store for her? She'd gain her mother, but lose Aidan?

"Let's not get ahead of ourselves," Kate said quietly.

Her answer satisfied Elizabeth enough. She couldn't—wouldn't—think of a life now without him. She stared down at her brandy for what seemed like an eternity before Gavin finally entered the room. She sprang to her feet as soon as she heard him.

"Elizabeth." He strode over to where she stood. She looked deep into his eyes, searching for answers to questions she couldn't bring herself to ask. "They've given him a healthy dose of laudanum so the doctor can get the bullet out," he said, a grim look on his face.

"But he'll survive?"

Gavin hesitated. "He's lost a lot of blood, Elizabeth. I'll let you know more when I can."

Elizabeth's heart stopped. That was not what he was supposed to say. She stared up at him, tears filling her eyes.

Gavin's mouth was set in a thin line, all the usual humor gone from his eyes. He reached out and squeezed her shoulder. "I'm sorry I don't have better news. If you'll excuse me, I have to get back to Aidan." He cupped her cheek. "Be strong."

He turned and left Elizabeth standing there trying not to fall to pieces. Kate came up behind her and wrapped her arms around her daughter. "If you are anything, it is strong. Have faith, my child. Everything will be fine, you'll see."

Elizabeth pushed her away. "I'm so stupid!"

"What on earth do you mean by that?"

"I love him, Mama. More than anything in the world. I think I've loved him since the moment he smiled at me when I was recuperating. And now he's asked me to marry him—twice—and because I couldn't let go of my past, I never answered him. I couldn't even admit that I loved him. And now I might lose him. Now he might die thinking I don't want to marry him! It was one little word. One. And I couldn't say it. Now he might never hear it—" Elizabeth dissolved into sobs and collapsed into her mother's arms. Kate was helpless to do anything but hold her daughter.

"I know Aidan loves you a great deal, Elizabeth. He's a good man, and a strong one. He'll not leave you without a fight, I can guarantee you that."

Elizabeth sniffed loudly. Kate pulled her down onto the sofa and cradled her in her arms. They remained like that for some time, until the Colonel came in to report that the fire had been contained and his men had been found.

"Couple of knocks on the head, the rest were chloroformed. Guess that was the easiest way to remove them without drawing attention." He spared Elizabeth a worried glance before he left again. Minute after agonizing minute ticked by until finally—*finally*—Gavin entered the room, pale as Elizabeth had ever seen him.

"Gavin?" she squeaked, trying to keep the alarm from her

voice. His snowy white shirt was spattered with a lot more blood than it had been the last time she'd seen him. She launched to her feet and grabbed him by his shirt front, crushing the fabric in a white knuckled grip. "What's wrong?"

He rested his hands reassuringly on her shoulders. "Nothing. Everything went well. The doctor was able to get the bullet out and stop the bleeding. He's dressing the wound now. I'm afraid it wasn't very easy on Aidan."

"Oh." Elizabeth's hand went to her throat.

"Poor dear," Kate said, her voice full of concern.

"He's resting comfortably now. Hopefully he'll sleep through the night." He turned his gaze back to Elizabeth. "He's going to be in a good deal of pain for some time, Elizabeth, and he'll be very weak for a few days. He's lost an alarming amount of blood, but the doctor thinks he should pull through."

"He's a tough bird, that Lord Ashby," the doctor said, coming into the room. He smiled at Elizabeth. "He should be just fine. Our biggest concern right now is infection, but other than that, with a little exercise and some help from you, he should be good as new in a couple of months."

"He's all right?"

"Yes, Miss. I think he'll be just fine."

Elizabeth stared at the doctor, still clinging to Gavin's shirt. "Thank you," she breathed, and then she collapsed against Gavin in a dead faint.

CHAPTER 38

*E*lizabeth sat by Aidan's bedside, holding his hand and studying his face in the lamplight. She couldn't believe it had only been a few short months ago when she hadn't known he existed. Now, her life would never be the same.

He looked so helpless lying there, pale and bandaged… not at all like the vibrant man she was used to seeing. She touched his bare shoulder, relieved to find it still warm. She blamed herself entirely for what had happened. If she hadn't been so reckless, if she'd listened to her mother…if only. There was nothing she could do now but wait.

She put her head down on the bed, resting her hand on his uninjured shoulder. She absently traced small circles on his skin with her index finger and closed her eyes, thinking of all the moments when he had made her laugh. She wanted a lifetime of laughter.

Something was tickling the back of her hand. She slowly became aware of her surroundings, and she realized she'd fallen asleep. She lifted up her head to find Aidan gazing at her, his eyelids at half-mast. He was running his fingers lightly over the back of her hand.

"Hello, love."

"Aidan!" Elizabeth snapped to attention. "Oh, thank God." She kissed his hand. "How do you feel?"

"Like I've been hit by a runaway carriage." He smiled languidly.

Elizabeth's eyes narrowed. "Very funny, my lord."

"Oh, no. I'm in trouble if we're back to that." He squeezed her hand. "I'm exhausted and my chest is killing me. Is that better?"

"No." Elizabeth's eyes filled with tears. "Aidan, I'm so sorry. This is my fault, I—"

"Sweetheart, stop. It is no one's fault. The important thing is you are safe, and Garrett…" Aidan closed his eyes, fighting against the laudanum. "Was anyone else hurt?"

"The guards have some bumps on their heads, but they are otherwise unharmed. Gavin and the Colonel…are understandably upset."

Aidan looked away, remorse in his eyes. "Garrett was family."

"They're not upset with you, Aidan. It's…it's just a loss." She kissed his hand again, trying to comfort him. She could see sleep tugging at him.

"Elizabeth, before I doze off, or another interruption occurs—"

"I love you," Elizabeth suddenly blurted.

Aidan gave her a drowsy grin. "That kind of interruption is acceptable."

"I'm sorry. It's just that I've waited far too long to say it and I wanted to make sure you knew."

"How much?"

"What?"

"How much do you love me?"

Elizabeth smiled at his question and gazed tenderly down at him. She captured his hand and kissed his palm, then rested it against her cheek. "With all that I am," she said, softly but emphatically.

"Then for the love of God, put me out of my misery and say you'll be my wife."

Elizabeth giggled. "If you insist."

Aidan smiled, closing his eyes. "I do."

"Then yes, Aidan. I'll marry you. Nothing would make me happier."

"Oh, thank God." He sighed, drifting off to sleep. "I love you, Eliza," he mumbled. Elizabeth leaned forward and kissed him on the forehead.

"I love you more," she whispered.

AIDAN SLEPT through the rest of the night and most of the next day as well. Elizabeth kept a close eye on him, dosing him with laudanum when he needed it. Thankfully, he did not develop a fever, and two days later, he was sitting up in bed, admiring his new fiancée.

"I'm afraid we can't be married for a couple of months, my love," he sighed. "I want to be fully healed before I take on the challenge of having you for a wife." His eyes danced as she shot him withering look.

"You'll need to be to handle me, my lord."

He chuckled and pulled her hand to his lips. He turned to kiss her palm and noticed the healing scrapes. "Did I do that to you?"

Elizabeth nodded. "I scraped them when I fell. But don't worry, I don't think it will scar, so we're hardly even," she said, kissing the faint line on his cheekbone. "Gavin is on his way up to see you."

"Good. Help me get up."

"Certainly not! You're not ready to be up and about yet."

"Elizabeth, I've been flat on my back for two days. I killed the man's brother. The least I can do is put on clothes when I face him. Be a good girl and fetch my trousers, will you?"

Elizabeth folded her arms across her chest and watched him struggle to sit up. "You are going to rip open your stitches, you stubborn mule." Her annoyance quickly turned to embarrassment, however, when he swung his legs over the side of the bed and flung off the sheets. She'd forgotten that he was naked under those sheets. He stood up shakily and grinned at her as she gaped at him.

"Enjoying the view?"

Elizabeth snapped her gaze up and narrowed her eyes at him. "Insufferable man," she grumbled, grabbing his drawers and trousers. He slid his arm about her shoulders as she helped him get them on. He trembled with the effort of dressing.

"Sit down before you fall over," she admonished.

"I just need something to hold onto," he replied, slipping his arm about her waist and pulling her close. She rested her palms against his chest, and he managed to get his left arm around her as well. "I can't put into words what peace overtakes me when I hold you in my arms," he said softly.

Elizabeth dropped a light kiss on his chest at the edge of his bandage. "You don't have to tell me. I feel it, too." She gazed up at him, wondering how it was possible to love a person so much that it felt like you would stop breathing without them. Aidan smiled at her tenderly, reveling in the fact that she was standing within the circle of his arms without the slightest hesitation. He leaned down to kiss her briefly, then she sighed and laid her head upon his shoulder. They remained as they were for a spell, simply enjoying the moment.

There was a knock at the door, and Gavin entered. He looked surprised to see Aidan on his feet. "What are you doing out of bed?" he demanded.

"Good to see you, too," Aidan replied with a chuckle. "Elizabeth, I'm starving. Perhaps you could see about getting me some breakfast?"

She took the hint and left the men alone. Gavin surveyed the bandage that covered Aidan's chest and shoulder. "How are you feeling?"

"Like hell," Aidan admitted. "Gavin, can you ever forgive me?"

Gavin's brows rose in surprise. "Forgive you?"

"Gav, I killed your brother. I can't imagine what you think of me."

"Aidan…" Gavin ran his hand through his hair and huffed out a breath. "Aidan, I've spent most of my life being ashamed of my brother, trying desperately to understand how he could have been such an evil man, and fervently hoping something would happen to turn his life around. I gave up hope when he shot me. I realized then that if he could kill his own brother, then nothing would save him. He's hurt—*killed*—so many people…I can't quite wrap my mind around what would drive a man to such…horrific acts. I couldn't stop him, but you did." He moved toward Aidan and put his hand on his shoulder. "You risked your life to save Elizabeth's and Kate's. Garrett would have murdered them both; I have no doubt of that. You didn't kill my brother, Aidan. He ceased being my brother years ago. Blood alone cannot make us brothers. But our hearts can." Gavin paused and swallowed hard. "The only brother I've ever truly known is you, Aidan. You're the one who's always been there for me, and the one I've loved my whole life. You were the one I was terrified to lose the other night. You're my family, Aidan…not Garrett. You. And I thank God for sparing you."

He smiled at Aidan with watery eyes. "There is nothing to forgive, my friend…my brother. So please don't ask me."

Aidan nodded, eyes bright with unshed tears. He clapped Gavin on the shoulder and squeezed. "Thank you," he choked out.

"I think I should be thanking you," Gavin replied, grinning at him. "After all, you've brought me a little sister to torment."

Aidan chuckled. "Go easy on her, Gav. She was an only child not too long ago."

Gavin smiled wickedly. "I'll be gentle, I promise." He paused. "By the way, did she ever say yes?"

"I was in a laudanum haze, but I believe that was the answer."

"Excellent. I wish you all the happiness in the world."

"Thank you. I believe I shall have it. But there is one thing that would make my happiness complete."

"What's that?"

"Marry Lainey."

Gavin let out a loud guffaw. "Good God, man, are you going to beg *all* of your friends to marry your sister?"

"Only the ones who I think are worthy of her." Aidan grinned.

Gavin snorted. "And you started with MacKavoy? I'll not insult her by repeating that. Time for you to sit, now," he said as Aidan swayed unsteadily. He helped Aidan into a chair by the fire. "Lainey's a good woman and perfectly capable of finding herself a husband. Give her time, Aidan. Lainey is looking for something special."

"Mm. Wish she would hurry up and find it," Aidan said, leaning his head back and closing his eyes.

Gavin sat across from him. "Have you told Elizabeth the news of Betsy?"

"Not yet. I want to surprise her. Betsy will be at the house when we return?"

"Yes, and more or less fully recovered. Smythe gave her a pretty awful beating."

Aidan grimaced. "I think it's time to do something about that man."

"I couldn't agree more."

"I'm just glad Blake was able to find her." A smile worked its way across his lips, and then he chuckled.

"What's so funny?"

"I was just thinking…we've found all the people Elizabeth has been searching for. She's not going to know what to do with herself now!"

CHAPTER 39

They stayed another week at the Mayfields' until Aidan was strong enough for travel. Garett's body had been buried in the family plot, a last effort from a father to his son. Kate was traveling to London with them to help with the wedding plans, and Mary was just about to burst with excitement over all the gossip she was going to get to tell the staff.

Elizabeth turned to Aidan as the coach pulled up to the town house. "I can't believe none of you ever told Lainey about me."

"We thought it best, dear," her mother replied. "Since I feared you might be in danger, we thought the less people knew of you, the better. It was generally believed that you were dead, and we wanted to keep it that way."

"Well, won't she be surprised," Elizabeth said wryly. She helped a tired Aidan up the steps, and Tibbs opened the door.

"Welcome home, my lord. My lady," he said, bowing to Elizabeth.

"Not yet, Tibbs, but thank you for the honor." She smiled, and the stoic butler winked—winked!—at her. Elizabeth stifled a laugh as he took her cloak. Lainey came swooping down from out of nowhere and launched herself at her brother.

"Oof. Easy, Lainey, I'm still sore."

"Thank heaven you're not *dead*. You stubborn, stubborn arse!" She turned and yanked Elizabeth into a fierce embrace. "I'm so glad you are safe and well. And so desperately happy that you are to be my sister!"

"I'm delighted, too, Lainey. And personally, I am glad that your brother is a stubborn arse, or he may have given up on me a long time ago!"

Lainey's brilliant smile faded when her eyes fell on Gavin. She took her hands in his and squeezed them. "I'm so sorry about your brother," she said softly. Gavin shook his head.

"Don't be. I believe he's better off now."

Lainey nodded, and finally noticed Kate. "Mrs. Mayfield! What a delightful surprise! What brings you here," she said, kissing her cheek. Kate exchanged glances with Aidan, and Lainey frowned. "What is going on that you are not telling me?"

"Lainey, I think we would all like to gather in the drawing room with some tea," Aidan said, ushering her toward the stairs. "We have a surprising story to tell you."

Tibbs cleared his throat. "Perhaps, my lord, you will allow me to inform Miss Townsend of her visitor?"

"I have a visitor?"

"Yes, Miss. In the drawing room."

Elizabeth glanced around. Everyone was smiling but Lainey.

"Don't look at me," she said. "No one would tell me anything."

Elizabeth headed for the drawing room and hesitantly opened the door. A young girl was standing by the fire, and Elizabeth gasped when she turned. "Betsy!" She charged into the room and gathered her friend into a crushing embrace. "Heavens, where have you been? I've been trying to find you for months! I was beginning to think something awful happened to you."

"Something did," she replied, studying her old friend up and down. "Cor, look at ye. A right toff now, y'are!"

Aidan stepped into the room, followed by the others. He introduced everyone and invited them to sit.

"Aidan, how did you know about Betsy?"

"Mary told me—don't be angry, she did the right thing. When that note arrived, she knew you were in some kind of trouble and wanted to help."

"The note! We still don't know who sent it."

"Actually, we do," Gavin supplied. "It appears it came from Peter Smythe."

"You were in on this too?"

"Will someone please explain what is going on here?" Lainey demanded. "What note?"

"Oh dear," Elizabeth said. "I'm afraid there's quite a bit you don't know."

And so the whole story was recounted while Lainey's eyes grew rounder and rounder. A long silence fell.

"My goodness," she finally managed. "That is quite a tale, Elizabeth. I suspected you came from a different background, but I never imagined…my goodness." She swallowed visibly. "And what of you, Miss Clarke? Where have you been all this time?"

"Recovering, same as Liz here."

"Recovering?" Elizabeth's throat constricted. "What on earth happened?"

"Smythe," she said simply, as if that explained everything.

"I'm afraid I don't understand."

"He never gave up wantin' ye, to be sure. He had a rat followin' me, gettin' hold of my letters to and from ye, so he knew where you were the whole time, the scum. I came across 'im in a tavern one night a few months back, and I heard 'im talkin' about ye with some bloke. Turned out to be yer man Garrett. Garrett said he was lookin' for a girl about yer age, and as I 'eard him tell Smythe his story, I knew he was talkin' about ye. He fed Smythe some tale about bein' a long lost brother and gettin' you and yer mum back together. Promised him some blunt if he could help find you. Bloody Smythe'd do anything for money, even hand you over, and I could see he knew who Garrett wanted.

"I didn't think Smythe knew where to find ye, so I thought ye'd be safe for a spell. I paid a little special attention to the bloke after Smythe left, and got 'im to talk. He asked me if I knew where to find ye. Said he knew you were looking fer yer mum and he knew where to find her. Somethin' in his eyes made me believe he was telling the truth, so that's why I wrote ye, hoping to make a plan when we met. Little did I know I led 'im right to ye. I'm so sorry."

Elizabeth squeezed her hand. "You couldn't have known, Betsy. You were trying to help me find my parents. But you never showed up that night. What happened?"

"Smythe got hold o' my letter to ye before it got sent on. The night I was supposed to meet ye, he met me first. I fought hard, but there was more o' them than me."

There was a collective gasp from the women. Elizabeth's eyes stung. "He beat you?" she breathed.

"Knocked the stuffin's out o' me. Left me lyin' in an alley in the rain. When I finally woke up, I couldn't remember my name, and I was horrible sick. A kind lady had found me and taken me in, and helped me get better." She gave Elizabeth a cheeky grin. "Things came back, tho, and now I'm right as rain."

Elizabeth just stared at her, horrified. "You almost died protecting me," she forced out past the lump in her throat.

Betsy shrugged. "I ain't ever had no one like ye, Liz. Ye taught me to read an' write, and ye treated me kind, always stickin' up fer me. Ye were worth protectin'."

Elizabeth's hand went to her chest, covering the acute ache there. Words completely eluded her, tears shimmering in her eyes. She couldn't believe she deserved a friend like Betsy. She couldn't believe she deserved any of these people who had fought so hard to save her. She smiled at her friend, seeing her with new eyes, and she decided right then and there that Betsy would have whatever it was she desired in life that Elizabeth could provide.

"Well," she managed, her fingers tapping her thighs. "Well." Her throat tightened to an alarming degree, and she could hardly draw a breath. "Ex...excuse me a moment." She slipped from the room before the dam inside her broke.

Aidan followed her into the hall, wordlessly pulling her into his arms. She fell against him as the torrent of tears sprang forth.

"My God, Aidan," she said after she'd calmed. "What unspeakable evil has followed me all my life. First Garett, then Smythe. How could he beat her like that and then just leave her to die?"

Aidan kissed her temple. "I don't know, but he will pay for it. He's been arrested for attempted murder and I am filing embezzlement charges. He'll rot in Newgate."

"Good. It's no less than he deserves." She sighed and lapsed into silence once more.

"There's something else I need to share with you." He set her away from him so her could see her face. "Burke is not who you think he was."

"What do you mean?"

"I mean Lord Burke never existed. Vincent made the title up, probably to attract women, or who knows why else. I'm afraid you've been fearing retribution all these years for naught. Vincent was just a common criminal, and it's doubtful anyone even questioned his death, much less mourned it."

Elizabeth went rigid, hands fisting at her sides, eyes bulging with anger. She worked her jaw in an effort to keep the words in, but to no avail. "Bloody *bastard!*" she spat.

Aidan laughed as she immediately clamped her hands over her mouth, shocked by her own outburst. Aidan took her face in his hands, still chuckling.

"My darling, I couldn't agree more!"

EPILOGUE

"Tell me again, Daddy," Liza begged, her little four-year-old fingers touching the scar on Aidan's cheek. She was sitting on his lap, smiling up at him expectantly. He kissed her fingers and she giggled.

"Oh, not that old story."

"Yes, again!" she demanded. Aidan laughed and hugged her close. She was a miniature version of Elizabeth, with a mass of dark curls and huge blue eyes that didn't miss a thing.

"Aw, Liza, he's told you a hundred times already. You know the story." Thomas James dug his toe into the dirt. He teased his little sister relentlessly, but the truth was, he adored her. He had inherited his mother's startling eyes, but his father's handsome features and his protective instincts. Liza would be well cared for her entire life.

"*I'll* tell you, even if your father won't," Lainey chided. Liza clapped her hands and turned her full attention to Lainey. Thomas James rolled his eyes and ran to play with his friends. It was, after all, his eighth birthday party.

"Well," Lainey began. "You have a very brave mother."

"What's this?" Elizabeth said, coming up behind her, carrying the newest addition to the family on her hip. Both she and Aidan had been thrilled to discover that she could, indeed, have children, and the three that they had were the light of their lives. Aidan believed that fate had intervened and prevented her from conceiving all those years, waiting until the time was right. Whatever the reason, Elizabeth was extremely grateful. "What have I done now?"

"Nothing," Lainey laughed. "Liza was just begging to hear the story of how you and Aidan met again, and your husband was being less than accommodating."

"Really?" Elizabeth said, arching her brow. "How very ungentlemanly of you, darling." She smiled, and her daughter cooed her agreement. "See that? Even Betsy thinks so."

Aidan rolled his eyes and looked at Gavin. "I think I'm hopelessly outnumbered."

"Yes," Gavin replied. "And you wouldn't have it any other way."

It was true, Elizabeth thought. Aidan loved all his women deeply. Elizabeth glanced around the table at her friends and family. It was a perfect July afternoon, the shade of her favorite oak tree protecting them from the heat of the sun while the breeze rustled the leaves overhead. Kate and the Colonel sat next to each other, holding hands and smiling at the scene around them. "Aunt Lainey, the story," Liza prodded.

"Oh yes, where was I? Well, your father had just crossed the street from where he had been talking to your mother, and he didn't see a carriage speeding toward him, so your mother gathered up all her strength and pushed him to safety."

"And you hit your cheek, right, Papa?"

"Yes, that's right, little one. But I think your mother got the worst of it."

"You think?" Elizabeth said dryly. Aidan winked at her over Liza's head.

"Mama was brave to save you!" she declared. "Was it love at first sight, Papa?"

Aidan chuckled, a distinct tenderness lighting his eyes. But it was Lainey who answered.

"Yes, it was, although neither of them knew it."

Liza collapsed against her father's chest with a sigh. "How romantic!" she exclaimed. That brought on a burst of laughter so hearty that Elizabeth found herself wiping tears from her eyes. She leaned over and kissed Aidan.

"I have to go round up our son and get him into some decent clothing. The painter will be here in an hour or so." They had commissioned a family portrait to be hung in the gallery where Aidan had first reached out to Elizabeth in friendship. She dropped a kiss on Liza's head. "I'll be right back."

She disappeared in search of Thomas, whom she sent off to the house, and when she returned to the ridge of the hill, her mother was waiting for her.

"You know, Liza is just like you when you were a child." She smiled at her daughter, some distant memory drifting through her eyes. Today was always a bittersweet day for both of them. Thomas James had been born on the exact date their lives had been torn apart so many years ago.

"I wish Papa could be here to see them," Elizabeth said softly, her throat tightening.

"He is here, Elizabeth, and he is very proud of you. I'm sure he is watching over every member of this family."

Elizabeth nodded. She believed that, too. "Sometimes, just once in awhile, I get angry still. We lost so much, Mama."

Kate put her arm around Elizabeth's shoulder and tickled Betsy under her chin. "But just look at what you've gained because of it."

Elizabeth gazed down the hill to the table full of people waiting for her...her family, her friends who had stuck by her when she had had a rough entrance to society...the people who mattered most to her in the world. Anne sat serenely with Lord Cranston while the Duke and Duchess looked on. Betsy Clarke appeared to be telling the Duchess a wild story, for a shout of laughter burst forth from the group. Will and Louisa were also there, as much in love as ever, though now their love encompassed their four children, as well. And of course, Gavin and Lainey had been her biggest champions. Elizabeth smiled to herself. Nowhere else could there be such a mixed gathering of people from all walks of life, who loved each other dearly.

And then there was the home in which Elizabeth now resided. She had taken one look at Rosecroft Manor ten years ago and fallen in love. She had understood perfectly why Lainey had preferred to spend most of her time here. The sense of peace that surrounded her when she was here was unmatched by anything—though how she could find any peace in such a lively household was beyond her. She and Aidan were hardly ever alone here, as family and friends were encouraged to visit often. They wouldn't have it any other way. Elizabeth sighed. "It was awful, Mama." She paused. "But I'd do it all over again to have this."

Kate kissed her cheek. "So would I. Now let me hold my granddaughter. I see your husband coming this way and I know that look in his eye. You've been away from his side for too long." She plucked Betsy out of Elizabeth's arms and blew a kiss to Aidan as she strolled back to the party under the oak. Aidan wrapped his arms around Elizabeth.

"You're taking too long. I miss you."

Elizabeth melted into him, laughing. "My mother knows you so well."

"What?"

"Nothing."

"Mmm," he mumbled, kissing her temple. "You seem to be in good spirits today, my love. Can I assume you and your mother were reflecting on the past just now?"

Elizabeth nodded against his chest. "But in a good way. She just reminded me of how I wouldn't have any of this if that night had never happened."

Aidan tightened his arms around her. "Fate has a funny way of trying to make things right. I've always said it had you in mind for me all along."

"Such a believer," she teased. "But I'm sure you're right."

Aidan set her back from him and looked into her eyes. "Can you believe it's been almost ten years since we married?"

Elizabeth shook her head. "It's gone by in a blink."

"The years do seem to fly faster as we get older." He gave her a rueful smile. "I noticed I'm starting to get a touch a gray at my temples. You may soon find yourself married to an old man."

"Hardly."

"Ah. So does that mean you still find me as attractive as you did then?"

"More so." She slipped her arms about his waist.

"And am I still as charming, too, or have the years worn at my polish?"

Elizabeth giggled. "Still devastatingly handsome, still undeniably charming. Anything else you are worried about?" She knew what was coming. It had become part of their daily routine. He pulled her in closer.

"Do you still love me?"

She twined her fingers into the hair at the nape of his neck. "With all that I am."

He smiled at her.

And then she kissed him with all that she had.

ACKNOWLEDGMENTS

I would like to thank the Romance Writers of America for giving me the opportunity to learn from some of the best in the industry. Many thanks to Victoria Pinder, Erica Taylor, Michelle Spray, and my other RWA friends for taking the time to answer my endless questions about all things self publishing!

Thank you, Kate, for doing way more than you were asked to do, single-handedly saving me from making egregious historical errors and giving me a stronger story. Thanks also to Karen Sidel, who, when I put about that I was looking for a good copy editor, held up a sign that said, "Will work for wine." And of course, my Drinking Divas, who are, if possible, even more excited about this debut than I am.

And to my friend Laurie Judd, who informed me I really should write historical romance. Thank you for putting me on this path. I think, perhaps, you were right.

But most of all, thank you to my beloved husband, who spent years encouraging me, yet did not live to see my name in print. There was no truer romantic hero than you, my love. I do this in honor of you.

ABOUT THE AUTHOR

copyright 2019 Sandy Puc Photography

Grace Hartwell is a lifetime resident of Connecticut and has been crafting stories since before she could hold a pen. Always a sucker for a love story and a firm believer in happily ever after, Grace picked up her first young adult romance at age twelve, and never looked back. She took a circuitous route to becoming an author that included a teaching degree, many years as an IV pharmacy technician, and a stab at portrait photography before the loss of her handsome prince spurred her into pursuing her lifelong dream of seeing her name in print.

Now she lives in their "castle" with their two cats, Lizzie and Bingley, who are largely uninterested in her writing. Grace loves to travel, has an ever-present cup of tea by her side, and when she's not writing, she can be found on stage (pursuing her other passion), or creating vintage-inspired jewelry. She is also obsessed with historical fashion and enjoys recreating hats, outfits and accessories from all different eras. Find out more at www.gracehartwell.com

f X O